S0-AHB-200

Elephant Secret

Elephant Secret

Eric Walters

Houghton Mifflin Harcourt
Boston   New York

Copyright © 2018 by Rule of Three Inc.

All rights reserved. Originally published in hardcover in the United States by Clarion Books, an imprint of Houghton Mifflin Harcourt Publishing Company, 2018.

For information about permission to reproduce selections from this book, write to trade.permissions@hmhco.com or to Permissions, Houghton Mifflin Harcourt Publishing Company, 3 Park Avenue, 19th Floor, New York, New York 10016.

hmhbooks.com

The text was set in Minion Pro.

The Library of Congress has cataloged the hardcover edition as follows:

Names: Walters, Eric, 1957– author.
Title: Elephant secret / Eric Walters.
Description: Boston : Clarion Books/Houghton Mifflin Harcourt, [2018] | Summary: Thirteen-year-old Sam and her father scrape by caring for rescued elephants until an offer comes through that may not only save the sanctuary, it may also restore an extinct species. Includes facts about woolly mammoths and cloning. | Includes bibliographical references.
Identifiers: LCCN 2017020600
Subjects: | CYAC: Elephants—Fiction. | Animal sanctuaries—Fiction. | Human-animal relationships—Fiction. | Woolly mammoth—Fiction. | Mammoths—Fiction. | Orphaned animals—Fiction. | Cloning—Fiction.
Classification: LCC PZ7.W17129 Ele 2018 | DDC [Fic]—dc23
LC record available at https://lccn.loc.gov/2017020600

ISBN: 978-1-328-79617-2 hardcover
ISBN: 978-0-358-20637-8 paperback

Printed in the United States of America
DOC 10 9 8 7 6 5 4 3 2 1
4500768101

Elephant Secret

CHAPTER

One

I LAY ON MY BACK ON THE INFLATABLE RAFT. THE WARM sun from above and the gentle rocking from below lulled me in and out of sleep. My arms hung down into the water, soothed and cooled. They needed it. Not just because it was a cloudless brilliant sky and the temperature was still above eighty, but because they were sore. I was sore in a lot of places. The tractor had broken down, and I'd pitched enough hay to feed an elephant. . . . Actually, a herd of elephants.

I hoped the tractor would be fixed by tomorrow, but there was no guarantee, nor that it wouldn't be broken again in a week or two. So much of what we needed to run this place seemed to be held together by duct tape, baling wire, and hope. Sometimes it felt like hope alone kept it all going, and sometimes even hope was in short supply. I knew I shouldn't complain. Things had been going a lot better since we got the —

I felt something brush against my left hand, and my left arm was wrapped up in a tight grip.

"Oh, no!" I gasped.

I was dragged off the raft and pulled beneath the water, unable to escape, powerless to fight as I was going down. Mouth closed and eyes wide open, I found myself staring into a gigantic dark eye shining through the murky waters no more than a foot away. As quickly and powerfully as I'd been pulled under, I was thrust toward the surface, shot out of the water, and propelled into the air.

"You big stupid—" I screamed before splashing back down into, and then under, the water.

I quickly rose to the surface to the sound of my father's laughter. He was standing at the edge of the pond, laughing so hard he was practically doubled over. Beside him on both sides were elephants slowly moving into the water or standing half submerged.

"I'm glad you found that so funny!" I yelled as I treaded water. I reached out and grabbed my wet baseball cap, which was floating on the surface, and put it back on my head.

"It's not just me, Samantha," my father replied, still laughing. He was the only one who called me Samantha. Everybody else called me Sam. I pretended it bothered me. Really, I kind of liked it. "You know, even though the elephants didn't laugh, they might have thought it was funny."

Off to my side was the tip of a trunk, the snorkel, of the culprit. I could identify the trunk, but even if that weren't the case, I'd know who had done this to me. It had to be Raja. Even if elephants don't laugh, this one certainly liked to play jokes.

Slowly the trunk started to rise, followed by a domed forehead and two brown eyes. Of course it was Raja. He turned slightly to the side, and I could have sworn that he winked at me. He sank back down under the surface, his trunk disappearing with the rest of him. I saw the ripples and knew what was about to happen. Knowing it didn't mean I could do anything about it.

Raja rose up beneath me, pushing against my feet and legs. I reached down to grab on, balancing, getting one leg on each side, until I was riding on his back. Floating forward toward the shore, Raja paddled along until I could feel the change in motion as his feet hit the bottom. His rolling gait carried him and me into the shallows, where he stood still.

"You're going to stop here?" I asked him. "Couldn't you at least take me to shore?"

He didn't answer, but he didn't move, either. I reached down and gave him a big scratch behind his left ear. That was his special spot, where he liked being scratched the best. Elephants don't laugh and they don't purr like cats, but if they did, Raja would have started to purr right then.

"If you keep rewarding bad behavior, you're only reinforcing it, Samantha," my father warned.

"Are you talking to me or Raja, Jack?"

"Jack?"

"Well, if you can call me Samantha, I can call you Jack."

"You know I'm going to keep calling you Samantha, so you have to decide what you're going to call me. My preference would be Dad, or Daddy, or Pops, or even J-Dog."

"J-Dog?"

"My rapper name."

I couldn't help but laugh. "You are the furthest thing from a rapper that I can even imagine."

"Yeah? Toss me your baseball cap," he said.

"What?"

"Toss me your baseball cap — you know, the thing that practically lives on top of your head."

I hesitated.

"You won't die if you don't wear it for a few seconds."

I took off the cap and threw it down to him. He caught it and put it on his head — backward. "Well, am I more rapper-like now?"

"You're a nut," I said.

"That's *Daddy nut.* Or you can just call me Dad."

"How about you take off the hat and I'll call you Dad?"

"I can agree to that," he said as he took it off. "You know I probably have a better chance of training the elephants to do what I ask than I do of training you."

"You don't train a daughter."

"Certainly not this one, anyway," he agreed.

One by one, the entire herd, all eleven Asian elephants, had entered the pond. Some had disappeared completely. Others were snorkeling, only their trunks and the tops of their heads visible above the water. Some waded in with their backs breaking the surface.

There were so many sounds coming from the elephants. True, they didn't purr or laugh, but they chirped, squeaked, squawked, clicked, and rumbled. People who get all their information from watching Disney cartoons think that elephants only trumpet. They do that — and it's amazing to hear — but they make many other sounds as well.

Still standing in the shallows was Daisy Mae. I wanted to go and see her.

"Down!" I said to Raja. He reached back with his trunk and helped me slide down into the waist-deep water. I sloshed toward the shore.

"Hey, Daisy Mae, how are you doing?" I gave her trunk a gentle rub.

Daisy Mae was a terrible name for an Indian elephant, but it was the name she responded to. Every elephant that wasn't born on the property had been rescued or donated by somebody in North America. Daisy Mae was from a private collector in Kentucky. He had a personal menagerie, and he'd thought that owning an elephant would be a good idea.

Of course it's never a good idea for somebody to own an elephant. To his credit, he'd had more than ten acres of property for Daisy Mae and a big-animal vet who treated her, and he'd managed to keep her alive and healthy for almost two years.

When he finally realized it was too expensive and just not right to keep an elephant on its own, he arranged for us to take her and paid for a special animal-transport company to bring her here. That was more than five years ago. Since then he'd made a donation every year to help pay for her upkeep. If other people were that considerate, we wouldn't have been so tight for money all the time.

Some of our elephants had lived through a lot before we got them. Some had been like abused children shut up in somebody's basement or attic. They'd survived without enough space and without a family or a herd. An elephant living on its own is like a prisoner locked away in solitary confinement. They're prisoners who have committed no crime except being an elephant.

"She's doing well, isn't she?" I asked. This was a comment, a question, and a concern all rolled into one.

"Daisy Mae's doing extremely well, and that's not just my opinion but Doc Morgan's, too." My dad handed me my baseball cap, and I put it on, tucking my hair under it.

"But things could have changed since the last time he examined her," I said. I couldn't help but worry about her.

"He saw her yesterday while you were in school."

"You didn't tell me he'd been here." I was surprised. There wasn't much that went on with the elephants that I didn't know about.

"I did. Just now. Do you have water in your ears from when Raja dunked you?"

"You and that elephant both think you're funny. You're both wrong. What did Doc Morgan say?"

"That she's healthy and progressing through the pregnancy just fine."

Daisy Mae was very pregnant — twenty-one months, or four weeks away from being ready to deliver. "And how is the baby?"

"Doing well. He let me listen to the heartbeat. It sounded like a drum."

"I wish I could have been there to hear that," I said. I'd heard it when he did his previous examinations, but still it would have been thrilling to hear it again. I felt like a niece or sister who was supposed to be there for all Daisy Mae's doctor visits.

"School does get in the way sometimes, but summer is almost here," my dad said.

"Ten more school days. I'm counting."

"The important thing is that you're going to be here for the birth."

"That *is* more important. I can't believe we're practically there. Why can't elephants be more like bunnies?"

He laughed. "A litter of elephants would be incredible."

"Even twins would be amazing."

"Amazing and extremely rare. We know she's carrying only one baby."

"Right. It's not so much the number of babies as the length of time it takes for an elephant to have even one baby."

"You know the rule of thumb — mostly, the larger the animal, the longer the gestation period. A mouse pregnancy is less than a month, and an elephant's is twenty-two months."

"Twenty-two months is ridiculous. A hippo isn't that much smaller than an elephant, and it gives birth in less time than a human. Blue whales aren't pregnant for that long either, and they're much bigger."

I knew about most animals, not just elephants. Part of the reason I liked being there when Doc Morgan examined or treated one of our elephants was because I wanted to be a vet when I grew up.

"It's size *and* complexity. Orca whales carry for about seventeen months, and giraffes about fifteen. And as you know, the closest relative to an elephant is a manatee, and they carry their young for about thirteen months."

"I wish elephants took thirteen months," I said. "I'm tired of waiting."

"It will be worth the wait. Scientists believe there's something about elephants and the complexity of their social structure that requires them to be born with fairly advanced neurological development."

"As opposed to the nine months a human is pregnant and the complexity of human social structure?" I asked.

"You have a point, but you know how I feel about most humans."

I did know, and I didn't feel any different. Elephants are loyal and kind and gentle, and while some people have those qualities, most don't.

We continued to stand at the edge of the pond as Daisy Mae waded deeper into the water until only the top of her head and her trunk showed above the surface.

"I want things to go well," I said.

"So do I. So do I."

Daisy Mae wasn't just pregnant. She was pregnant by means of a special program. Money had been invested in our sanctuary, money we needed badly, on the condition that three of our elephants were artificially inseminated—artificially made pregnant. I found the idea a bit strange — okay, *really* strange — and gross until my father explained it to me. He said that the best way to guarantee the survival of elephants is to create genetic diversity. Since you can't easily ship elephants around to be mated, artificial insemination is the answer.

It might be weird, but some wealthy eccentric investing money to create new elephants wasn't the worst thing in the world. Rich people do stranger things with their money, and this made more sense to me than buying a fancy yacht or building a bigger mansion. My father had heard rumors that ours wasn't the only sanctuary where this offer had been made.

Unfortunately, Daisy Mae was the only one of our three elephants whose pregnancy was successful. Raina's didn't "take" to begin with, and Tiny had carried for about a year. That was very sad for all of us. I wasn't surprised that Daisy Mae had managed to carry her pregnancy all the way. She was already the proud mother of Bacca, "baby" in Hindi. Bacca was more than two years old and completely weaned. Still, he never strayed far from his mother. Right now he was off to the side, rolling around in a mud wallow, having fun and watching his mother with one eye.

My father was unusually secretive about the details of the program. He talked to me about almost everything, but not much about this. I'd pressed him for more information, but he said he really didn't know much himself. When the project started, two years ago, he told me that they wanted things to be kept quiet, so the money was shrouded in mystery. But what more did I need to know? They gave us money and the chance for a new baby elephant. How bad could any of that be? Anybody willing to invest money in elephants had to be a pretty good person.

The best thing so far about us being in the breeding program was that it meant an infusion of money for our sanctuary. We'd been getting by on donations, admission fees from visitors to the sanctuary, and whatever my father could make working at the local diner as a waiter. None of that income was guaranteed. The additional money wasn't a fortune — it certainly wouldn't pay for a tractor that didn't break down all the time — but it was enough to help keep us going. We could pay the mortgage on the property, and we weren't scrambling for food for the elephants.

Elephants eat almost continually. Each of ours could have eaten up to three hundred pounds of food a day. Some of it they foraged, but most had to be brought in and distributed, sometimes by hand. Today it had been *my* hands — and arms and shoulders and back. We owned more than two hundred acres of open land with trees, creeks, and, of course, the pond. Our property was the size of almost two hundred football fields. It was big, but even an area this size wasn't big enough to allow the elephants to free feed. Without the bales of hay we brought in, they would have destroyed every tree, shrub, bush, and blade of grass.

Our sanctuary was the only place I'd ever lived. I hoped that like Bacca and the new baby, I'd never have another home. Why would I want to live anyplace else? When you have paradise, you don't up and leave it. And right here by the pond was my favorite place on the property.

"I better go to work," my father said.

"You don't work on Saturdays."

"Barney's out sick, and a shift is a shift. We can always use the money. Are you okay with being left alone?"

"I'm fourteen, not four."

"Don't you mean you're thirteen and not three?"

"I'm fourteen in less than three months. Right after that, I'm going to start saying I'm fifteen, because technically I'll be in my fifteenth year."

"Don't rush away the years, Samantha. Someday you'll be as old as me."

"About two hundred years from now."

"Careful, there — show some respect. I'm only ninety-nine years older than you. I just feel bad leaving you alone, especially at night."

"Night or day, I have a herd of elephants to keep me company and a twenty-foot fence to guard me, so I'm not too worried."

"Speaking of fences, I need to do a perimeter check tomorrow. That storm may have done some damage."

The weather was heating up quickly, and over the past few weeks, we'd been hit by a series of thunderstorms. Thank goodness none had developed into a tornado, but yesterday's thunderstorm had threatened to. Instead it was just massive rain, big winds, and enough lightning to light up the night. My father was afraid that some of the fences on the far side, by the creek, might have been weakened or washed away.

"I could have a look," I volunteered.

"You should think about hanging out with friends occasionally."

"Actually, I was hoping to just hang around here with friends, if that's all right."

He looked unsure. "I guess that would be okay. How many people are you talking about?"

"There will be twelve of us altogether, but only one of us is a *people*."

"So you want to stay home with the herd instead of going out with friends?"

"I *will* be with friends."

"You could invite a few human friends over," he said.

"I see them at school."

He shrugged. "Who am I to argue? It's not like I spend a lot of time with people. Are you all right fixing yourself dinner?"

"As all right as I usually am."

"Point taken," he said.

I didn't mind cooking for myself. I made more of our meals than he did — nothing fancy, but he didn't much care what he ate. Sometimes I thought he'd be happier grazing with the herd.

My father gave me a little peck on the cheek and headed for the house. I turned back and watched the elephants. They were splashing and swimming and spraying one another and themselves. They were rolling in the mud on the bank and playing. Dinner could wait.

CHAPTER

I CLOSED THE FRONT DOOR QUIETLY SO AS NOT TO WAKE my dad. He hadn't gotten home from work until almost three in the morning. I knew because I didn't sleep soundly until he came in. Not that I'd ever let him know, because he'd worry. He could sleep late now while I finished checking the fences. I'd started the job after he went to work last night, but darkness fell before I could finish. Having it done would be a nice surprise for him when he finally got up.

I walked past the big barn where the herd used to sleep. It was really old, in terrible shape, and we were afraid that parts of it — or the whole thing — might collapse in the next big windstorm. My father had barred the doors and didn't let the elephants in anymore. The barn needed to be replaced, or at least torn down, but there wasn't enough money or time right now to do either.

Next I went down to the pond. I hadn't expected them to be here. They usually only went to the water either in the middle of scorching days or toward the evening, when the temperature was more moderate. The pond was a favorite place of the herd, but they had serious business to do before going there. Every day, for up to eighteen hours, they ate. Elephants are eating machines. They have to eat constantly to get enough nutrition into them to live. Sort of like teenage boys, except elephants are way more sensitive and pleasant than the teenage boys I knew.

Elephants are amazingly intelligent, much more than cats and dogs. They are considered the smartest animals, along with dolphins and the great apes. Elephants can solve problems, use rocks as climbing platforms, and break branches to use as tools — although they do that mostly to swat at flies, but still, a tool is a tool. They learn from their own experiences and by watching other elephants. The leader, usually the oldest female, uses the wisdom she acquires as she gets older to make sound decisions, and the others learn from her.

In our herd, the matriarch was Trixie. She was the oldest, biggest, and wisest. She most often stood where she could see all the other elephants. She always watched for danger and would place herself between the herd and anything she thought was a threat. Though there was no danger at the sanctuary, she constantly stood guard, watched, assessed, and made decisions.

Through the trees, I glimpsed the herd in the distance. They were, as I'd expected, close to the place where their food was stored. They were smart animals, and they were always hungry animals. And the evidence of that was visible on the property. Most of the trees had a browse line — leaves above the level an elephant could reach, and only stripped branches below that. Some trees had their bark stripped off and were dying. Others had simply been knocked down.

The closer I got, the more of the herd I could see. Trixie suddenly stopped eating and looked around. I wasn't surprised that she was the first to become aware of me. I would have been surprised if she hadn't been. She took her job very seriously.

She had probably smelled or heard me. Elephants have a powerful sense of smell and an acute sense of hearing. When I was younger, I used to try to sneak up on the herd. It never worked. You couldn't move too quietly for them to hear.

Trixie swiveled her head, her big ears flapping. That was her way of pinpointing where the noise was coming from. It's also a way an observer can tell that an elephant is excited about something.

Within seconds of Trixie reacting, there was a ripple of response from the other elephants. They stopped eating and started looking around. Bacca, who was now almost as big as a compact car, had been pressed against Daisy Mae. If he'd been smaller, he would have tried to shelter between his mother's legs.

Almost automatically I started to count them — maybe

Trixie wasn't the only one who had to watch everything. Raina, Selena, and Tiny were clustered by the far end of the storage area. They were almost always together, and if they strayed too far from one another, then they were still talking to one another. They'd come as a group from a traveling circus about eight years earlier and were almost like a sub-herd within the herd. All three were gentle and calm.

In the distance were Jumbo and Ganesh, who was named after the Indian elephant god. They were younger than the girls and had been with us two and three years, respectively. Jumbo was about four years old. When he was thirteen or fourteen, he'd begin spending more time foraging and exploring alone, although up until his twenties, he'd still spend most of his time among the herd. Even when he separated from the herd almost completely to live independently, our property would be big enough for him to coexist on the same piece of land. Of course Raja's turn would come first, since he was almost nine. That was still a long way in the future, and I didn't even want to think about it.

There were only three whom I couldn't see yet. I knew they couldn't be far. They never wandered any distance from the herd.

"Good morning!" I called out.

All the elephants I had located turned in my direction. A couple, including Trixie, raised their trunks so they could "see" me better by smelling me. I raised my arm in the air, not to wave but to imitate their gesture. Satisfied it was me, they went back to the very serious business of eating.

My father used to kid me that I had spent so much of my childhood growing up with the elephants, I copied elephant behavior at least as much as I did human behavior. That only made sense. We two humans were always outnumbered by elephants.

The elephants were standing among the remains of yesterday's meal. There wasn't much left, just enough loose hay for a breakfast snack.

Getting closer, I saw Hathi and Stampy in the trees. Hathi was named for the elephant in *The Jungle Book,* and Stampy was the elephant on *The Simpsons*. We would have loved to change that name, but that's what he came with and what he answered to.

That left only Raja unaccounted for. Why wasn't he here? I looked around and saw movement at the far side of the storage enclosure. Rather than eating the available scraps of hay, Raja was reaching his trunk through the bars of the storage area, trying unsuccessfully to get at new hay bales. So much for *all* elephants being smart.

Then again, Raja the prankster might have been playing a game with the bales — sort of like me trying over and over to sneak up on a herd of elephants, even though I knew it was impossible. In many ways, Raja was my peer. Elephants live about two-thirds as long as people, so if you took his age — nine — divided by two, and multiplied by three, we were both thirteen and a half. That meant that we were the two teenagers in the herd, closest in age and attitude. I liked him a lot, even when he was annoying. Kind of like most of the boys I knew — especially the annoying part, not the liking-them part.

I learned in health class that males and females mature at different rates. My nana — my mother's mother — confirmed it. She told me that generally little girls roll over, crawl, walk, talk, and are toilet trained earlier than boys. She said the boys eventually catch up — at about age seventy-five — and they are so shocked, they die! I knew she was joking but kind of serious at the same time. I missed her. She'd passed on three years ago.

My dad was a wonderful father and a great guy, and one of the smartest people I knew — *the* smartest about animals — but sometimes I felt like I was the parent in our family. I did more cooking and housework than he did, not that either of us did much. There were always things to do around the property and with the elephants that were more important than the chores around the house. Sometimes his head seemed to be somewhere else, even when he was right beside me. Maybe elephants have it right. Formally put a female in charge, and everything works well.

As I got closer, the elephants started to move toward the storage area, ready for breakfast. They had to be fed, and the tractor was still broken because my father hadn't had time to fix it, so it wasn't going to be any help.

I took the key from its hiding spot and unlocked the gate of the enclosure. It was locked and chained to keep the elephants out. The food inside was theirs, but if they got in, they'd make a real mess and probably eat more than they should — more than we could afford.

I wasn't looking forward to feeding them this morning. The bales were heavy, and my arms were still sore from the day before, but what choice was there? It wasn't like they could feed themselves. . . . *Wait.* Maybe there was another possibility.

"Raja!" I called out.

He was still off at the side of the area, snaking his trunk through the bars. He was, if nothing else, persistent. He stopped what he was doing, raised his head, and turned in my direction. He looked a bit guilty, like he'd been caught doing something bad.

"Raj, come here!"

He tilted his head to the side like he was thinking about what I wanted. He probably knew but was deciding whether or not to listen to me. He hesitated a few more seconds and then lumbered over in my direction.

"If you want to get what's in here, you'll fit better through the gate," I said as I opened it up wide enough to allow him to pass through.

He didn't need a second invitation. He slipped through the gap, careful not to touch the sides of the fence or brush against me. Now we'd find out if this was a good idea or the stupidest thing I was going to do the entire day.

I backed into the enclosure, pulling the gate closed behind me. Trixie and some of the others were watching my every move. I wrapped the chain back around the bars to keep the gate shut. I didn't want anybody else in here. At the sound of the chain, Raja turned around, his ears flapping. He looked uneasy. New situations always make elephants anxious, and this was new. He had never been inside the enclosure — no elephant was ever allowed in here — and now he was separate from the rest of the herd. Well, with the exception of me.

Raja, the broken tractor, and I were standing in a large open space. In the middle, under an overhanging roof, were the bales — thousands and thousands of square bales of hay piled, in some places, two or three times my height. About half of them had been purchased and the other half donated by local farmers. Donations often weren't in cash but in kind. Bales of hay weren't worth their weight in gold, but they were as good as cash.

Moving slowly, I approached Raja. "No worries," I said.

"I'm just going to put you to work. Think of this as payback for tossing me into the water."

I grabbed one of the bales and dragged it to the fence. Almost instantly Trixie moved over, stuck her trunk through the bars, pulled at the bale, and was rewarded with a trunkful of hay.

I turned back around. Raja had already grabbed a bale from the pile, ripped it apart, and started eating. For him, the sixty-pound bale weighed next to nothing.

In parts of Asia, elephants have been used as work animals for more than four thousand years. Today they are mostly used to give tourists rides, but in rural areas, they are still used to haul lumber and transport crops. I'd read somewhere that a *mahout* — the man who trains and rides an elephant — can communicate with a worker elephant using more than a hundred different words that the elephant understands. The trainer can point at things, and the elephant knows what needs to be done or does it simply because it already knows the steps that follow. I'd never seen that happen, but I believed it. I knew how many words our elephants understood. Would Raja listen to me and understand what I wanted him to do?

I pointed to the ground, right in front of the bars. "Bring that bale here! Put it right here!" I shouted. "Right here, put the bale down!"

Raja stopped eating. He turned his head so he could see

me, and once again he looked like he was trying to figure out what I was telling him. He picked up the bale he'd been eating and started walking toward the fence. Had he understood me?

"Here, here, right here!" I yelled, jumping up and down and pointing.

He moved up until he was right beside me, towering over me.

"Attaboy, Raja. Now just put it down. Put the bale down." I crouched down and patted the ground. "Right here!"

Raja turned his massive head so I could look into his eyes. At this short distance, I had no doubt that he was thinking.

Suddenly he reached his trunk up, still holding the bale.

"No, put it down. Don't —"

He tossed the bale into the air. It soared over the fence and landed on the other side, among the rest of the elephants.

I turned to Raja. He looked amused, like he was thinking, *Isn't this a better way?* He turned and trotted back over to where the bales were piled. He grabbed a second one, quickly returned, and tossed it up and over the fence. Trixie voiced her approval in a series of clicks and chirps.

Then, rather than go back for a third, Raja reached down and grabbed the remains of the bale I'd brought. He gathered up the hay and tried to toss it over, but it was loose, and hay showered down around me like rain. Was he trying to fix my mistake — not tossing it over — or had he deliberately decided to cover me in hay? It could have been either or both. He was off again.

I felt proud. Of myself, for coming up with the idea, but more of Raja, who not only understood but was doing the heavy lifting. Of course, for him, it wasn't heavy lifting.

This is one of the things people don't understand about elephants. They not only live in groups; they also care for one another in family groups. Here was Raja, taking care of the others in his herd before he took care of himself. They were communicating with one another. I wouldn't have been surprised if Trixie was counting the bales as he tossed them.

This is how they live together, caring and in harmony. Elephants are one of the most powerful species on the planet, and they can be deadly, but mostly they go out of their way not to harm any other animal unless they are threatened.

Elephants show empathy in a way that only humans and one other species — chimpanzees — do. Elephants grieve for their dead. A herd doesn't just stay with a sick or injured member to protect it, but stays on after it dies. They gently push and prod the dead animal, caress it with their trunks, and even visit the remains long after its death. I'd read about this — I'd read everything about elephants I could get my hands on — but sadly, I'd also seen it happen.

We'd only ever lost one elephant. His name was Peanut,

and he was so old when we got him — my father figured he was at least in his early sixties — that his teeth and tusks were worn down. My father assumed he was sent to us because he was older and close to dying. That was also probably why he had been allowed to be part of a herd instead of forced to live the solitary life of a bull. Trixie had allowed him among the other elephants. At least he got to spend his last months with us as part of a herd, a far better place than the private zoo where he'd lived most of his life.

We knew Peanut wasn't well, but it was still a shock one morning to see him down on his side and unable to get back up. My father called in our vet. Doc Morgan examined Peanut and said there wasn't much he could do. Sick could be fixed sometimes, but old was incurable.

The herd had surrounded Peanut. Some were watching him, and others were facing away, eyes and trunks outward, as guards. They stayed like that all day. Nobody ate. Occasionally, one or two at a time, they left to drink from the pond and then returned.

When he finally died, they remained. They gently touched him with their trunks and moved him with gentle nudges until they were sure he was dead. As they moved off, they passed right by me and my father. We had stayed too. Elephants don't really cry, but they do have tear ducts, and liquid flows out to cleanse their eyes. Every single elephant had liquid running from the eyes that day. I'd never seen that before, and I've never seen it since. It doesn't matter what the books say — they were crying. They were sad, grieving for the loss, for Peanut. He had lived alone, but he died as a member of a herd, surrounded by a family who cared for him.

That's one of the things that makes it so cruel to keep elephants in captivity instead of in a sanctuary like ours where they can live in a herd and wander through hundreds of acres. Some zoos are better than others. But there are carnivals and roadside attractions and private collections where elephants are often isolated and abused, and mothers and babies and families are broken up as animals are traded or sold. I knew all about that, because most of our elephants came from those places.

Some people argue that places like our sanctuary shouldn't exist either — that all elephants should be returned to the wild. How can you return animals to the wild when they were never in the wild to begin with? How can you return them to a wild that doesn't even exist? How can you return one elephant when elephants need a herd to live in? Trying to return an elephant to the wild would mean sentencing it to a slow death by starvation or a quick death if it clashed with local people.

I heard the sound of an engine and turned to see my father driving up. Normally we weren't supposed to let the elephants inside the food storage area, but I couldn't see him being upset about this. Actually, I hardly ever saw him upset. In some ways, in many ways, he was like an elephant. He even looked like an elephant. He was really big, with graying hair, a shaggy beard, and big brown eyes. Sometimes I wished my eyes were elephant brown too, but they were blue. Oh, and one more way he was elephant-like was that he was eating almost all the time. He always had an apple, a granola bar, or trail mix stashed in his pockets.

Trixie and the herd stopped feeding for just an instant as he approached. They had made sure it was him and his truck and knew there was nothing to fear. He didn't like to bring the truck too close, so he stopped at the edge of the clearing. He climbed out, chomping on an apple. No surprise.

I heard his laughter before I could see his smile as Raja tossed another bale over the fence.

"Samantha, you are amazing!" he called out.

"I'm not the one doing the work."

"But you're the one who trained him to do the work."

"I'm not too sure of that. He just seemed to know what to do."

Dad moved among the members of the herd. He spoke to them by name and gave each a pat or a rub on his or her special scratching spot.

He took one more bite from his apple and then offered the core to Trixie, as usual. She gently took it from him with her trunk and slipped it into her mouth. He always spent extra time with Trixie or gave her a special treat or both. I thought of them as the matriarch and the patriarch. Together they were in charge of the herd, keeping everybody safe and fed and watered. I believed that Trixie saw things the same way.

He leaned against the fence. "So now that you've got him started, have you figured out how to get him stopped?"

"I told him to stop when he reached sixty bales."

"I didn't know he could count that high."

"Maybe I'll leave the stopping part to you, since you're the expert on elephant behavior."

"I'm an expert on their behavior, but I bet nobody knows more about how they think and feel than you do," he said.

I shrugged, trying to be elephant calm, although I was really happy to hear him say that. "It's not complicated."

"Maybe not to you, but I guess it makes sense that you'd know them so well."

He was right. I was born and raised with elephants. My first word wasn't *Daddy*; it was *Ella,* which is what I used to call them. My father had never been much for taking pictures, but almost all the pictures of me growing up had an elephant in them. When I drew pictures of my family in the early years of school, I always included me, my father, and the rest of our herd. I guess if anybody knew how elephants thought and felt, it should be me.

"That looks to be about the right amount of bales," Dad said.

Raja had been very productive. He'd done effortlessly in less than thirty minutes what would have taken me two or three painful hours of hard labor. He was coming back with another bale. I undid the chain and pushed the gate all the way open. Raja didn't need to be told. Still carrying the bale, he lumbered through the opening and out to join the herd.

"I thought you were leaving it up to me to get him out."

"Raja and I decided against it." I went through the gate and closed it behind me.

Dad pulled another apple out of his pocket and tossed it to me. "Be sure to share the core with Raja."

"I will."

He glanced at his watch. "We have some time before we open. We should head back and eat something as well."

We opened the sanctuary from noon until five every Sunday. For ten dollars per person or a family pass for twenty-five dollars, visitors were allowed in to see the elephants. They had to stay in their vehicles and keep to the dirt roads, and they weren't allowed to come close to or chase the elephants.

We could have made more money if the hours were longer, or if we added Saturday viewing, or if we let the cars go off the roads so people could get closer, but none of those would have been good for the elephants. In fact, if we hadn't needed the money, we wouldn't have let people in at all. Having to let in visitors — customers — bothered my father a lot. He said we were a sanctuary, not some sideshow. During the entire time there were visitors, my dad was out in his truck, cruising around, watching, making sure the rules were being followed by our guests.

"Do we have much help today?" I asked. A number of volunteers gave their time to help us keep the place running.

"I believe we have three volunteers."

"Volunteers? Or Joyce?"

"Joyce is a volunteer."

"Is she a volunteer today?"

"She's one of them. Mr. and Mrs. Patterson are coming too."

"I like the Pattersons."

"I don't know why you don't like Joyce."

"She's okay . . . for a lawyer."

"What do you have against lawyers?"

"They spend half their time helping guilty people get free."

"And the rest of their time is spent helping innocent people stay free. I'd sure like her on my side if I was ever in trouble with the law."

"What would you be charged with — not having a license for your elephant?"

"That would be eleven elephants and eleven charges."

Joyce was a volunteer. She was a lawyer. And she was dating my father. I'd seen that coming the moment she'd started volunteering here, six months earlier. I got the feeling that she didn't like the elephants anywhere near as much as she liked the man who owned them. Dad was completely unaware. I saw what she was doing, all the smiling and tilting her head to one side and hanging on his every word and chuckling at his jokes. He was a really smart guy, but human interaction was as confusing to him as elephant interaction is to almost everybody else. I wasn't the least bit surprised when he told me that she'd asked him out on a "date" to see a movie together. He'd asked me if it was all right, and what was I supposed to say, that it wasn't?

"She's a good person. Just try to be nice to her," he said.

"I always try."

"Try harder. You're a kind person, so be kinder to her."

I didn't say anything more, because I didn't want to lie. I didn't want to try any harder. I really didn't have anything against lawyers, only this specific lawyer. Not that I didn't want him dating. He'd gone out with other women over the years. I just didn't want this one to be the woman he was dating now. There was something about her that made her different from the others. Or maybe there was something different about the two of them together, or about him. I'd noticed the way he watched her when he didn't know I was looking. I'd heard him laughing and giggling when he was around her. Laughing was one thing, but giggling — it was strange to see somebody as big and old as him giggling. I suspected he liked her more than he'd liked any of the others, and that scared me.

Joyce was tiny — I guess she was what people would call petite — and she and my father side by side looked ridiculous. Most people would probably consider her pretty. She smiled a lot. She had perfect teeth, white and shiny and straight. Somehow she seemed to have more teeth than humans were supposed to have. Her hair was blond — or at least dyed blond — and it always looked like she'd spent way too much time on it. That and her makeup. Who wears makeup to throw bales of hay or shovel elephant dung? And then there was her clothing. Her outfits matched and fit like they were made just for her. Even her work clothes were always clean and ironed.

That smile of hers was probably what bothered me the most. If my father was an elephant, then she was a crocodile. That crocodile smile wasn't fooling me for a second. If I were an Egyptian plover — birds that clean crocodile teeth — I would never clean her teeth, because I wouldn't trust her not to eat me, and I'd tell all the other plovers, and none of them would clean her teeth, and she'd get cavities, and —

"Joyce is going to come a bit early today."

I gave him a questioning look.

"She said she was going to bring in lunch for us. If you'll eat the food she brings."

"I can eat the food," I said. I just wouldn't help clean her teeth.

CHAPTER

Three

"IT LOOKS LIKE A GOOD CROWD," JOYCE SAID, GESTURING toward the front gate and offering me one of those perfect, shiny crocodile smiles.

"It's okay, I guess." I deliberately offered no show of teeth back.

I'd done a quick count. There were already twenty-two cars waiting, and it was still ten minutes before opening. I'd gone to the little rickety admission booth to get ready to open, and Joyce had tagged along with me. She hadn't realized that I was going there early to try to get away from her.

"Are you all right?" she asked.

"I'm fine. Why are you asking?"

"You didn't eat much at lunch, and you've hardly said a word all day."

"I have lots on my mind." And she was lucky what was on my mind wasn't being said aloud.

"What's his name?" she asked.

"What?"

"The boy you were thinking about. What's his name?"

"Why would you assume I was thinking about a boy?"

"I was fourteen once."

"Yeah, but that was *so* long ago."

"How old do you think I am?"

"I don't know. It's hard to tell once people get to a certain age."

"And what certain age do you think I am?" she asked.

She looked bothered, and I felt a sense of pride in bothering her. I continued, "I guess you're probably about five years older than my father."

"I'm seven years *younger* than your father. I'm only thirty-five."

"Really? I never would have guessed."

She looked even less happy. Actually she looked younger than thirty-five, but I certainly wasn't going to give her a compliment.

She looked hurt, but she wasn't going to give up. "Some people aren't good at guessing ages."

"Yeah, some people," I agreed. "But I'm really good at it."

I was thinking about adding something, like maybe she'd spent too much time in the sun, or how stress aged people and I was sure her job was stressful, but I thought that crossed well over the line of mean. I really wasn't a mean person, and my father had asked me to be kinder. This was far from kind.

She looked hurt, but that expression softened. Part of me felt bad for hurting her and another part felt sorry that it hadn't hit her harder.

"I know it's hard to have your father dating somebody, but I'd like you to know that if you ever have anything you want to talk about, I'm always here for you."

"You're only here a few times a week, so you're not always here."

"I'm only a phone call away if you want to talk."

"My father is usually *less* than a phone call away. He's here. He's my *father*."

That emphasis was meant to remind her that he was my father and that she was not my mother. Although he had been dating her longer than most of the women he'd gone out with, and he did seem goofier than usual when he was around her. Was there something more to this one? Was that why she bothered me more than the others had?

"It's just . . . I know that there are some things a girl can't talk to her father about. Woman things."

I worked hard to avoid gagging.

"For example, let's say you wanted some advice on what to wear two Friday evenings from now."

"I'm wearing this," I said, indicating my jeans and T-shirt, baseball cap, and running shoes.

"You're wearing that to the end-of-the-year school dance?"

"How do you know about that?" I asked.

"It's written on that big sign out in front of your school."

"It's happening, but I'm not going to the dance."

"Won't all your friends be going? It *is* the eighth-grade graduation dance, isn't it?"

"You don't have to go to it to graduate."

"Oh, oh . . . okay . . . I understand."

"Good. Wait — what is it that you understand?"

"This is so delicate. I know it's embarrassing to go if you don't have a date."

"What makes you think I don't have a date?" I demanded.

"So there *is* a boy," she said. She looked pleased with herself, like she had just caught a witness in a lie.

There wasn't any boy, and she wasn't that clever.

"You know, it's not like *your* generation," I said. "A group of girls in my class are going together. We don't need a male to define who we are or what we can do or where we can go."

"I'm sorry if that's what you thought I was implying," she said, tripping slightly over her words. "I agree with you. I'm a lawyer. I'm a feminist. I've fought my whole life for those rights, and I'm sorry if I said something to offend you."

I bit my tongue so I wouldn't tell her she didn't matter

enough to offend me. She moved in closer and put a hand on my shoulder. Why were some people so touchy-feely? I had to fight the urge to brush her hand away. Then I had an idea.

"Look, there is something I wanted to talk to you about," I said.

"You can talk to me about anything," she said, giving my shoulder a squeeze.

Her hand felt heavy, and there was almost a burning sensation where she was touching me.

"Anything."

"I need help," I said.

"What is it?" she asked.

She looked so concerned and caring and hopeful.

"Over there," I said, pointing off toward the house.

"You want to talk somewhere else, in private?"

"No, I have to stay here to open and do the admissions. I didn't get a chance to clear the inner yard, and I *need* you to go and clean up the elephant dung."

She didn't look caring or hopeful anymore. She just looked hurt.

"Sure, if that's what you want me to do." She removed her hand, turned, and walked away.

I suddenly felt bad. Bad for her and bad for doing what I'd done. Did she really deserve that? But I didn't have the time to think about it, and really, what could I do about it now?

It was time to start admitting visitors. I unlocked the gate, slid it open, and motioned for the first car to come forward. As I returned to the admission booth, the car pulled up to the window with a father and mother in front and three little kids in the back seat.

"Good afternoon," he called out.

"Good afternoon. That's twenty-five dollars."

He held out a credit card.

"Sorry, we're a cash-only business," I said, pointing to a sign tacked to the side of the booth.

"Oh, I didn't see that."

"It's all right. I have cash," the wife said.

She dug into her purse and pulled out bills and some change. She handed it to the man, who counted it out as he passed it over. I dropped it into the cash box.

"Thank you. Please drive slowly, stay on the dirt roads, don't drive too close to the elephants, and do not get out of your vehicle. You can roll down the windows to take pictures."

"Believe me, we're not getting out," he said.

"And please don't, under any circumstances, feed them."

"We wouldn't do that. But wait — they're not going to get close enough for us to even think about that, are they?" the woman asked.

"They sometimes come right up to the vehicles, but they won't harm you."

"Or my car?" the man asked. He seemed more worried about his car than about the safety of his family.

"They won't hurt the car." *Although they could flip your precious car and roll it onto its roof if they wanted to,* I thought. Some things are better to think than to actually say. "Just turn off the engine and let them pass by. No worries," I said instead.

"Thank you."

I leaned out so I could look at the kids in the back seat. "The elephants are really kind and gentle. Don't worry about a thing."

"We're not worried," the eldest of the three said.

"Thank you so much for being so kind and reassuring!" the wife said.

As they drove off, the next car came up to the window.

Car by car, I collected the money. Many held familiar faces, people who had visited often. Some of them gave more than the admission fee as a donation to the sanctuary. I always gave new people the same information and warnings.

Loud music was coming from a vehicle a few cars back. The music got louder as it got closer. As the car pulled up, I recognized the occupants, four guys who had gone to my school and were now in high school. I didn't know them personally.

The driver turned the music down but not off. "Hey, Elephant Girl!" he called out, and the other three guys laughed. I cringed and hoped they hadn't noticed.

Kids called me Elephant Girl when I started school. Back then, I liked it. After all, what could be a bigger compliment than being compared to an elephant? But it wasn't a compliment anymore. To some people, I was no longer the girl with the elephants but some sort of freaky elephant-girl hybrid. I should have taken it as a compliment even if it wasn't meant that way, but I couldn't.

"That will be forty dollars," I said.

"Forty? But it says that a family admission is twenty-five," the driver said.

"You're not a family."

"Sure we are. I'm the father, and Donnie there is the mother, and these are our kids," he said, and they all laughed again.

What jerks. "Forty dollars."

"How about giving us a friends' discount?"

"You're not my friends. Forty dollars or turn around and leave."

He grumbled and swore under his breath as they gathered up the money. He handed it to me. "There you go, Elephant Girl. Buy yourself some peanuts." All four of them laughed at his lame joke.

"You know, you are *so* funny, like I've never heard that before."

I gave them the whole lecture about staying on the path,

staying in their car, and not chasing the elephants, and then decided to add something else.

"You need to turn your music off."

"What?"

"Elephants have very sensitive hearing. Turn it off."

He turned off the music. "Is that because they have such big ears?"

"That's part of it." The other part was that I didn't like their music any more than I liked them.

They drove off with no extra noise, and the next car glided up to the window to pay admission.

CHAPTER
Four

THE SCHOOL BUS HIT A BUMP, AND WE ALL FLEW SLIGHTLY
out of our seats to an accompaniment of screams and laughter.

"I still can't believe you're not going to the dance," Stacy
said as we settled back in.

"I still don't believe you can't believe it," I said.

"But it will be fun," Lizzy offered, leaning over the seatback
until she was almost on top of me.

"Standing in a stuffy, smelly, hot gym wearing uncomfortable clothes isn't my idea of fun."

"You'd be with *us*," Stacy said. "How could that not be fun?"

"And it's the last time we'll see each other until after the
summer," Lizzy added.

"That's not true. You know you're both welcome to come
out to the sanctuary anytime you want."

"You know we'll come out there," Stacy said. "But it's different than seeing each other at school."

"It's *better* than seeing each other at school," I said.

"For sure," Lizzy agreed, "but still, you really should come to the dance."

"Will you at least think about it?" Stacy asked.

I nodded. What I didn't say was that I was starting to have second thoughts about not going. Part of the problem was that I didn't have anything to wear.

The bus slowed down as it came up to my stop. I got to my feet and said goodbye to my friends.

"Think about the dance!" Stacy called out as I weaved my way down the aisle.

I waved over my shoulder without looking back. All the school bus kids might have heard her yelling that out. Talking in public about going to a dance seemed so personal and a little bit embarrassing. What did the boys on the bus think about me going or not going? Did they think anything about it? Were my friends the only ones sad that I wasn't going? Did anybody else even care?

The bus came to a stop, and the door opened.

"Sam, you say hello to the elephants for me," said Mrs. Shaffer, the driver.

"I will."

She said the same thing to me every day when she dropped me off. She was a nice lady, and sometimes she came to see our elephants and brought her grandchildren with her.

I went down the stairs and stepped away, and the door

closed behind me. The bus took off, and I was left behind in a cloud of dust. I watched it drive away and thought that I'd miss Mrs. Shaffer. Next year I'd be going to high school on a different bus with a different driver. I'd miss a lot of things about my school — the school I'd gone to for nine years! — and there was now less than two weeks before it would all be over. Maybe I really should try to go to the school dance.

I walked along the outer fence. Our property had two fences. The outer one kept people from looking in and from coming in. It was high, metal, and impossible to climb. The inner fence kept the elephants in. It was only four feet of concrete topped by three strands of wire. The top strand could be electrified, carrying a high enough charge to discourage an elephant from trying to go farther. We hardly ever turned the current on, partly because the electricity was expensive, and besides, our elephants didn't try to go through it. Their world and what they needed were all inside the walls.

The real obstacle wasn't the wire but the concrete wall. While it was only four feet high — low enough that a determined eight-year-old child could have climbed over it — it was too high for any elephant. Elephants don't jump, and they don't climb. Although they can be trained to climb on barrels and stand on only their front or back legs, they would hardly ever do so voluntarily.

I punched the numbers — my birth date — into the

combination lock to open up the first gate. The lock buzzed and popped open. The second gate had a key lock. I opened the gate and went through, closing it behind me.

I strolled across the yard and into the house. "Hello!" I yelled. There was no answer, and that was no surprise. My father usually wasn't indoors. There was always elephant work to be done.

I heard the TV playing in the other room. Dad liked to have background sound when he left or came in. It was on, and it was really, *really* loud. I went in to turn it down and saw a sheet of paper taped to the screen. In big letters it read, *New arrival — come to the isolation pen!*

* * *

I RODE MY BIKE AS QUICKLY AS I COULD ACROSS THE property. I startled a coyote, who gave me a sideways glance like I'd annoyed him, and a family of armadillos, who waddled away. I hadn't come across the herd, so I figured they were up by the forest or down by the pond. You hardly ever saw just one elephant. You saw all of them or none of them. They would spread out while they ate but never moved too far away to see the others.

New arrivals were put into an enclosure on the north part of the property. It was deliberately distant and isolated. That way the new elephant would have quiet time away from the herd, and if it was carrying diseases or parasites, they wouldn't spread to the other elephants. Having one sick animal was bad. Having a herd of sick animals would be much worse.

I saw a transport truck slowly bumping along the road toward me. I recognized it, and I knew who was driving it. Yes, it was Tim.

Tim's truck was specially designed for animal transportation and had been modified with cages and harnesses. It was sort of like a horse trailer that could be adapted to all sorts of animals. He was called in when an exotic animal had to be shifted from one location to another. It wasn't like you could send a tiger by UPS or FedEx. He had brought us three elephants over the years. More than just a driver, Tim was an animal lover. Whenever he was passing near our sanctuary, he'd drop by to have coffee and look at the elephants. Sometimes he would eat supper with us, and he'd slept over more than once. I knew my father enjoyed their talks. Tim said that of all the animals he transported, elephants were his favorites. How could they not be anyone's favorites?

The truck stopped, and I went up to his window.

"Good afternoon, Sammy," he said with a little tip of his cowboy hat. He, his smile, and his hat were so big, I was always surprised they fit in the cab of the truck.

"Afternoon, Tim. Good to see you."

"Good to be here, although I'm a little tired. I drove basically nonstop — nine hundred miles in fourteen hours."

"You were really moving."

"No choice. My passenger wasn't happy. He was kicking up a fuss back there."

"Young or old?" I asked.

"Come on, Sammy, how often are they young?"

Of course he was right. Young elephants are too valuable to give away.

"Old or really old?"

"Somewhere in the middle. He's a big male, about twenty-five years old. Can you do me a favor?" Tim asked. "I want you to be careful with this one."

"I'm always careful."

"No, you're not. This elephant — well, he has a story behind him. Your father will tell you."

"You could tell me. Maybe you could tell me over dinner."

"There's nothing I'd rather do than share a meal with you and Jack, but I'm going to have to eat on the run. I just got another call. I'm moving a lion from San Diego to San Francisco."

"It sounds like *you* should be the one who's careful."

"I always am." He paused. "As far as I know, the lion has never hurt anybody."

That could mean only one thing — this elephant *had* hurt somebody. I shouldn't have been surprised. Old *and* complicated is what we usually got.

"You'll be careful, right?"

"I'll be careful."

He tipped his cowboy hat, put the truck into gear, and pulled away. I pedaled off in the other direction.

Soon I could see the isolation pen. I followed along the outer fence that enclosed it. It was made of twelve-foot-tall sections of corrugated metal, painted in a dozen colors — whatever paint my father could find at the dump or had been donated — and streaks of rust had come through. There was no real strength to the fence, and an elephant could have pushed through it easily. It was intended as a visual block so that an animal inside couldn't see what was outside. Within it was the second wall, exactly the same as the inner wall that lined the entire complex — low concrete topped by wire.

The gate to the corrugated section of the fence was open. My father's truck and Doc Morgan's van were just inside. The two men were standing at the edge of the inner wall. I skidded to a stop right beside them. They both nodded at me to acknowledge I was there but didn't stop their conversation.

Then I saw the elephant. He was fifty yards away, partially hidden behind some trees. He had long tusks and he was big, although with no comparison point, I couldn't tell how big. He was, of course, gray, with darker patches on his body.

"What's that on his skin?" I asked.

"Body sores," Doc Morgan said.

"That's awful!"

'They're all over him," my father said. "I'm hoping that fresh air and sunshine will help them heal."

"That's about the only thing that will, unless you're going to let me tranquilize him," Doc Morgan said.

"He was sedated to be transported," my father said.

"And if we knew what he was sedated with and the dose, then I could figure out what he needs now. I can't believe the vet didn't send that information along," Doc Morgan said.

"I don't think it was a vet. Judging by his condition, I don't think he's seen a vet in a long time. That's why I wanted you to see him right away."

"For me to see him from any closer than this, we'll have to tranquilize him."

"You know better than I do the possible health risks and complications of tranquilizing him a second time," my father said.

"It's not only the elephant's health I'm worried about. I can't do more than a long-distance visual examination, no treatment, unless he's tranquilized and secured. Did you get me here to do an examination or sightseeing from a distance?"

"He's been through so much, I hate to put him through

anything more. Could you at least use a low dose of tranquilizer?"

"You know me well enough to know I *always* use as low a dose as possible. So, do I go ahead?"

My father nodded.

Doc Morgan went back to his van.

"Doc doesn't trust this elephant," I said.

"That's understandable. It's a combination of what we know and what we don't know."

"What do we know?"

"He's a twenty-three-year-old male, and his name is Burma."

"That's not a bad name. It used to be the name of an Asian country."

"He came from a roadside attraction where he was kept in a small pen, received very questionable medical treatment, and was probably abused."

"Is that why we've got him? Did the authorities take him away?" My father didn't answer. "Were they forced to give him up, or was there something else?"

"There was a fatality. A trainer was killed."

"He killed someone?"

My father nodded. "Crushed him."

"You always say there's a risk, that accidents can happen with large animals, especially in a small space," I said.

"This was no accident. It was very deliberate and very thorough."

"Then the man probably deserved it. He was probably the one abusing Burma."

"Possibly, but it doesn't matter. Burma was going to be euthanized if we didn't take him."

"And that's why it happened so fast?" I asked.

"There wasn't much choice. It was us or a death sentence. The world can't afford to lose any more elephants."

"Or to lose animal sanctuary owners or their daughters," Doc Morgan said as he returned. He was carrying a very large rifle — a tranquilizer gun. "Or for that matter, it can't afford to lose any vets willing to work with elephants."

"Especially ones we can afford," my father added.

"Especially those, because they are a very rare species, almost extinct," Doc Morgan agreed.

"We'll all just be careful."

"Do you think he can get along with other elephants?" I asked.

"He's a big male, so he will tend to live independently from the rest of the herd most of the time, but there's no reason he can't coexist in the same sanctuary with the others," Dad replied.

"It would be awfully good if you could take over the

adjoining property," Doc Morgan said. There was a vacant, unused, undeveloped parcel of land — about five hundred acres — on our north and east sides.

"It would be nice, if we only had a couple hundred thousand dollars to buy it. You don't have that kind of money on you, do you, Doc?" my father asked.

"I think I left that money in my other pants."

"How did he get along with the other elephants where he was before?" I asked.

"From the information I was given, I don't think he's ever even *seen* another elephant," my father said.

"Ever?"

"He was the only elephant there. He was held in solitary confinement."

"But he had to have seen some other elephants at some point . . . at least his mother."

"He could have been taken from her when he was less than twelve months old," my father said.

"That's barbaric."

"You know that's the method some trainers use to gain control over animals. The early separation breaks the animal's spirit and makes it completely dependent on the trainer."

Of course I knew that. It didn't make it any less barbaric.

"And if he can't get along with the herd?" Doc Morgan asked.

"It's a big property. He can live independently, either out in the larger area or in the isolation pen."

"The pen isn't that big," I said.

"It's almost fifteen acres. That's enormous compared to what he's used to," Dad said. "He's lived his life in a pen that wasn't as large as our barn."

"That's just so awful, so terrible, so —"

"So abusive," Dad said, cutting me off.

I stared out at the elephant. He was big and strong, and at the same time alone and fragile, and he must have been scared. And then there was a bang and a swoosh, and the elephant ran away, the tail of the tranquilizer dart that had been fired at him showing as a hint of orange feathers on his backside.

"Direct hit!" Doc Morgan said. "The animal world is lucky I use my hunting skills only for the forces of good."

Burma ran all the way to the far side of the enclosure.

"How long do we have to wait?" I asked.

"It will start to take effect within twenty minutes, but we'll have to judge the reaction to know when it's safe — well, *safer* — to enter the pen."

Five

BURMA HADN'T MOVED IN ALMOST TEN MINUTES. HE had been standing by the creek, drinking, and that was worrisome. If the drug took effect and he fell into the creek, he could drown. We were all relieved when he moved back. Now he was doing nothing except standing . . . and rocking. He was definitely rocking back and forth. The thick tree-trunk legs were starting to give way.

"What's the worst thing that can happen?" I asked Doc Morgan.

"That we didn't give him enough medication and he kills one or all of us."

"I meant for the elephant."

"Believe me, that would be the death of the elephant as well. As you know."

I guess I did. Killing a second person would remove any hope of rehabilitation.

"The potential danger for the elephant is that he could

experience a cardiac episode — a heart attack — or respiratory distress, meaning he'd stop breathing. In humans, this type of medication can result in lowered heart rate, lowered blood pressure, and of course slowing of the breathing. With an elephant, the complication is that when he goes down, the weight of the animal compresses the lungs."

"What a terrible way to die," I said.

"Probably a better way than how he lived," my father said. "I'd love to put those people in a closet for a month or so and let them know how it feels."

"You'd probably be arrested for that," Doc Morgan said.

"They're the ones who should be arrested," I snapped.

"It won't happen. There are lots of regulations around the care of exotic animals. They vary from state to state and are so confusing and poorly enforced that it's difficult to get a conviction," Doc Morgan said.

"It shouldn't be long now," my dad said.

Almost as if the elephant was listening, he swayed back and forth and then toppled over onto his side, throwing up a cloud of dust.

"Let's get in there!" Doc Morgan ordered.

The gate had already been unlocked; the chain removed for us to enter. As we raced forward, Dad stopped me with a hand on my shoulder.

"Maybe you should wait out here," he said.

"If it's too dangerous for me, it's too dangerous for the two of you."

"She has a point," Doc Morgan said.

"Besides, if there's a problem, I can easily outrun both of you."

"She has a second point," Doc Morgan said.

"Please?" I gave my father a pleading, pathetic look.

"You are hard to say no to. Come on," he said.

To prove my point, I ran in faster than the two of them. To be fair, they were both carrying equipment needed for the examination. And maybe getting there sooner wasn't smarter. I slowed down and let them go first.

"Get his trunk extended to help with respiration!" Doc Morgan ordered.

I hesitated for a split second, then reached out and touched the trunk. If there was going to be a problem, it would happen right now. There was nothing, no reaction. That was good — or terribly bad. Had he stopped breathing? Was his heart still pumping? I couldn't tell.

I grabbed the trunk and pulled it out straight as far as it would go. Then I heard air going in and out. Burma was breathing. Thank goodness.

Then I caught sight of one brown eye. It was watching me. It looked terrified. How could the elephant not be terrified?

"It's all right," I said. I slowly moved my hand so that it

was cupped around the eye, offering it shade from the bright sunlight.

"I was just going to suggest that you cover the eye with a piece of cloth to protect it," Doc Morgan said.

"I am protecting it, but I don't want to cover it completely. That would be even scarier . . . and you're scared, aren't you, big guy?"

"You're right. I am a little scared," Doc Morgan said.

"I was talking to the *really* big guy."

"I thought you were referring to the extra fifteen pounds I've packed on."

"He can see and hear, right?" I asked.

"And smell and feel. He just can't move. He might go deeper under the drugs, but even then, keep talking. Hearing is the last sense to go, because it's passive."

Keeping one hand cupped over the top of the eye, I moved closer to the ear — not so he could hear me better but because right behind the ear was the tender spot where most elephants liked to be rubbed. If he sensed touch, I could communicate with him that way.

"It's all right. We're all just trying to help you." I scratched right behind the ear. "I hope that feels good. You have to know that you're among friends here. Are you all right being called Burma? It's a nice name. My name is Sam. Some people call me Elephant Girl."

"I call her Samantha," my dad said. "Or Sweetie."

"And you can call him J-Dog," I said.

"J-Dog?" Doc Morgan asked.

"Long story," Dad said.

I turned back to Burma. "We know you're not well, so the doctor is examining you. He'll draw some blood for testing."

"Already done that," Doc Morgan said. He was holding a large vial of dark red liquid.

"What do you think in general?" my father asked.

"The skin patches are fungal. You're right: the sun and open air will help, and I'm going to apply a topical balm. That should clear it up in a week or so."

"Good."

"There's an infection in the back right ankle. It looks like the place where a chain was attached. It was too small — likely it wasn't adjusted when the elephant grew. I'll apply a topical antibiotic cream and give him an antibiotic injection."

"A double approach seems prudent," Dad agreed.

"Especially since it's not like we're going to be tranquilizing him again in the immediate future. I'm going to go with a wide-spectrum antibiotic to assist with the skin infection. I'm pretty sure he has parasites as well, and I want those eliminated."

He pulled a big plastic bottle out of his bag and handed it to my father. "Slather this on wherever you see the skin rash."

"But what about the side that's on the ground?" I asked. "The side we can't get to?"

"Unless one of us is going to pick him up and roll him over, I think we're going to let those be treated by air and sun, with a little help from the antibiotic."

Doc Morgan pulled out another container, opened the top, and with his gloved fingers applied clear goop to the wound on the foot. Next he filled a big syringe with a clear liquid and injected it behind the ear.

"Can you tell us anything else right now?" my father asked.

"His muscle tone is poor, and he's definitely underweight."

"I thought so too," Dad said. "Probably he was underfed and denied exercise. That can be corrected. How about the teeth?"

Doc Morgan shifted over and peeled away the lips to reveal the elephant's teeth. "They're worn down but within acceptable standards for an elephant this age. This is probably only his second or third set."

I knew that elephants get six sets of molars during their lifetime. They never need to go to the dentist because when one set wears down, another one is on its way.

Doc pulled his stethoscope out of his bag and put the two plastic pieces in his ears. He put the other part against the elephant's side, moved it around, and —

"This is not good."

"What's not good?" I asked.

"His heart rate is down . . . dramatically. Do you hear the way he's breathing?"

"I thought the breathing rate was slowing," my father confirmed.

Now I was paying attention. Burma's breathing was shallower than before.

"You have to do something!" I exclaimed.

"I am." Doc Morgan rummaged around in his bag and pulled out a big hypodermic needle, bigger than the one he had used to draw blood. He took out another bottle.

"What are you doing?" my father asked.

"I'm going to give him a shot of adrenaline," Doc said as he filled the hypodermic from the bottle. "You two have to get out of here."

"I'm not leaving," I said.

"We can help."

"You can help by taking my bag, getting out of here, and getting out of my way when I run."

We hesitated.

"This will revive him. It could work really fast, potentially within seconds. Get out of here. Now!"

We both got to our feet. I reached back and grabbed the bag. It was surprisingly heavy and awkward to carry. As we ran, I looked back over my shoulder to see what the vet was doing. With two hands, he drove the hypodermic needle into the elephant's side.

Doc Morgan jumped up and took off, the now-empty needle in his hand. He was moving fast, gaining on us. That gave me a reason to move even faster.

I heard movement and glanced back again. The big elephant started to move his legs and then staggered to his feet. He looked uneasy, as if he was going to topple over.

"A little more speed!" Doc Morgan yelled, coming up right beside us and grabbing his bag from my hands.

Together the three of us reached the gate, and the two men let me through first. I turned around and looked back. The elephant was not only up but charging in our direction.

Doc Morgan and my dad came through, and my dad slammed the gate shut and chained it in place. Burma wasn't that close, but I was closer than I'd ever been to a charging bull elephant.

"How much did you give him?" my father asked.

"Possibly more than I should have. I just guessed. I gave him enough to kill a horse but, luckily, enough to save an elephant."

Burma slowed down from a run to a trot to a walk and then stopped altogether. He shook his head repeatedly and then turned to look at us with one eye. I couldn't tell if he was trying to remember who had saved him or who had almost killed him. Either way, he was an elephant and he wasn't going to forget what had happened. Neither would I.

CHAPTER
Six

"OKAY, ALL THE PAPERS HAVE BEEN SIGNED," JOYCE SAID.

"Thanks for your help in finalizing this," Dad said.

"So Burma is now officially ours?" I asked.

"Lock, stock, and history," Joyce said.

"The history is the reason we have him," my dad replied. "And by the way, thanks for making dinner."

Joyce had come over after work to bring the legal papers. She had correctly guessed that we had been so occupied that we hadn't eaten. She'd brought some groceries with her and had rummaged through our fridge and cupboards, and there was a meal waiting for us when we walked in. She'd made meals for us before, and I had to admit — at least to myself — that she was a good cook. Maybe it was just that anything I didn't have to fix tasted good.

"I should get going," Dad said.

"Going where?" Joyce asked.

"I'm going to spend the evening and night by Burma."

He always did that when we had a new animal. She'd never been here for a new animal, so she didn't know that.

"Okay, well, you get going and I'll clean up," Joyce offered.

"I can do it. You should get going too," I said.

My father got to his feet and came to my side. "I'll have my phone on, so just call if you need me."

"Good to know, in case there are any boogeymen or ghosts that I need you to save me from."

"I'm always there to save you, even if you don't need to be saved." He gave me a kiss on the forehead. "See you in the morning."

That was so true. He always was there for me.

Joyce followed him to the door. They exchanged some words that I couldn't hear. Then she took his hand and he bent down and they kissed. I knew they kissed and stuff, but they were usually careful not to do anything in front of me. I didn't know if that was his idea or hers, but I was grateful. They continued to speak quietly, kissed once more. I couldn't deny that she did seem to make him happy.

Dad's gear was in a pack by the front door. He grabbed it, gave me a wave and a smile, and left. I heard the engine starting and the truck driving away. Finally it was just me and Joyce — and the awkward silence in the room.

Joyce started clearing away the dishes.

"I said I'll take care of it," I said.

"More hands make for quicker work."

I wanted her to go home, but I didn't really want to do the dishes by myself. Lazy won. Besides, I actually did want to talk to her. I'd thought this through and argued with myself both ways, but in the end, she was the only person I could turn to.

"Thanks." I got up and collected more dishes.

She ran water into the sink and squeezed in some dish soap, swirling the suds around with her hands. How could her nails always be so perfect?

"You're very brave," she said.

"Dishes aren't that scary."

She laughed. Louder than that joke merited. "I meant about staying alone. There's no way I would have been brave enough to stay in a house by myself when I was thirteen or fourteen, or even a little older."

For a second, I thought about taking a shot at her age, something about how dinosaurs were really scary, but I didn't. It was counterproductive to try to annoy somebody you wanted a favor from.

"I'm not really that brave. I'm locked in a house that's surrounded by two walls. One of them has electric current. I have a herd of guard elephants inside the fence. I'd be more worried if I were you, driving home at night."

"That's sweet of you to worry about me, but I really need to get home, because I have an early court date tomorrow."

"I didn't mean that I wanted you to sleep over—"

She laughed. "Don't worry. I'm going to leave right after the dishes, I promise."

She washed, and I dried and put things away. There was silence, but it was a little less awkward. It was my turn to break it.

"Could I ask you a question?"

"Of course."

"It's just—well, I was thinking about maybe going to the graduation dance next week."

"That's wonderful!" she exclaimed. "What made you change your mind?"

"I just thought it would be good to spend some time with my friends, that's all."

She nodded but didn't say anything.

"But now my father is going to be pretty busy with the new elephant."

"I'd be happy to be here more to help, or to give you a ride to and from the dance," she said.

"Thanks for the offer, but I can get a ride. It's just . . . maybe I shouldn't even ask."

She turned away from the sink and toward me. "Ask away."

"It's just that it would take a lot of time, and I know you're busy with that trial and all."

"Not so busy that I can't find time for you."

That was, well, sweet. It made me suspicious. There'd been more than one girlfriend who thought the best way to my father's heart was through me.

"So what can I do?" she said.

"I was wondering, do you think you could help me — you know, go with me — to pick out something that I could wear to the dance?"

"You want me to go dress shopping with you?"

Hearing those words said out loud made the whole thing sound even stranger, but I nodded ever so slightly.

"Of course I will! Thank you so much for asking me!" She threw her arms around me. I could feel her soapy wet hands on my back. "We'll find you the perfect thing to wear, and your hair . . . what about your hair?"

"Um, I thought I'd wash it."

She let go of me. "Your friends are all getting their hair done, aren't they?"

I nodded. Some were even getting their fingernails and toenails done.

"If you'd like, I can arrange an appointment with my

stylist," she said. "Unless you have somebody else you normally go to."

"Nobody regular." It was usually whoever was taking the next customer at Supercuts.

She reached over and removed my cap. She'd taken me so much by surprise that I hadn't even tried to stop her. "You have such wonderful hair."

"I do?" I felt embarrassed.

"It's thick and full and has a natural curl. I wish my hair had that curl."

Her hair was always done nicely. That was actually one of the things I sort of disliked about her.

"How about if I pick you up right after school tomorrow?" Joyce asked.

"I'm not sure. With the new elephant and all, my father might need me here."

"The dance is coming up fast," she said. "Your hair probably should wait until next Friday, right after school — I'll schedule an appointment for you — but I think we should look for the dress as soon as possible. I'll be waiting outside your school at the end of the day tomorrow. Just look for my car."

"That would be nice. Thanks." I felt such a sense of relief — at least about the dress. There was still one other area that had me worried. "I have one more question."

"I'm sure you have lots of questions about what we'll —"

"It's about Burma."

She looked down. "Your father is probably a much better person to ask than me."

"It's more of a legal question. What do you think about us taking in this elephant?"

"It sounds like you're a little worried," she said.

"Do you think it was a good idea?"

"I'm just a volunteer around here."

"But you're also a lawyer. You aren't happy about this elephant being here, are you?"

She looked uncomfortable.

"Please, I just want to know more about what happened."

She shrugged. "I know Jack will tell you all of this, so it's not like I'm doing anything wrong in telling you."

"Thank you."

"You know this elephant comes with a lot of history."

"Like Dad said, we only get elephants that have a history."

"This one has *more* history."

"So much history that you don't think we should have taken him?"

Joyce looked like she wanted to answer, but she didn't.

"I really want to know your opinion," I said. "Please. You said to me if there was ever anything I wanted to talk about, I could talk to you. I want to talk about this."

She slowly nodded. She still didn't look happy, but I'd

pretty well given her no choice. "As a lover of elephants, I understand why your father took him in," she said. "But as a lawyer, I see the potential for problems with liability."

"He'll be careful," I said.

"I know he will, that both of you will, but the best prediction of future behavior is past behavior."

"Isn't everybody entitled to one mistake?" I asked.

"One mistake, yes. Three is two mistakes too many."

"Three?"

"Maybe I shouldn't have said anything. I should leave this to your father."

"You started, so you need to finish."

Again she hesitated before speaking. "There was another trainer, two years ago. Burma threw him against a wall and broke his arm."

"And the third?" I asked.

"It was a visitor to the amusement park," Joyce said. "A ten-year-old girl."

Somehow it being a little girl made whatever she was going to say that much worse.

"Burma stuck his trunk through the bars and pushed her backward with such force that she fell over and struck her head."

"She should never have been allowed that close to the bars," I retorted. "We don't let people get that close."

"I don't know all the circumstances, but if somebody were to get out of their car here, what would happen?" Joyce asked.

"We don't let cars go in the isolation pen."

"And is that where he's going to spend the rest of his life?" she asked.

"No, of course not. Besides, you know we always tell the visitors to stay in their vehicles."

"None of which would matter to a judge. If a visitor to the park were injured, your father would be sued. If the animal had a history of violence — like this one — then he could be successfully sued, and there could also be criminal charges of reckless endangerment."

"The elephant would be charged?"

"Your father would be charged."

"That doesn't make sense."

"From a legal position, it makes perfect sense. He would have created a situation in which a person is placed at substantial risk of death or serious injury. He would have, in essence, done nothing to prevent the problem, which is what is meant by reckless endangerment. A conviction could bring a jail term from two to seven years."

"That could happen?" I gasped.

"Very possibly. Regardless, even if criminal charges were not brought or a conviction obtained, the lawsuit would undoubtedly be successful, and you would lose the sanctuary."

I felt stunned. How could that happen? It wasn't that I didn't believe her — I didn't want to believe her.

"You've got to tell my dad all of this."

"I've told your father everything that I said to you just now, and he said there was no choice."

"Of course there was a choice. He could have said . . . no, I guess he couldn't have said no, if it meant Burma was going to be put down," I said.

"You have to think of your sanctuary as a lifeboat," she said.

"I don't understand."

"In a sea of uncertainty, you have provided a lifeboat for eleven elephants."

I couldn't help picturing a herd of elephants in a lifeboat wearing oversize life jackets. I almost giggled.

"There is only so much space in the boat. By taking in this latest elephant, you risk the lives of the others already in the boat."

That thought sank in, and there was no humor involved. "I understand."

"Good. Now if only your father understood that concept a little better. You've been lucky so far, but you don't want to depend on luck forever."

"I can talk to him."

"Do you think he'll listen?" Joyce asked. "Do you think he'd turn the new elephant away now that it's already here?"

I shook my head. "Of course not, but I can try to convince him to be more careful and maybe think harder the next time."

She finished up the last of the dishes and pulled the stopper from the drain.

"I think I need to ask you a question too," Joyce said.

"Is it a legal question?" I asked.

"No, it's — you're joking."

"Apparently badly. I've been told I have my father's sense of humor."

"It's actually about your father." Again a long pause. "We've been dating for around six months."

I hadn't known the exact length of time because I think it had sort of started before I knew it had. I did know she'd been around longer than any of his other girlfriends.

"He and I have been talking about where we're going in our relationship."

I didn't like where any of this was going.

"We've been talking, nothing definite, but talking about where things are heading."

"What does that mean?"

"We're just trying to figure it out. Neither of us is getting any younger."

I bit my tongue rather than blurt out something mean about her age.

"And I guess because we're not kids, we're talking about what might happen eventually," she said.

I really didn't like this at all.

"I guess you just hoped at some point I'd leave," she said.

How could she possibly have known what I'd been thinking?

"I'm a lawyer, so I have to be able to read people," she said, as if she'd been reading my mind. "Your father is a wonderful person — you know that — but he thinks you'll be fine with anything we decide. I told him I was glad he can read elephants better than he can read people, because I know you have some doubts."

I couldn't stop myself from laughing.

"I'm assuming he hasn't mentioned any of this to you."

I shook my head.

"I'm sorry about that. He should have. I've told him that because we're not just a couple, because there are three of us, anything that's going to happen moving forward has to be done with your knowledge . . . and agreement."

"You're looking for my permission?" I asked. I was more shocked by this than by the idea of them "moving forward."

"I don't know if 'permission' is the right word. It's important for you to be aware of what's happening, to be part of the discussion along the way."

"You're both adults, so you can decide what you want to do. It's not up to me."

"Look, I understand," Joyce said. "I understand that you're protective of your father. Believe me, I understand how you feel. I understand *completely*."

"What is it that you think you understand?" I asked. How did she think she could possibly understand how I felt?

She let out a sigh. "I don't talk about this much, but my mother died when I was nine."

"I didn't know that. I'm sorry."

"I know your situation was different. You were so much younger —"

"A lot younger."

She nodded and looked appropriately sad, the way people always looked when they found out. I *hated* that look.

"But I still think I know some of what you're feeling."

Thank goodness she'd put in that word *some*, or I would have screamed.

"I was worried about the people my father dated. There were some real losers. Funny, he was a smart man about most things, but not things like that," she said.

I laughed. "That does sound like my dad. He's one of the smartest dumb people I've ever known."

"He's a very smart man, but he's so gentle and sweet and kind, and sort of innocent. It would be nice if he did understand people the way he understands elephants."

"Sometimes he forgets they're people and starts thinking they're like elephants."

"Even elephants can be bad."

"Or abused to make them bad," I said. I was still trying to defend Burma, though I hardly knew him and wasn't even sure I wanted him around.

"Or abused," she agreed. "As a criminal lawyer, I spend a lot of time with people who have committed crimes."

"Not a very nice crowd," I said.

"Not the nicest. I stopped being surprised a long time ago about how many of the people I defend have suffered horrific family situations and gone through terrible things."

"Like Burma."

"You may find this hard to believe, but even what he went through is nothing compared to what I've seen with some people."

"That is hard to believe," I said.

"Knowing the backstory helps us understand why they act the way they do, but that doesn't mean we can change the way they will act in the future."

I had the same concern about Burma. It made me anxious to think that Dad was out there alone with him, even if they were on opposite sides of the fence.

"Getting back to what we were talking about, I was worried that the women who wanted to date my father were also trying to replace my mother," she said.

"You can't replace what you've never had," I said, my voice barely a whisper. I felt close to tears.

She placed a hand on my shoulder. At least it was wiped dry now. "I have some pretty clear memories of my mother, but of course, you couldn't possibly remember yours."

I shook my head. "We have some pictures of her." They were in our cedar chest. I hadn't looked at them in a long time, but it was good to know they were there. It made her more real — at least as real as pictures ever could.

"Your father told me about the pictures. He also told me there's not one picture of you and your mother together."

"There wasn't time," I said, my voice barely a whisper. I bit down on my bottom lip to keep myself from crying. How did causing pain to yourself stop tears? I let out a big sigh.

"I'll say this again. If you ever want to talk about things, girl things, things you can't talk to your father about, you can call me. Even if I'm not here or not dating your father anymore or a volunteer here at the sanctuary anymore."

"I like you being a volunteer." I paused. "I even like you dating him."

"Thank you for saying that."

I was surprised that I'd said that, and even more surprised that I really meant it. When did that happen? Where had those feelings come from so suddenly?

"Then for now, your father and I will continue to date. Nothing more for now. I'll tell him that we talked but not all of what we talked about . . . if that's okay with you."

I nodded.

"Nothing is going to happen too fast or without you knowing. Life can throw us surprises that we can't see coming. Terrible surprises. Nobody is going to surprise you about things that are happening between Jack and me."

"Thank you."

"In the meantime, we have a dress to buy for you, and you have a new elephant to be careful around," she said.

"I'm not sure which of the two scares me more."

She laughed. "I promise you we'll find the right dress. You have to promise me you'll watch out for yourself and your father, okay?"

"I can do that."

I couldn't help wondering what we had gotten ourselves into. And I didn't mean just with the new elephant.

CHAPTER

Seven

MY DRESS WAS RED WITH LITTLE GOLD FLECKS. IT WAS floor-length because Stacy's and Lizzy's dresses were both floor-length. I liked the feel of it, soft and silky, and it sort of shimmered when I moved.

It hadn't been the first or the second or even the tenth one I'd tried on. Coming out of that dressing room wearing the first one had been, well, uncomfortable, but somehow Joyce had made me feel okay. In the end, the ritual had gotten to be almost fun, almost playful. When I tried this one on, I was pretty sure it was the one, and the way Joyce and the saleswoman reacted confirmed it.

After we bought the dress — and some shoes to match — we had a late dinner at a really nice restaurant. We talked about the elephants and TV and a movie we'd both seen and her first school dance, and about her becoming a lawyer and how I wanted to be a vet. It was nice and easy and nothing about it seemed awkward or strange. She said we should do this regularly, and I didn't argue.

Now I hesitated at my bedroom door, almost afraid to go out into the living room, but it was either go to the dance or wait in here all night. It was time.

"My goodness, you are beautiful!" Joyce gushed.

"As opposed to how I usually look?"

"You know that's not what I meant — different from your usual dirty jeans and your hair hidden under a baseball cap."

"I was thinking about wearing my baseball cap."

"And risk ruining that beautiful hair? Not a chance."

I'd had my hair done right after school. Joyce had driven me to the salon and then back home again. It had been nice and relaxing and sort of indulgent to have my hair washed and cut. The stylist was really friendly, and she had such nice things to say about Joyce — she'd known her for years. When we left, my hair was sort of piled up and curled and there was even some hairspray holding it in place.

"I'll burn your hat before I let you wear it tonight!" Joyce finished.

A week ago, I would have grabbed my hat and put it on just to defy her. Tonight I didn't. I walked over to the mirror on the wall.

"I don't look too stupid, right?" I asked.

"You look beautiful!"

"Well, I *feel* stupid."

"You're feeling that way because you look different. That's going to throw some people, because different always does. I just figure that any girl who isn't afraid of eleven animals weighing thousands of pounds shouldn't be afraid of what a bunch of eighth-grade boys think."

"I don't care about what they think," I protested.

"You must care a little, or you wouldn't be going to the dance to begin with."

"Maybe I shouldn't be —"

"You're going. Your friends are expecting you, and you want to spend time with them, right? Even if the boys don't matter."

"I did — I mean, I do."

"And I think you made the right decision about wearing flats instead of heels," she said.

The shoes were almost the identical color of my dress and were leather and fancy. Much fancier than anything I'd ever owned before.

"Heels are stupid. I don't know how anybody gets around in high heels," I said.

"You learn," Joyce said, looking down at her mile-high heels.

"I didn't mean *you* shouldn't wear them," I said, surprised that I was concerned about offending her.

"With your father being so tall, these help to even things up a bit. Besides, you don't want to tower over the boys too much when you're dancing."

"I don't know if I'll be doing any dancing," I said.

"You'll be dancing. Just be careful they don't step on your toes too often. When are you being picked up?" Joyce asked.

"Stacy and her parents will be here in about thirty minutes."

I heard the front door open, and my father walked into the room. He gasped.

"You look . . . you look . . ."

"I think we've agreed on the words 'different' and 'beautiful,'" I said.

"I was going to say you look so much like your mother."

I hadn't expected that.

"I think there's a picture of her with her hair up the same way," he said.

I hadn't been in the cedar chest in such a long time that I hardly remembered what she looked like, but I did remember she was pretty. Maybe it was time to look again — even if it did make me a little sad. It always made me happy in a different way.

"It's uncanny. I guess I just hadn't thought about the resemblance, and as you get older, you grow into looking more like her."

"I'm certainly glad I don't grow into looking like *you*, Jackie Boy," I said.

"As far as I can tell, the only thing the two of you share is temperament," Joyce said. "I'm not sure which of you is the more stubborn."

My father and I pointed at each other.

"We should take some pictures of you," Joyce said.

"We have lots of pictures," I said.

"None of you dressed up, and very few that don't feature an elephant. You have thirty minutes, and I have a really good camera — so let's just do it."

"Um . . . could I excuse myself for a minute? I have to make a phone call," Dad said.

What phone call couldn't wait a few minutes? "Who are you calling, and why do you have to excuse yourself to make the call?" I asked.

"It's nothing."

"If it's nothing, then answer my questions . . . please."

"I'm just going to give Doc Morgan a call."

"About what?"

"It's not important," he said.

"If it wasn't important, you wouldn't be calling him on a Friday night," I argued.

He hesitated. "Look, I'm just a little worried, I repeat *a little* worried, about Daisy Mae."

"What's wrong with her?"

"Nothing. It's just that she just seems a bit *off.*"

"Off?" Joyce asked.

"She's lower-energy than usual, she seems a little listless."

"She is twenty-one months pregnant," Joyce offered. "Doesn't she deserve to be a little listless?"

"If you're worried, then maybe I should—"

"You're going to the dance!" my father declared, so forcefully that he surprised me. "I'm sure Joyce is right."

Because she's a lawyer and you're an elephant expert, I thought but didn't say.

"What I was going to say, before I was interrupted, was that I should go out and see Daisy Mae before I leave," I said.

"Oh, that would be all right," he said.

"But maybe *you're* right, and I shouldn't go to the dance."

"You're going to the dance," he said again. Not as loud this time, but still determined.

"I won't enjoy myself if I'm worried about her."

"Look, how about you go, and I promise if there's anything more, I'll let you know right away," he said.

"Promise?"

"Promise," he said.

That was all I needed. My father's word was as good as gold. "Thank you. Maybe I'll just go and have a look at her now."

"They're on the far side of the property," he said. "You're being picked up soon, and we haven't taken pictures yet."

He was right.

"Besides, you going out there dressed like that, smelling like that, might confuse the elephants so much they'd stampede."

I knew he was just joking about spooking the elephants, but the last thing I wanted to do tonight was to smell like an elephant. Elephant Girl wasn't going to the dance; *I* was.

There was a bottle of perfume from forever ago tucked away in the back of the bathroom cabinet. When I was little, I asked my father about it, and he told me it had belonged to my mother. I had opened the top and smelled it. Today I put some on for the first time. I smelled good. I smelled like my mother.

"Fine, I'll go, but remember, if there's anything, you let me know. I have my phone with me, and I'll keep it on."

"Guaranteed. You'll know if anything happens."

* * *

THE MUSIC WAS SO LOUD THAT I COULD HARDLY HEAR myself talk, let alone anybody else. I wanted the DJ to turn it down at least a little, but I wasn't going to be the one to say it was too loud. There was only one couple dancing—Donnie and Dawn. They'd been dating since preschool—for ages, anyway—and everyone expected they'd get married someday and have two kids and name them Donnie Junior and Little Dawn. But nobody else was dancing. The boys were all clustered on one side of the floor and the girls were on the other side and nobody seemed brave enough to cross the open divide in the middle.

"Doesn't the gym look wonderful?" Lizzy yelled.

I shrugged. "It's about the same as usual, except louder and darker."

"But what about the balloons and streamers and signs?"

I suddenly remembered that Lizzy had been in charge of the dance decorations committee. "They really add to the atmosphere," I yelled back. "It's really lovely!"

One song ended, and before the next started, there was a brief silence. It sounded so good.

I hadn't told my friends about Daisy Mae, but that hadn't stopped me from thinking about her. I knew my father would keep his promise. No news was good news.

Another song came on, much quieter. Somebody had turned down the volume. Thank goodness.

"Your dress is beautiful!" Stacy exclaimed.

"So are both of yours." Stacy was all in gold, and Lizzy's had blue and green flowers. They both had their hair up the same way I had mine. Stacy was balancing uneasily on really high heels. A couple of times, I thought she was going to topple over.

"Everybody looks so grown up," Lizzy said.

"Well, at least the girls look grown up," I responded.

"You're right; the boys still look like, well, *boys*," Stacy said.

A couple of boys had suits that actually fit, but most were lost inside jackets that were too big, probably borrowed from their fathers. They had badly tied ties, and many had on sneakers with their dress pants. Apparently suits and jackets were easier to borrow than dress shoes.

"When I heard you got a new elephant, I thought there was no way you were going to show up tonight," Stacy said.

"Not to mention getting a new dress and having your hair done. It looks wonderful."

I shrugged. I felt embarrassed.

"And you're wearing makeup," Lizzy said.

"A little bit."

Joyce had helped me do my makeup. Actually, she did it. She was careful not to put on too much, and I was grateful. She had bought me a couple of things — lipstick and mascara and some foundation — but she'd also used some of her own makeup. It had been strange having her put it on me, but nice, too.

"How is the new elephant doing?" Stacy asked.

"His name is Burma. We're taking it slow and spending a lot of time with him."

My father was still sleeping beside the isolation pen, and I'd sat and talked to Burma when Dad had to be elsewhere. He'd turned down some shifts at the diner, which meant money we really couldn't afford to lose, but it was part of Burma's rehabilitation to be in the company of caring humans as much as possible.

Yesterday after I sat there by myself for a few hours in silence, Burma came closer than he'd ever come before. I offered him an apple through the fence. He moved really close, so close I thought he was going to take it, then suddenly retreated. He did that again and again, coming closer each time and then moving away. Finally, about the fifth time, we both reached out — arm and trunk — and he took the apple. He was so gentle. I hadn't told my father about hand-feeding Burma because I figured he'd worry.

"Hi, girls." Brendan had come up to us. I wasn't surprised that he was the one brave enough to cross the floor. Brave and stupid were often close cousins, and he had never been guilty of being too smart. He could be loud and as obnoxious as any of the other guys, but he was never mean-spirited. He was a goof, but a nice goof.

He tried to make conversation, which was hard over the music and his obvious nervousness. Why was he so nervous? We'd all known one another since kindergarten. He was practically swimming in his oversize jacket, and there was sweat dripping down the sides of his face. To top it off, he was wearing enough after-shave to prepare for the first few years when he did actually start to shave.

"You look different!" he yelled at me while Stacy and Lizzy looked on.

"Unfortunately, you don't!" Those words popped out, and I almost instantly felt bad.

"What?"

Good thing he hadn't heard me. "Nothing."

"Do you want to dance?"

"With you?" I asked.

"Who else?"

"Do you even know how to dance?"

He shook his head. "Not really. How about if you lead?"

I laughed.

"Well?"

I thought about what Joyce had said. "If you promise not to step on my toes."

"I don't like to make promises that I can't keep. Come on." He offered me his hand, and I took it. He led me out into the middle of the almost-empty floor until we were standing beside Donnie and Dawn. He put his arm around me, and we began to dance — okay, we began to shuffle.

"I didn't think you were coming to the dance," he said.

"Neither did I."

"What changed your mind?"

"I thought I might have the chance to dance with you," I said.

He leaned back, and his eyes widened. "Really?"

"Of course not, you idiot."

"Oh, of course," he stammered. He looked embarrassed, and I felt bad again. Why was I being so hard on him? Maybe he wasn't the only one who was nervous.

I noticed that three more couples had come onto the dance floor. Somehow us being out there had signaled that it was safe.

"But I'm glad you asked me to dance," I said.

"I'm glad you said yes. You look really nice. I don't think I've ever seen you in a dress before."

"What did you expect me to wear, my jeans and baseball cap?"

"That's what I'm used to seeing you in." He paused. "Actually, you're about the only girl who can pull off wearing a baseball cap and make it look good."

"Yeah, right."

"No, I mean it," he said.

The music ended, and he kept shuffling. "I think the dance is over."

"Oh, of course, sorry." He let go of me. "Maybe we could have another dance later on."

"That might be—"

I caught sight of Joyce standing in the doorway, beside our principal, Mrs. Wexler. Dad hadn't called; he'd sent Joyce. That could only mean something bad. Was it Daisy Mae, or was it my father?

"CAN YOU DRIVE ANY FASTER?" I ASKED.

"Not unless I want to put us in the ditch," Joyce said.

"Okay, sure, you're right." I took a deep breath and tried to calm down. "Thanks for coming to get me."

"I knew you'd need a ride back, and I wanted to tell you in person."

"And thanks for telling me right away that my father was all right."

"I knew you'd be worried about Daisy Mae, but your first thought would be that something had happened to your father," Joyce said.

"How did you know that?"

"I know from my own life that when you've lost one parent, you're always one parent away from being an orphan. I remember what it was like."

"How bad is Daisy Mae?" I asked.

"I'm a lawyer, so I'm not the best person to ask."

"It must be bad, or Dad wouldn't have sent you to get me."

She didn't answer, which really was an answer in itself.

"Can you tell me what you do know?"

"Doc thinks that the baby might be coming early."

"But it's not even that early. Humans have premature babies all the time. I was three weeks early."

"I think it's more than that," Joyce said. "Doc said her blood pressure was down, and there was some concern about heart rate."

"Hers or the baby's?"

"I'm not sure. They were talking fast and in medical terms, and I'm afraid I just got lost. And it was a bit unnerving, the way all the other elephants crowded around."

"They were crowding you?"

"Not just me, but Doc Morgan as well. Especially Trixie. As if she were trying to get between us and Daisy Mae."

I knew Trixie was trying to protect Daisy Mae, or maybe to protect the baby that she knew was on the way.

"Trixie seemed okay with your father being there, but nobody else."

"That makes sense. She sees him as a member of the herd, so Daisy Mae doesn't need to be protected from him. Trixie would see him as offering protection," I explained.

"They see you that way too," she said. "You're one of them."

"That's why I need to be there. I can help."

"What do you do for a premature elephant?" Joyce asked.

"I'm not sure."

"It's not like you can put them into an incubator. It's not like you have an intensive-care unit — Wait. I shouldn't be saying any of this. I guess I'm worried too and not thinking straight. This could all mean nothing except a little baby elephant coming early."

The headlights outlined the fence around our property. We came up to the entrance, and I took the remote from the dashboard and hit the button to open the outside gate. The inside gate was already open, and we rolled right through. I closed the outer one behind us.

"I'll drive you to the house to get changed," Joyce said.

"Just drive me to where they are."

"But your dress — your shoes will get ruined."

"I can go barefoot, and the dress doesn't matter. Just get me to —"

The elephants were straight ahead, caught in the glare of the headlights from my father's truck and Doc Morgan's van.

"Oh, look, she's resting," Joyce said.

"Resting? What do you —" And then I saw Daisy Mae between the legs of the others. She was on the ground.

"She must be getting ready to give birth," Joyce said.

"Elephants give birth standing up."

"But that is her, right? That is her, lying down?"

It was her. There are only a few reasons an elephant would ever be on the ground like that, and most of them aren't good.

CHAPTER
Eight

I JUMPED OUT OF THE CAR ALMOST BEFORE IT HAD stopped. I took a few steps and kicked off my fancy shoes. Daisy Mae was down on her side, her legs pointing toward me, surrounded by the rest of the elephants. Bacca was pressed right against her, holding his mother's tail in his trunk. My dad looked up at me. His expression — upset, anguished, worried — scared me.

"Tell me what's happening, please," I pleaded.

"She's in distress," Doc Morgan said. "Her breathing is shallow and slow, and her heart rate is fluctuating wildly."

"And the baby?" Joyce asked.

"Its heart rate is equally erratic."

"What can you do?" I asked.

"We've given her medication to raise her blood pressure, but the breathing is the big problem," Doc Morgan said.

"She has to get up or at least sit up," Dad said. "But there's no way of making her do that."

"What about the tractor? We could push against her back and . . . that wouldn't work, would it?"

"It would just stress her more. I'd worry about causing internal bleeding or breaking bones," Doc Morgan said.

"Not to mention what it would do to the baby," Dad added.

"Can you save her?"

"I don't know," Doc Morgan said.

"Can you save the baby?" Dad asked.

"We can only save the baby by saving Daisy Mae. I don't have the knowledge or the equipment to do an emergency caesarean section."

"So what do we do?" I asked.

"We wait and hope and maybe even pray a little," my dad said.

I left the two men and circled around to Daisy Mae's head, giving Bacca a reassuring word and a pat on the side as I passed. As I got close, Daisy Mae followed me with her eye.

"I know you're scared," I whispered in her ear. "I'm scared too."

In response, her ear flapped slightly, as if she was letting me know she not only heard but understood.

"We're all here for you. We're trying to help you and help your baby."

I wanted to tell her it was going to be all right, but I didn't know that, and I couldn't bring myself to lie to her. I pressed myself against her, laying my head right beside her ear. I reached up and scratched her in her special spot behind the ear. It was the only thing I could do.

* * *

MY EYES POPPED OPEN, BUT I COULD MAKE NO SENSE OF my surroundings. There was a horn blaring and I was outside wearing a dress, and the sun was just starting to peek over the horizon. It was like a bad dream. And then I remembered. It was worse than a dream; it was a nightmare. I was near our house, surrounded by elephants. Daisy Mae was still on her side, and my father and Doc Morgan stood over her.

I got to my feet. My dress was wet from the morning dew. In the background, the horn was still sounding, long and loud. Whoever it was, they were certainly persistent.

"How is she?" I asked.

Doc Morgan shook his head.

"Is she . . . is she . . ."

"She's alive, but just barely," my dad said.

"Can't we do *anything*?"

"She at least deserves to have quiet," Dad said. "I'll go to the gate and tell those people, whoever they are, to shove off—"

"Let me go," I said. "I'll take care of it."

I didn't want my father to go because I wasn't sure I could count on him to keep his temper. I'd rarely seen him angry, never with me, but he was so big, he could be scary-looking when he did get mad.

Passing by my dad's truck, I reached in and grabbed a gate remote from behind the sun visor. As I ran, sharp stones and twigs pierced my bare feet. I grimaced in pain but tried not to slow down. I needed to silence the noisemakers and send them on their way before my dad decided to do it himself.

Coming up to the gate, I hit the button. The gate started to slide open, and I skidded to a stop. A woman and a man were standing in front of a truck. She was short and had a shock of short red hair, and he was much taller and thinner and had darker skin, like a great tan. Despite it all, I couldn't help but think he looked like somebody from a TV soap opera. Behind the truck was a gigantic shining silver trailer.

"We're closed!" I yelled at them. "Go away!"

"You don't understand!" the woman yelled. "We're here to help!"

"Help what?"

"We're veterinarians," the man said.

It was then that I noticed they were both wearing white lab coats.

"But how did you—" It didn't matter how or why. Only one thing mattered. "This way, please. Follow me."

They climbed into the truck, and it rolled forward. I waited for them to clear the gate, then hit the button to close it. The truck raced past me. The vets didn't need directions—they could see where the elephants were. As they passed, I caught sight of my reflection in the long, shiny silver trailer. I'd forgotten I was still wearing my dress.

For a split second, I thought I should run to the house and change. It would only take a minute.

Maybe that was more than Daisy Mae had left.

I ran after the truck, reaching Trixie's side as the newcomers climbed out. My father and Doc Morgan came toward the truck. Dad looked upset and angry.

"Which of you is Mr. Gray?" the woman asked.

"Me, I'm Jack Gray."

"And I'm Doc Morgan. I'm a vet."

"My name is Dr. Grace, this is Dr. Tavaris. We're vets too."

"We're from the San Plato Zoo," Dr. Tavaris said. "We're large-animal specialists."

"We were sent to offer assistance in the treatment of your elephant," Dr. Grace added.

"Sent by who?" my father asked.

"I assume somebody associated with your facility contacted us," Dr. Grace answered.

"We didn't call anybody—Wait! I did send an e-mail

about it to our backer. That must be it. I just didn't expect this," my father said.

"We received an urgent request —" Dr. Tavaris began.

Dr. Grace interrupted. "Actually, it was an order from the head of the zoo."

"Yes, we were roused out of bed and told there was an emergency," Dr. Tavaris said.

"We drove through the night." Dr. Grace didn't seem happy. "Please, Dr. Morgan, bring us up to date."

His response was a lot of medical words that meant nothing to me. If I hadn't known already what was happening, I would have been completely in the dark.

"This is very serious," Dr. Tavaris said.

"We came instantly, but we still might be too late unless we act immediately," Dr. Grace said.

"Act how?" Doc Morgan asked. "What do you have in mind?"

"We need to do a C-section," Dr. Grace said. Dr. Tavaris nodded in agreement.

"If this were a cow, I would have started already," Doc Morgan said. "But I don't have the equipment or the expertise necessary to operate on an elephant."

"We have the equipment with us," Dr. Grace said quickly.

"But you'd need all the equipment associated with an operating theater," Doc Morgan said.

"Our trailer is a mobile surgical suite."

"But it's still an elephant."

"Dr. Grace and I have operated on elephants many times," Dr. Tavaris replied.

"As well as hippos, a musk ox, and a particularly nasty rhino," Dr. Grace added. "Like my colleague said, these larger zoo animals are our specialty."

"So you've done a caesarean on an elephant?" I asked.

Dr. Grace shook her head. "That would be unusual."

"But you know what to do, right?" I asked.

They both nodded. Neither looked too confident.

"How risky is this procedure?" my father asked.

"Risky," said Dr. Tavaris. "Very high-risk."

Dad turned to Doc Morgan. "What do you think?"

"I don't have the experience or expertise to know the risk factors. What I do know is the certainty factor. If something isn't done soon, Daisy Mae and her baby are going to die."

"Then there's no choice," my father said. "It's the only hope of saving them."

"Unfortunately not," Dr. Grace said. "We have no chance of saving them *both*."

"We're going to have to sacrifice the mother to try to save the baby," Dr. Tavaris explained.

"But in a C-section with a human, aren't the mother *and* the child saved?" I asked.

"This is not a human. This is an elephant, in great distress, in an open field, depending on a mobile operating theater," Dr. Grace said.

"So there's no chance of saving Daisy Mae?" my father asked.

"Sorry," Dr. Tavaris said. "If we could do anything else, we would, but we can't. All we can try to do is save the baby."

"And there's no guarantee we can even do that," Dr. Grace added.

"With every second we wait, the chances of saving the baby go down. So what do we do? Do we have your permission to do the procedure?" Dr. Tavaris asked my dad.

"Doc?" Dad asked Doc Morgan.

"What they're saying makes sense."

Dad turned to me. "Samantha, if there was any other way, we'd do it."

"I understand," I said. At least I understood in my head.

He nodded. "Dr. Grace, Dr. Tavaris, you have our permission."

"I'll get the equipment ready," Dr. Tavaris said, and headed for the trailer.

"We have to do a preliminary examination, but we can't do that until the area is cleared," Dr. Grace said.

"You want us to leave?" I asked.

"We want the other elephants to leave."

"They'll want to stay," my dad said.

"They want to be here to comfort her, to take care of her," I added. "They're a family."

"And a family would never be allowed in the operating room if it were a human," Dr. Grace replied. "Especially not a family that could crush the doctors doing the operation."

"She's right," Doc Morgan confirmed. "There's no telling how they will react when they see the doctors operating on Daisy Mae."

"We can't have them interfere. If we're interrupted mid-procedure, the baby will die," Dr. Grace said.

Everything they were saying made sense, but how did you explain that to the elephants? How did you convince them they had to leave? It went against their natural instincts, against their herd mentality, against their whole social structure to abandon a member who was in distress.

"We have some cattle prods in the van," Dr. Grace said.

"What?"

"Sticks that have electric charges, used to control large animals."

"We don't use things like that here," my father snapped.

"Then how are you going to move them away?" she asked.

"We'll move them. You get your equipment ready."

Dr. Grace and Doc Morgan went toward the trailer.

"How are we going to do this?" I asked my dad.

"I'm not sure. Maybe I can convince them they can do the surgery with the herd still here and we can keep them calm. You stay here with the herd, and I'll be back as quick as I can."

And he was gone, running toward their truck and trailer.

I suddenly felt scared, not for me but for Daisy Mae. Soon the procedure would start. Soon she would be dead as the vets made a desperate attempt to save her baby. She needed to know. Somehow I had to let her know that even if the others left, I'd still be there. That no matter what happened, her baby would be safe and cared for.

I circled back toward her head. The eye I could see was closed. Was it too late? Was she already —

The eye opened. She looked directly at me. That soft, gentle brown eye was staring right at me. I expected her to be panicked or pleading. Instead she was calm.

"I'm here, Daisy Mae. I'm here for you."

Her ear quivered slightly in response to my words.

"What's going to happen is to save your baby. I know if you could make the decision, this is the decision that you'd have made. You were always such a good mother."

I looked over at Bacca. He was still holding on to his mother's tail. He had shuffled a bit but hadn't let go of his grip since before his mother tumbled to the ground. I realized that he'd need almost as much help as the baby would. For him, it would be even harder. He had known his mother. The baby would never know his or hers.

Then I realized. This was what it had been like for me, for my mother. This is what had happened to me, *for* my mother, *to* my mother, for me.

"I'll be there for your baby, for both of your babies," I whispered in her ear. "I promise."

She blinked, and I saw something behind her look. It felt like she not only understood but was trying to offer me reassurance. She was trying to comfort *me*.

"We don't have much time." Dr. Grace had come up behind me. "The herd still has to be moved."

"Didn't my father talk to you about it?"

"He's still trying to persuade Dr. Tavaris to let them stay, but I'm not going to operate until I know we won't be interrupted or harmed."

She started to examine Daisy Mae, moving her stethoscope up and down her side.

"I'm not going far," I said to Daisy Mae. "I need to talk to the other elephants."

I stood up and walked to Trixie. "We're going to need you to move the herd off," I told her.

She stared at me but didn't move, didn't respond. How could I expect anything different?

"We'll stay with Daisy Mae, but you have to have everybody leave."

"What did you say?" Dr. Grace asked.

"I was talking to Trixie."

"You know she doesn't understand what you're saying."

"She knows how bad things are," I said.

"She knows on some level, of course."

"She knows on every level. Trixie is the leader. Even if she doesn't understand all the words, she still understands the situation."

"You have to be careful not to project human characteristics onto the elephants," Dr. Grace said firmly.

"I'd never do that. They're much *better* than humans."

Dr. Grace laughed. "I agree with that. If she really understands what you're saying, then have her move the herd away so we can get started."

"My father will be able to do that."

But maybe I could do something before he came back.

I moved up right beside Trixie. She reached out her trunk and touched my face. She was trying to connect with me. I wondered if she was also trying to comfort me.

"I'll stay, but you need to go . . . you need . . . water," I said. Maybe she didn't understand everything, but she knew that word, and the herd did need water. Nobody had left Daisy Mae's side since she'd fallen. That was almost ten hours ago.

"Water! Go and get water," I said to her.

The other elephants had also heard. Tiny and Selena turned their heads to the side, trying to understand. Raina's ears were flapping wildly. They were all looking at me, listening — to me and to the others. There was a sudden burst of noises as they talked to one another.

"Go to the pond. Get water!" I yelled.

Raja didn't need to hear any more. He took a few steps away and then skidded to a stop. He turned and looked directly at Trixie. He wanted water, but he wasn't going to go without her permission, without her leading the way or at least coming along. She was the key. The herd would leave only if Trixie led them away.

"Trixie, you have to take them to water." I gently took her trunk in my hand and pulled ever so slightly. She didn't budge. She looked at me, then at Daisy Mae, then back at me. She nodded. It could have just been my imagination; it could have been her just stretching and flexing, but I didn't think so. She knew.

I released her trunk, and she started walking away, toward the pond, and the others started moving too. Raja, already ahead of the rest, began trotting, and Stampy, Hathi, and Ganesh ran to catch up to him. That seemed to energize the rest, and they all moved faster.

"It looks like they understood," I said loudly, so Dr. Grace could hear.

"That doesn't mean they're going," she said. She pointed, and I turned around.

The elephants had stopped moving and were looking back at us.

"Go, go to the water!" I yelled.

"The big one is coming back," Dr. Grace said.

Trixie was trotting toward us.

She angled around Daisy Mae, and there was Bacca, still clinging to his mother's tail. I'd lost sight of him, hidden behind his mother's haunch.

Trixie went to the little elephant and lowered her head until her forehead was pressed against Bacca's. Trixie began clicking and chirping. I imagined her talking, explaining things, but Bacca couldn't understand. He was too young and too scared and too worried for his mother.

Trixie moved slightly forward, leaning into Bacca, pushing against him until he released his grip on his mother's tail. Trixie moved into the gap so that she was between mother and child. Bacca desperately tried to go around the big elephant to get back to his mother, but Trixie shifted to block his way. Once again she lowered her head until it was pressed against Bacca's. Once again she was trying to communicate with him. Trixie gave a low rumbling noise, and Bacca chirped in reply.

Trixie turned around. Bacca reached out and grabbed Trixie's tail with his trunk. Trixie walked off, trailing Bacca behind her. They reached the other elephants, still waiting, and Trixie led the herd away toward the pond.

"Anything else you want to say?" I asked Dr. Grace.

"If I hadn't seen it with my own eyes . . ."

"Just save the baby. We're counting on you. Daisy Mae is counting on you."

CHAPTER

Nine

I SAT WITH MY BACK PRESSED AGAINST DAISY MAE. The vets, my father, and Joyce had all tried to get me to leave. That wasn't going to happen. I had positioned myself right by her ear, where I could talk to her and look away from what was to come. I had to be there — I needed to be there — but I didn't want to see it. Daisy Mae had been given a shot to put her to sleep. I remembered that with Burma, Doc Morgan had said that the last sense to go would be hearing. So I figured that even after she was knocked out, she might be able to hear me.

From my position, I would see the herd coming if they returned from the pond. So far they hadn't appeared, but if they did, I'd have to try to intercept them, stop them from coming closer. This was a delicate operation, and I understood that it couldn't be done with the herd crowding around and maybe misunderstanding or defending.

I wasn't watching the surgery, but that didn't mean I

couldn't hear it. Not just the doctors talking but the sound of the incision — I could hear them cutting into Daisy Mae. I started talking to her more loudly, trying to distract myself and let her know she wasn't alone. Nobody should be alone at the end — an end that I was starting to think might have already come. I couldn't hear her breathing anymore. Her eye was closed. I couldn't feel her breathing. Was she gone?

"There it is!" Doc Morgan yelled.

I braced myself to look. I turned. Daisy Mae's whole side had been cut open, and there was blood everywhere. The two vets were practically inside the incision, their arms and upper bodies not even visible.

"We need help!" Dr. Grace yelled.

My father, who had been standing slightly off to the side, rushed over. He reached down, and I could see the strain in his face. He straightened up, and in his arms was a mass of wet, brown matter — he was holding the baby elephant!

"It's not breathing!" Dad yelled.

"Suction, get me suction!" Dr. Tavaris ordered.

Dr. Grace was wielding a long tube. It looked like a vacuum cleaner — suction; that made sense. She moved the wand around the mouth of the baby and it sucked away the mucus surrounding it. Next she suctioned off the trunk, and all at once the elephant was moving, its legs pushing and its trunk thrashing. Then there was a noise, almost more like a vibration than a sound. It got louder, and there was a soft chirping, a cry to let us know the baby was here and it was alive.

I stood up, and my legs almost collapsed under me. It wasn't just that they were numb and cramped from sitting. I was overwhelmed by what I was seeing. Daisy Mae was there, all cut open, the ground stained with blood. I couldn't allow myself to look again. I had to focus on what was still important.

Eyes aimed straight ahead, I took a few steps and then a few more until I was close to my dad and the baby. It was wet and gray, with a fringe of red hair around its head and little ears plastered down to the sides of the head. Its eyes were closed. Although it was a baby, just born, it was larger than me, filling Dad's arms. I could tell it was a heavy armful. I reached out and placed my hand against the baby.

"I'm going to have to put it down," he said.

Slowly, carefully, he let the baby's feet touch the ground. The legs looked as if they were going to buckle, but somehow it managed to stand, supported by my father's arms.

Doc Morgan put a stethoscope against the baby's side. "It's breathing, and the heart seems strong."

"That's so good. It's going to be all right, right?" my father asked.

"I've never seen a newborn elephant before," Doc Morgan said. "Bacca was up and moving before I got here." He turned to the other two vets.

"I have, but not born this early. How premature is it?" Dr. Grace asked.

"About three and a half weeks," my father said.

"That would explain why it looks so — well, odd," Dr. Grace said.

"I think it looks beautiful," I said. "Is it a girl or boy?"

"It's a girl," my father said. "A *beautiful* little baby girl."

"A girl, yes," Dr. Grace said. "But I don't know about beautiful. It is a very strange-looking little elephant."

"Luckily, this isn't a beauty contest," Dr. Tavaris said. "I think she's doing well, all things considered."

The little elephant was now standing on its own, although Dad was still offering his arms as support. Its trunk was moving around, its eyes were partially open, and it was looking at me, or at least trying to. I wasn't sure the eyes were able to focus yet.

"I guess we have one more problem," Dad said. He turned to me. "What should we call her? Samantha, what do you think she should be called?"

"You want *me* to name her?"

"Yes. You picked out the perfect name for Bacca. Do you have a name in mind for this one?"

"I have to get to know her, but I'll come up with something."

*   *   *

MY FATHER PICKED THE BABY UP AGAIN AND CARRIED her into the enormous shiny trailer. The vets guessed she weighed almost two hundred pounds, but he was able to carry her, even so. Sometimes I lost track of how big and strong he was because he was so gentle. Then I'd see him standing beside somebody—especially somebody small like Joyce—and remember his size. Like right now. He towered over two of the three vets and was still taller than Dr. Tavaris.

Once in the trailer, the vets washed the baby off with a little hose and dried her. They used special heat lamps, and I helped with a towel. Normally the mother would have cleaned her, but now it was up to us. Everything was up to us.

The baby had been weighed—177 pounds—and measured. She stood 2 feet 8 inches at the shoulder. Dad said that Bacca had been a bit bigger, but the vets said those numbers were good for a premature baby.

She seemed to be getting steadier and stronger with each passing minute. Now she was able to stand on her own without wobbling or being in danger of toppling over. Her eyes were fully open, and her head and trunk were moving around constantly. I knew she was trying to figure out what was going on. I wondered if she was looking for her mommy.

Doc Morgan, Joyce, and my father had gone off to make up some formula to feed her, leaving me with the other two vets.

"How do you think she's doing?" I asked.

"Remarkably well," Dr. Tavaris answered.

"All the vital signs are strong," Dr. Grace said. "Strong heartbeat and good respiration."

"Those are always at risk when a baby is premature or the birth is forced," Dr. Tavaris explained.

"I've never seen one with so much hair," Dr. Grace said.

The newborn did have a lot of hair. Bacca was born practically naked compared to her. "Don't some human babies have less hair and others have more?"

"She has a point," Dr. Tavaris agreed. "One of my nieces was born with lots of hair all over her body. It fell off within a few weeks."

"Hers is so long, it's like she's wearing a woolly sweater," Dr. Grace said.

I laughed. "That's it!"

"What's it?"

"Her name. She's going to be called Woolly."

"It certainly fits," Dr. Tavaris said. Dr. Grace nodded in agreement.

"Hello and welcome to the world, Woolly the Elephant," I said.

"Now that she's named, let's just make sure she stays here," Dr. Tavaris said.

I had a rush of fear. "But you said she looks fine, right?"

"So far, but it's too soon to know if she has brain damage caused by oxygen deprivation. Only time will tell."

I looked into Woolly's eyes. They were clear, and inside, behind them, I thought I could see intelligence looking back at me. Almost as if she could read my mind, she reached out her trunk and started to run it all over my face.

"She's going to be fine," I said.

"I'm not going to make that guarantee yet. What I do know is that she seems to like you a lot," Dr. Grace said to me.

As I stood there, Woolly had taken my left hand in her mouth and began sucking it.

"She's trying to feed," Dr. Tavaris said. "She has the suckling reaction — another good sign."

"But that means nothing if we have nothing to feed her," Dr. Grace countered. Why did she always have to add a negative to any positive?

"They'll be back soon with the formula," I said.

"Elephant formula is a very complicated mixture. It's not like you can give her straight cow's milk," Dr. Grace said.

"I think we know the difference between a cow and an elephant." I said it sarcastically and then felt bad. Dr. Grace had been part of bringing the baby into the world alive.

"I'm sorry. I didn't mean to imply you didn't," she said. "It's just that a baby elephant can only absorb certain proteins and

117

nutrients. It isn't enough to get the formula into them. They have to be able to break it down and utilize it."

"You know, my father raised a baby elephant that had been rejected."

"We didn't know that," Dr. Grace said.

"Was it a newborn?" Dr. Tavaris asked.

"It was before my time. My father did the raising." And my mother. I wasn't born yet. "She's out there now. Hathi. She was three months old when she came, and she was fed the same formula he's mixing now."

"Zoos, professional vets, and nutritionists struggle to come up with the right mixture," Dr. Grace said.

"*We* didn't. The elephants told us what to put in it."

Both vets stared at me curiously.

"Joking. Just joking. Dad made contact with a sanctuary in Nairobi that raises orphaned elephants, and they shared their recipe."

"Those would have been African elephants."

"It worked for us then, so why wouldn't it work now?" I asked.

The two of them looked at each other and shrugged.

"By the way, do you always wear a prom dress to the birth of an elephant?" Dr. Grace asked.

I'd forgotten what I was wearing until she mentioned it.

I looked down at the dress. It was covered with dirt and mud and elephant afterbirth. Somehow the gold flecks still sparkled. I didn't expect to be wearing it again.

"I was at the eighth-grade graduation dance when this all happened, and I didn't have a chance to get changed."

"You could go and get changed now," Dr. Tavaris suggested.

"Not yet. I'm still needed."

Woolly continued to suckle on my hand. She was obviously hungry, and we needed to get food into her soon.

On cue, my father, holding a gigantic bottle of what looked like bluish-white milk, returned, accompanied by Doc Morgan and Joyce.

"Perfectly mixed and ready to go," Dad said.

"And warmed to the body temperature of an elephant," Doc Morgan said. "Ninety-seven-point-seven degrees."

"How is she doing?" Dad asked.

"She is doing well, and Sam has decided on a name," Dr. Tavaris said.

"And that name is?"

"Woolly," I announced.

"Brilliant choice!" Joyce said.

"And now Woolly needs to eat," Dad said. He held the bottle out to me.

"You want me to do it?"

He pointed at my hand, which was entirely inside Woolly's mouth. "She's already trying to feed from you. Let's make it official."

I pulled my hand free of her mouth. It came out with a sucking sound. I took the bottle with both hands.

"This is the moment of truth," Dr. Tavaris said.

"If it doesn't work, we'll have to tube feed," Dr. Grace said.

"What does that mean?" I asked.

"We take a tube, like a hose, and we insert it into the mouth, down the throat, and directly into the stomach, then pour the liquid through the tube," she explained.

I felt myself gag. This had to work.

I held out the bottle, offering it to Woolly. She felt it with her trunk. I lowered it, trying to insert the nipple of the bottle into her mouth, but instead she tried to get my hand into her mouth again.

"Come on, girl, you can do it," my dad said.

"Are you talking to me or to Woolly?" I asked.

"Both of you. I have faith in both of you."

I withdrew my hand and turned it palm up. I handed the bottle to Dad. "Squeeze some formula onto my palm."

He dribbled formula into my hand, making a little pool.

I slipped my hand, dripping with formula, into Woolly's mouth. She started suckling again.

"That's working," my dad said. "I'm going to position the bottle so the formula dribbles down your wrist and onto your hand, then into her mouth."

He placed the nipple against my wrist, just outside of Woolly's mouth. The formula ran down. Some of it dripped onto the floor of the trailer, but it looked like most was leaking into her mouth.

"Is it working?" Dr. Tavaris asked.

"I'm sure it is," my father said.

I pulled my hand out slightly so I could see the heel of my palm. Dad understood and shifted the bottle down so the nipple was touching my hand. He squeezed the bottle, and a small river ran into my palm and into Woolly's mouth. I could feel the suction increase as she suckled even harder.

"That was better," Dr. Grace said.

"We can do even better," my dad said.

He shifted the bottle again so that the nipple was in Woolly's mouth. I pulled most of my hand out, leaving only my fingers inside. Woolly coughed, and formula dribbled out of her mouth.

"I squeezed too hard," he said. "Samantha, can you handle the bottle now?"

"I'll try."

He balanced it against my left arm and wrist, and I held

the nipple end with my right hand. I could feel the suckling on my fingers and see bubbles rising into the bottle as the liquid level went down.

"I think we'd better mix up a second bottle," Joyce suggested.

"You better mix up a lot more than a bottle. She'll drink close to two gallons of formula every day. I'll help," Doc Morgan said. He started out of the trailer and stopped. "The herd is back," he said.

The others got up to look. I wanted to look, but I couldn't move. "What are they doing?" I asked.

"They've surrounded the dead elephant," Dr. Grace said.

"Her name is Daisy Mae," my father said.

"Sorry, I didn't mean anything by that. Yes, they're surrounding Daisy Mae," she said. "They're examining the body."

"They're doing more than that," Dad said. "They're grieving the loss. They're saying goodbye to a family member."

CHAPTER

Ten

"CAN YOU LEAD HER OVER TO THE SCALES?" DR. GRACE asked.

I walked away, and Woolly trailed after me without being asked. My legs and back were sore. I'd been squatting in the trailer, feeding the baby, for the past three hours. I had sticky formula all over my arm, as well as a large wet spot on my lap where it had dribbled down. I didn't think I could have ruined my dress more if I had rolled in the mud wearing it. Moreover, Woolly had drenched my feet in urine. Dr. Grace had said that was a good sign because it showed that her urinary system was working.

Woolly, Dr. Grace, and I were the only ones in the trailer now. Everybody else had gone off to grab some breakfast and clean up. I wasn't hungry, and there was no point in even trying to get clean. Besides, Woolly had gotten upset when I'd tried to leave to grab another bottle.

"Just get her to step right onto the platform," Dr. Grace said.

With a little bit of nudging, I was able to get her onto the scales.

"One hundred and eighty-nine pounds," she announced.

"That can't be right. That's twelve pounds she gained."

"You fed her more than two gallons of formula, and each gallon weighs eight pounds or so. That's about right."

We'd fed her until she stopped wanting more. That didn't happen until she had swallowed twenty-one bottles of elephant formula. I gave her a dozen of them, but my arms got too tired to continue. Everybody else took a turn, feeding her two or three bottles each. It was amazing to watch it happening, and even more amazing to actually feed her.

"Can I ask you a question?" Dr. Grace asked.

"Sure."

"This backer — the person with the deep pockets, the one who had enough money and influence to get us and our equipment here for the birth — who is he?"

"I have no idea. I'm not even sure if it's a he or she or a corporation. It was all done on the internet. I don't know if my father has even talked to anybody on the phone."

"That's very strange."

"I just figured I like anybody who likes elephants and

wants more of them. That's why they wanted the three elephants to get pregnant," I said.

"You have two more pregnant elephants on the property?" Dr. Grace sounded worried.

"The other two didn't carry to full term," I said.

"Neither did the third." She said the words and then looked sad that she'd said them. "Sorry."

"Is that unusual, to have the same thing happen to all three?"

"Elephant gestation has been studied for years, but our knowledge is limited. We know the length of time, obviously, twenty-two months, but we don't know the carry rate. Perhaps elephants carry only one out of three or four pregnancies to full term and lose the others in the early stages. We just don't know." She paused. "I'm sorry, really sorry we couldn't save the mother."

"I know you did the best you could. Daisy Mae was a good elephant, and she was always such a good mother."

"Woolly is going to make your lives much more complicated. She will need constant care and feeding," Dr. Grace said.

"I'm home for the summer now, and my father will be here when he's not working, and we have a whole lot of volunteers who help out."

"You're going to need all the help you can get. Will the backer send more people?"

"I don't know, but we'll do fine either way," I said.

"I'm sure you will, but obviously he or she has lots of money, so you can probably get more help if you need it. Having us come here wasn't cheap, not to mention the cost of inseminating the elephants to begin with."

There was also the money that had been invested in the sanctuary to help keep us going. Dr. Grace didn't know about that, and I wasn't going to tell her.

"I'm going to go in and grab some food," She said. "Will you be all right here by yourself?"

"I'm not by myself. I'm with a baby elephant."

Dr. Grace left.

"You'll never be alone," I told Woolly. "We'll be with you a lot, and you'll always have your herd with you."

How was her herd doing?

I walked out of the trailer, and Woolly trailed behind me. I stopped where I could see the body of Daisy Mae. The herd, as I anticipated, was still surrounding her. They had come back from getting water hours ago, but they still hadn't left the body. The same thing had happened when Peanut died. They were touching Daisy Mae with their trunks, pushing their heads against her to try to move her.

Bacca stood stone-still, holding Daisy Mae's tail with his trunk. It made my heart break. He was big and almost completely weaned, but sometimes he still nursed from his mother. Never again.

Trixie raised her head and her trunk even higher. She looked all around. She tilted her head to the side and stared at me and Woolly. She started toward us, and the entire herd was drawn along, all but Bacca, who was still holding tightly to his mother's tail.

I had an irrational urge to scoop up Woolly and go back into the trailer — to hide her or protect her from the herd — but of course that made no sense. There was no place to hide and no need to protect her from her family. In fact, they would be there to protect her.

As the herd came closer, it was Woolly who decided to hide. She moved behind me and tucked her head against my bottom. She was like a little kid, closing her eyes and thinking that if she couldn't see them, they couldn't see her.

Trixie stopped directly in front of me. The other elephants were farther away. Were they giving Trixie a chance to meet first and investigate?

I looked over and saw that my father and the other people had come out of the house. They had stopped at a safe distance where they could watch. It was me and Woolly and Trixie.

I had to say something. "Trixie, this is Woolly. She's Daisy Mae's baby."

Trixie inched forward and reached out with her trunk.

I thought she was going to touch the baby, but instead she touched my face with her trunk and then started to stroke my hair. She was comforting me. I knew that, and I was grateful. I needed her touch.

Woolly moved, and her trunk shifted slightly. Almost by chance, the two trunks touched, and Woolly's withdrew. Trixie's did too. Gently she pushed me aside until I was standing beside Woolly instead of in front of her. Trixie ran her trunk all over Woolly, feeling and smelling the baby elephant. She would have known by the smell that Woolly was Daisy Mae's offspring.

"That's right, she belonged to Daisy Mae, and now she belongs to the herd," I said.

Trixie lowered her head until she was eyeball to eyeball with the baby, making a series of low chirping sounds. Woolly wasn't answering.

More sounds were coming from the rest of the herd. Were they saying hello or asking permission to come closer?

Dad didn't feel he needed permission and came over, leaving the other humans behind. He stood next to Trixie. That seemed right, the elephant matriarch and the human patriarch examining the newborn member of their herd.

"What's going to happen now?" I asked him.

"Whatever it is, it will be the right thing."

My father's arrival seemed to be a signal to the other

elephants that they could come closer. One by one, they came until we were surrounded, with a safe cushion of distance on all sides. It was like being enclosed and protected by a wall of elephants. I was sure that this was what they would have done in the wild, putting the newborn in the center, where it was protected from tigers.

Raina, the second-oldest female, was the first to break through that cushion. She edged forward, shifting her gaze from Woolly to Trixie to my dad. She was curious about the baby and was seeking approval and permission from the other two. When there was no opposition, she came right up to Woolly. Woolly slipped behind me again and grabbed my hand with her trunk, and this time she didn't hide her face. Raina held her trunk out, Woolly released my hand, and the two touched. Raina made the same chirping sound that Trixie had.

I expected the next-highest-ranking female, Selena, to come next, but instead Raja jumped his place in line. Woolly stepped forward to meet him, and they touched trunks. Was she less afraid because this was the third elephant or because Raja wasn't quite as big as the first two? Regardless, Woolly seemed less apprehensive this time.

The members of the herd moved in until they were all close enough to reach out and touch Woolly. Every one of them had been gentle. I hoped she felt safe and protected.

With the arrival of the herd, the rest of the humans felt like they could come too. They approached, staying outside the inner circle of elephants and me and my dad. I thought that was respectful and wise. None of them were members of our herd.

"This is your family," I said to Woolly. "This is your herd . . . all of them."

"Not all," Dad said.

I looked closely. There were only nine elephants plus Woolly. Bacca was missing. I looked past tree-trunk legs and towering bodies to try to see him. He was where I thought he would be, standing beside the lifeless body of his mother, still holding her tail with his trunk, still waiting for her to rise.

"I'll be back," I said softly. My father nodded.

I sidled a few steps away from Woolly, not wanting her to notice my departure. I was relieved and a little bit disappointed that she didn't. I moved around the herd, heading toward Bacca and the lifeless body of Daisy Mae.

I cleared my throat as I got closer. I wanted Bacca to know I was coming, and I also wanted permission to invade their privacy. Bacca obviously heard me but didn't look up. He was still holding his mother's tail in his trunk, and he had rested his forehead against her side. My heart felt like it wanted to break.

"Bacca, she's gone."

He didn't react. I let out a deep sigh, and my whole body shuddered.

"Daisy Mae is gone."

Hearing his mother's name, he looked up at me. Liquid was dripping down from his left eye. I knew it wasn't really a tear, but knowing that didn't stop the heartache for him and for me. Liquid was dripping out of my eyes too. Maybe I was just cleansing my eyes.

I offered my hand. Slowly, hesitantly, he released his mother's tail, then reached out and tentatively took my hand with his trunk.

"Come and meet your new half sister," I said. "Her name is—"

I was cut off by the sound of trumpeting. I spun around. Trixie had her trunk in the air and was calling out loudly. Within seconds, she was joined by another and another of the herd until they all were calling out. I'd heard of this happening, but never seen it. They were welcoming the newest member of the herd.

Bacca released my hand, raised his trunk, and joined in the chorus. There was only one thing to do. I tilted my head back and began calling out, imitating him, imitating them, and welcomed the latest arrival to their herd—to *my* herd.

CHAPTER
Eleven

MY FATHER AND I FINISHED OUR DINNER AND WENT OUT to the front porch. I'd finally had a chance to change out of my dress and into jeans. My hair was tucked back into my baseball cap. I'd tossed the dress directly into the garbage can. My friends had been right—the dance was a never-to-be-forgotten experience, although not the way anybody could have predicted.

Joyce and Doc Morgan were standing among the herd. I'd started noticing that the herd had become more comfortable with her in their midst. Joyce was feeding Woolly. She had offered to take a feeding shift so that I could eat. I was already grateful when anybody else provided the bottle. Caring for Woolly was indeed going to be demanding and time-consuming. Dr. Tavaris knew what he was talking about.

He and Dr. Grace had been pacing back and forth beside the house for thirty minutes. It was getting darker, and while he was starting to fade into the dark, her bright red hair continued to shine through. I'd watched this odd little couple out the front window as they'd taken turns speaking on the phone. I thought they should have been spending more time watching Woolly, but the phone seemed to be their priority. As they paced, their voices got quieter and louder depending on their distance from the house. They were close enough for me to hear agitation, disagreement, and at times anger, but they were always far enough away that I couldn't make out the words.

"Who exactly are they talking to?" I asked my father.

"Somebody from the zoo," he said.

"It doesn't sound like the conversation is going well."

"I don't know why there would be a dispute." Dad looked puzzled. "Doc said they did a remarkable job. Without their assistance, there's no way that Woolly would have survived."

"If only Daisy Mae could have lived too."

"I wish that could have been possible," he said with a sigh. "The work we have ahead of us is going to be tremendous."

"I guess it's lucky I'm free for the summer and can help out every day."

Doc Morgan left Woolly and Joyce behind and came up onto the porch. Great; we had a lawyer looking after the baby. That would work well if a lawsuit broke out.

"How's she doing, Doc?" I asked.

"Couldn't be better."

"I was just telling Samantha that it's going to be day-and-night work," Dad said. "Caring for a newborn is a twenty-four-hour, seven-day-a-week process."

"I guess you've had experience with that," Doc Morgan said.

"Well, Bacca wasn't that much work," I said.

"Bacca had his mother. I meant you," he said, pointing at me.

I felt a rush of embarrassment and discomfort.

"It was similar, but she didn't need two gallons of formula every day," Dad said.

"But I still had to be fed. You had to do that," I put in, making that connection for the first time. "You had to do everything. How did you do it all?"

My father hesitated. I'd just broken an unspoken agreement that we didn't talk about my birth and what happened afterward. I wasn't sure how he'd feel about my crossing the line any further.

"I had help. Both your grandmothers practically moved in."

"But Grandma Cora and Grandpa John live on the other side of the country."

"Those are my parents," he said to Doc Morgan. "They flew in a few days before Samantha was born and stayed."

They were nice people. I knew them through phone calls and letters and the occasional visit. The last visit was more than three years ago. Grandpa said he was just too old for regular travel after that.

"I always had one or both of your grandmothers here, from the day you were born until you were more than six months old. I couldn't have done it without their help."

"We're herd animals too. Just like them," Doc Morgan said, indicating the elephants.

There were many questions I wanted to ask my father about that part of my life, but now wasn't the right time. Maybe it would never be the right time. Besides, it was Woolly's turn to be fed and cared for.

"This herd can't raise Woolly without our help," my father said. "We need a lot more helpers. Joyce has offered to put together a feeding schedule that will assign volunteers to feed Woolly."

"I can do a lot of the feedings. I can handle a lot of things," I said.

"I know you can. You've always been so strong. Hey, it looks like their phone call has ended."

Dr. Grace and Dr. Tavaris came to the edge of the porch.

"Glad to see you've changed," Dr. Grace said to me.

I was in what my father called my uniform — jeans, T-shirt, and, of course, my baseball cap. It felt good to be in my regular clothes.

"I was thinking I'd have to get a tux to meet the dress code around here," Dr. Tavaris said.

"*This* is the dress code around here," I replied.

"I don't think we're going to be around long enough to test that out. We're leaving tonight," Dr. Grace said.

"We're just so grateful you came," my father said. "You have our thanks."

"Ours and Woolly's, too," I added.

"You know, you don't have to leave right away. You're more than welcome to stay the night," Dad went on. "We have five bedrooms, so there's plenty of space for the two of you."

"Thanks for the invitation," Dr. Tavaris said.

"But we have to get back to the zoo," Dr. Grace said. "With the two of us away, the animals would be vulnerable if something were to happen."

"And, unfortunately, they'll continue to be somewhat vulnerable for at least a few weeks after we get back," Dr. Tavaris added.

What did he mean by that? I wondered. *Were they going someplace else?*

"Just thankful you were here," my father said.

"We all are," Doc Morgan said. "It was killing me to stand and watch what was happening but not be able to help, to save either mother or child. You saved the life of that little elephant."

"Just doing our jobs," Dr. Grace said.

"We owe you," my dad said.

"Perhaps you could start paying us back by giving us a ride into town."

"A ride?" my father asked. "Why don't you drive your truck?"

"Apparently we no longer have a truck," she said.

"Or a trailer," Dr. Tavaris added.

My father and I looked at each other in confusion.

Dr. Tavaris held out a set of keys. "Here, these are yours."

"Ours?" Dad asked.

"You didn't know?"

"Know what?"

"The truck and the entire medical trailer now belong to your sanctuary," Dr. Tavaris said.

I gasped. "You're giving it to us?"

"Not giving. It's been purchased. We were told to leave it here."

"There's got to be a mistake. We could never afford anything like this," Dad said.

"If you *could* afford it, I've been a fool all these years for giving you a discount," Doc Morgan said. "Just judging from the cost of the equipment —"

"State-of-the-art equipment," Dr. Grace said, cutting him off.

"Yes, state-of-the-art equipment. I'd estimate it would be worth more than three hundred thousand dollars."

"I put this trailer and its contents together. The amount is closer to half a million," Dr. Grace said.

"But why are we getting it?" I asked.

"Your backer must have incredibly deep pockets," Dr. Grace said. "Apparently he made a donation to the zoo of almost double the value of the trailer on condition that we leave all the equipment here when we go."

"So you'll be able to buy another one," Doc Morgan said.

"You don't just *buy* something like this," Dr. Grace said.

"You'd have to purchase and assemble the individual components, some of which would have to be custom-made, so it would take time to put it together," Dr. Tavaris said.

"Which means that the entire population of our zoo will be vulnerable until we replace this equipment."

"You must have some other equipment," Doc Morgan said.

"Not enough to provide for the possible needs of an entire zoo filled with more than four hundred species and four thousand animals," Dr. Grace replied. "Animals could die."

"But that's not right," I said.

"That's what we were arguing about on the phone," Dr. Grace explained. "We couldn't believe what we were being ordered to do."

"I don't think it's right either. We can't take your trailer." My father tried to hand back the keys.

"It isn't your decision or ours," Dr. Tavaris said. "The trailer and truck are yours. They're going to stay here whether you want them or not."

Dad turned to Doc Morgan. "Are you familiar with this equipment?"

"Not all of it."

"We can give you a crash course," Dr. Grace offered.

"I wouldn't turn that down. Greatly appreciated," Doc Morgan said.

"It's the least we can do," Dr. Tavaris replied. "There's no point in your having the equipment if you can't use it."

"I don't know what to say about any of this," my father said.

"There's nothing to say," Dr. Grace said. "The trailer stays here. But I do have a question. Who exactly *is* this backer of yours?"

"He's more a partner than a backer," Dad said.

That was the first time I'd heard the word *partner*.

"Okay, who is your partner?"

"I'd tell you if I knew."

"You've never met him?"

Dad shook his head. "It's all done through lawyers, accountants, and e-mails."

"Well, regardless, you're a very lucky man, and that's an even luckier elephant," Dr. Grace said. "Dr. Morgan, perhaps we should get started on the tutorial so we can be on our way."

"Once we're done, I'll drive you into town," Doc Morgan said. "Consider it a professional courtesy."

The three of them moved toward the trailer.

"I knew we had a backer, but I didn't know we had a partner," I said.

"A very silent partner, who owns a very small share of the place."

"How small?"

"Ten percent, and believe me, they really overpaid for that ten percent. You know that's where all the extra money has come from over the past two years." He paused. "To be honest, I'm not sure we could have survived without it."

"And the only condition was that we had to allow three of our elephants to be pregnant?"

"That was it."

"So he or she or they now own ten percent of Woolly."

"Correct. But as long as we own the other ninety percent, there's nothing to worry about."

I didn't feel that confident. He must have sensed my concern.

"Samantha, we've had this arrangement in place for over two years, and it's worked well. It will keep on working fine."

I nodded agreement, but that didn't mean I really agreed.

* * *

"ARE YOU SURE YOU'RE ALL RIGHT WITH THIS?" MY father asked.

"Why wouldn't I be?"

"Well, you're going to be bedding down on an examination table in a medical trailer in the dark in the middle of the night, isolated and on your own."

"Are you *trying* to make me nervous?"

"I'm just putting all the facts out there."

"First off, the trailer has electricity, so I'll have light. I have my phone and I can instantly get you, so I won't be that isolated. I'm surrounded by a herd of elephants outside the trailer, so I'm certainly safe, and to top it off, I am definitely not alone."

At my side, holding my hand with her trunk, was Woolly, my trailer mate. She was wearing a big red blanket that covered her entire body and hung down so that I could see only her feet.

One of the greatest dangers for a young elephant is pneumonia. It sinks into their lungs fast and hard, and from what I'd heard the vets say, I knew that it could cause death so suddenly that the elephant was dead before you even knew it was sick. I didn't want to think bad things could happen, but among the things I knew about elephants was the mortality rate for babies. Although Dr. Grace and Dr. Tavaris were gone, I reminded myself that Doc Morgan was only a phone call and a short drive away.

"You call me if you need anything or you just want to talk. Try to sleep as much as you can," Dad said.

"I'll sleep as much as Woolly will let me."

"Since she's just been fed, you're probably good until the middle of the night. I wish I could stay with you."

"Burma needs you."

My father was still spending at least part of every night outside Burma's pen. We hadn't expected it to take this long for Burma to settle in. After three nights, my father had thought it would be fine to leave Burma alone overnight. The next morning he found Burma agitated and bleeding from a cut on his forehead. He'd been butting his head against the gate, trying to get free. Dad or me being there seemed to calm him. Still, neither of us had risked going inside the pen with him.

I hadn't been into the pen—I wouldn't do that without my father giving permission and being there—but I had gone on giving Burma apples from my hand as part of his adjustment process. He was always gentle. Still, I couldn't get away from thinking about him pushing that girl down and hurting her. Or worse, what he'd done to that trainer. It wouldn't take much for an elephant to kill a person.

When I looked into Burma's eyes, he seemed like a sad, gentle soul who needed to be loved and cared for, talked to softly, rubbed behind the ear, fed and watered, and included in a herd. Well, at least allowed to share space with the herd. As a male, as a mature bull, he'd always have to live on the outside.

Of course that couldn't happen yet. He still needed to be in a completely separate enclosure. I was starting to wonder how long it was going to be. A number of times we'd brought the other elephants close to his enclosure so they'd start getting to know one another, but he'd run to the far side of the enclosure and tried to hide behind the trees.

"You know I'm going to call you a couple of times," Dad said.

"I'm going to turn off my phone so the calls don't disturb Woolly. I think we all need to sleep. Including you," I said.

"You're probably right, but remember to call if you need anything or want to talk to me."

*   *   *

I SHIFTED UNEASILY, TRYING TO GET COMFORTABLE ON the cold metal table. I pulled the blanket up and tucked it under my chin, being careful to keep one hand outside. When

I tucked it under the blanket, I was awoken by Woolly feeling around to find it.

The temperature wouldn't drop below seventy tonight, but there was a coolness to the wind and I'd left one of the windows open. I could hear the other elephants shuffling around outside. I was always amazed by how quietly elephants moved, considering their great size. Still, in the silence of the night, I could hear them, not just moving but chirping and clicking. I wondered if they were talking about me and the baby. Once, I thought somebody might be rubbing against the trailer.

I knew they could see, hear, and smell our presence, and I knew how important that was, especially for Trixie. The separation was distressing to her, but it wouldn't be safe for me to sleep out there with them — a stray foot could accidentally crush me — and it wasn't like they could get in here with me. Besides, keeping Woolly inside and warm was important. My father figured this separate sleeping arrangement would only be for a week, two at most. Then again, he hadn't thought he'd still be sleeping out beside Burma.

Woolly released my hand again. She'd done this a dozen times before. The first few times, I'd followed her with a flashlight and watched as she walked to the window and touched trunks with the elephants on the other side. It was reassuring to them and to her, and I guess to me as well.

Sleep wasn't coming easily—not entirely because of the hard metal table. Disturbing thoughts kept going through my head. Who was this partner we had? Who would invest that kind of money to produce one little elephant? I knew from experience that animal lovers could be a bit nutty, but then again, who was I to talk? People undoubtedly saw my father and me as totally insane. Sometimes I thought they might be right.

* * *

I AWOKE WITH A START, SAT UP, AND ALMOST FELL OFF the table before I regained my balance. It wasn't morning, but it wasn't night any longer. There was enough light to see that Woolly wasn't in the trailer with me.

Dad must have opened the door. I kicked off the blanket, rolled off the table, stumbled to the open door, and saw Woolly. She was standing among the other elephants, with Trixie on one side and Bacca on the other. As I watched, she nuzzled into Bacca.

"Good morning," I said as I stepped out of the trailer.

The whole herd turned at the sound of my voice, and Woolly trotted over to me. I was thrilled that she was so happy to see me. She barreled into me, bumping me backwards and practically knocking me off my feet.

"I'm glad to see you, too," I said.

She took my hand into her mouth. "Oh, yeah, you're hungry, that's what it is."

I went back inside the trailer with Woolly still holding my hand hostage in her mouth. There were two more bottles of formula in the warmer. I pulled my hand free to open the cabinet door, removed one, and offered it to Woolly. Instantly she began suckling from the bottle. Little bubbles rose up and the level went down quickly.

"You are one hungry baby."

There was a noise, and the trailer shook. Was somebody rubbing against it again? Then it shook even more. I had to stop whoever it was before some elephant damaged the trailer.

"Come on," I said to Woolly.

I pulled the bottle from her mouth and walked toward the door, Woolly chirping in protest as she followed after me. I figured she wouldn't let me or the bottle get too far away.

I stopped in shock. Bacca was at the door of the trailer — actually halfway through the door. He was trying to force himself inside. In response to seeing us, he pushed harder, and the trailer shook once again.

"Bacca, stop — you can't come in here! You're too big!"

I pushed against Bacca, trying to make him move backward. Of course I couldn't budge a nineteen-hundred-pound elephant. If anything, he was pushing harder to get in. He reached out his trunk and grabbed the bottle from my hand.

"What are you doing, Bacca? That's Woolly's bottle."

And then it dawned on me. Bacca had still occasionally nursed from his mother. He'd watched me feeding Woolly, and he wanted to be fed too.

I pulled the bottle away from Bacca, turned it around, and pushed the nipple into his mouth. I squeezed the bottle to force formula out. He sputtered and coughed and then began suckling.

Woolly started chirping. She wanted her bottle, but that wasn't going to happen right away. Bacca would finish this one quickly, and then I'd give Woolly the one that remained in the warmer.

Bacca's bottle quickly emptied. He continued to suckle, but this was all he was going to get. I pulled the bottle free and showed him that it was empty. He understood, backed out of the doorway, and joined the rest of the herd.

We were responsible for two babies, not one. I'd make sure that both of them would be cared for. I'd promised Daisy Mae.

My thoughts circled back to my situation—to my own birth. I couldn't help but wonder if my mother had had a chance to know that I'd be cared for. Did she make my father promise that while she still could?

CHAPTER

Twelve

I WATCHED CLOSELY AS MRS. PATTERSON FED WOOLLY her bottle. I liked and trusted Mrs. Patterson. She was always kind and treated the elephants well. There was no reason to doubt that she'd do the right thing. Still, I needed to watch.

She held the bottle up high. It was empty, and she was beaming.

The news that we'd had a baby elephant had spread throughout the community in the week since Woolly's birth. We'd had to close the sanctuary to visitors the day after Woolly was born, since we were so busy taking care of her. But instead of having a hundred or so visitors the next Sunday, we might have had two or three times that many. People love baby elephants. So many visitors would mean a lot of money, but it would also mean a lot of work—not just preparing the grounds, but keeping an eye on everyone. And we'd have to throw a tarp over Daisy Mae's body. We couldn't do anything with the body yet, but visitors wouldn't understand. I could barely look in that direction myself.

My father was on the computer, giving a progress report on Woolly. Apparently one of the conditions of the agreement with our "partner" was twice-daily reports about any babies that were born, including any medical concerns and height and weight figures. Woolly had gained another six pounds today. That was important right now, because it proved that she was absorbing the formula, not just drinking it.

Dad came out of the house. "We're going to have a visitor tomorrow," he said.

"I was figuring more like three hundred visitors."

"We're not opening for business tomorrow."

"But why not? It would mean a lot of money."

"We're being given an amount equal to the admission fees of five hundred visitors on the condition that we don't open."

"Is our partner giving us the money?"

He nodded.

"I wish I knew more about him or her, or them, or whoever they are," I said.

"I wish we both knew more, but tomorrow will answer some of our questions. Our visitor is our partner."

"Really?"

"So we have a lot to do to get the place ready."

"Especially with you having to go to work tonight," I said. "Don't you have an extra shift?"

"I'm not going to be working at the diner for a while."

"But don't we need —" I stopped myself from saying anything more, but it was too late.

"We do need the money, but that won't be a problem. Our partner is also paying me to not go to work."

"That's amazing!"

"I thought so. Do you think you could go and feed Burma?" he asked.

"I guess I could."

"I know you want to stay with Woolly, but I have things to do that only I can do, and I don't trust anybody else to be around Burma."

"I understand."

"That's my girl. Do you want to take the new truck?"

"The zoo truck?"

"Why not? You've been driving around the property for years, and it's our truck now. Fill the back with hay and feed Burma."

* * *

AS I STARTED TO DRIVE AWAY, JOYCE CAME RUNNING toward me, waving her arms in the air. I stopped the truck, and she came up to the passenger-side window. As always, her hair and makeup and clothes were perfect. Somehow it didn't seem to bother me as much as usual.

"Do you want some company?" she asked.

"Yeah, I guess that would be okay," I said. "Especially if that company doesn't mind riding with a thirteen-year-old driver and helps to toss bales of hay."

"No objections to one, and I can do the other."

She jumped in, and we started off. We passed by the remains of Daisy Mae. Raina, Tiny, and Selena were close by. I tried not to look.

"How long do you think they'll be visiting her?" Joyce asked.

"It was almost a week with Peanut, but it's already longer this time. They were closer to Daisy Mae," I said.

We drove along in silence. The last part was on one of our worst sections of road, and while I wanted to rush back to Woolly, I made sure to take it slow with our new truck. There was no point in risking a busted axle.

"How do you think Burma is doing?" she asked.

"Not as well as we expected in this amount of time, and now we'll have less time than we need to devote exclusively to him in order to integrate him," I said.

"And if he can't be integrated?"

Up until a few days ago, I would have said that of course he could be integrated. Now I wasn't so sure. The process wasn't moving nearly as fast as it should have been. "I guess if he can't be let out with the others, he'd stay in the isolation pen."

"And what happens when you want to bring in a new elephant and the isolation pen is permanently occupied?"

"We could build another one."

"It took a lot of money to build the one you have now," she said.

It did. More money than we should have spent. In fact, more money than we had.

"And will your father move out permanently to sleep beside Burma?"

"Of course not. It's just a matter of time."

We drove along in silence for a while. What she was saying made sense. That didn't mean I wanted to hear it.

"How much is an elephant worth?" Joyce asked.

"They're priceless."

"Really, how much *money* is an elephant worth?"

"Burma's not worth anything, so there's no point in even thinking about selling him," I said.

"I wasn't talking about selling Burma. I just want to know what an elephant is worth in dollars and cents."

"There are lots of factors."

"Such as?" she asked.

"Trained elephants and tame elephants are worth more

than untrained or wild elephants. The older the elephant, the less it's worth. A fifty-year-old isn't worth nearly as much as a ten-year-old."

"And a baby elephant? I guess I'm asking how much Woolly is worth."

"We're not selling Woolly!" I exclaimed.

"Of course you're not. I just want to know what she's worth."

"I can't really say, but a lot, a whole lot."

"Is she worth somewhere between a million and a million and a half dollars?"

"Nobody would pay that much for . . ." I let the sentence trail off. I knew exactly what she was thinking, because I'd been asking myself the same questions.

"We know what the trailer, the truck, and all the medical equipment are worth, and that the zoo was given that amount twice, so that's a million dollars. Add in what was paid to buy into the sanctuary—and we have no idea what that amount was—and what you were given to compensate for closing the sanctuary to visitors and for your father to stop working, and you have well over a million. Is that little elephant worth that much money?"

"There were supposed to be three babies," I said.

"But there aren't. There's only one, and it was after that one was born that the emergency medical trailer was sent here and then purchased for you. I just feel — well, suspicious."

"You're a lawyer. Aren't you always suspicious?"

"Yes, but just because I'm suspicious in general doesn't mean I have no reason to be suspicious now. You have to admit that you're at least a little suspicious," she said.

"You're wrong. Not a little suspicious; a lot. Dad expects that some of our questions will be answered tomorrow."

"I hope so, but experience leads me to believe that questions are answered only if they are asked. We have to ask questions. You and me, because I don't think your father will," Joyce said. "He's just too . . . well . . ."

"Trusting," I said. "By nature, he really is an elephant more than he is a human."

She nodded. "It's a wonderful way to be, and one of the reasons I care for him so much. Sometimes it seems like he takes care of the elephants, and somebody else has to take care of him."

I almost said, "That's my job, not yours," but I held my tongue. It wouldn't be bad to have help.

As we drove up, I couldn't see Burma at first. Then I caught sight of him hiding in the corner. I realized he wouldn't recognize this truck, and that would unnerve him. I pulled the truck to a stop. Joyce jumped out and opened the gate in the outer fence. I drove through the gate and pulled the truck up twenty feet until I was right beside the wall. The closer we were to the inner fence, the shorter the throw would be.

The entire bed of the pickup was filled with bales of hay piled eight high. We were going to put food for a couple of days inside the wire. Thank goodness water wasn't a problem. A creek ran in on one side of the enclosure, pooled, and ran out the other side. I wondered if one day Burma would be free to use the pond, maybe when the other elephants weren't bathing.

I got out, and without being asked, Joyce climbed up onto the pile. She pulled on a pair of work gloves over her red nails. I pulled on my work gloves as well. Part of me thought doing your nails like hers was silly, but another part wondered if Joyce could show me how to do it one day — just for fun.

Given Burma's past, we couldn't take any chances with him until we were more confident, so the wire around the isolation pen had been switched on. "Be careful of the top wire," I said. "It's live."

"Thanks for the warning."

Joyce tossed the first bale high and over the wire. She was certainly a lot stronger than she looked. There were lots of things about her you wouldn't know if you just saw the surface.

I started to climb up the pile.

"How about if I do the tossing and you go and see how Burma is doing," she said.

I wasn't going to argue.

I wandered down the inner fence, trying to get as close to Burma as possible. I called out to him. I could see enough of him through the trees to observe that his ears were twitching and that he was looking in my direction. As I got closer, he came out of the trees and headed directly toward me. His head was turning from side to side, and his ears were flapping. He was anxious, but not so anxious that he didn't want to come to greet me. He wanted either the contact or the apples that he knew would be in my pockets. Or both. He knew I never came without apples.

He slowed his pace but kept moving until he was right beside the concrete wall. We were separated by only a few feet — the length of a trunk and an outstretched arm.

"Good afternoon, Burma. How are you doing today?"

In response, he extended his trunk, careful to avoid the wire. That meant that he'd probably had contact with it at least once.

His skin had certainly improved since he arrived. The sore spots had healed, and those areas were only slightly discolored. The place on his ankle where he'd been chained was almost completely healed. Did he know we had done that for him?

"I know what you want."

I pulled an apple from my pocket and started to reach out and hand it to him, then stopped myself. I turned around and looked down the fence for Joyce. She was still atop the pile of bales, facing away from me, so she wouldn't see me hand-feeding Burma. Maybe it would be safer if I just tossed the apple into the pen — but what would Burma think? Would he feel like I didn't trust him? Did he want my touch and faith as much as he wanted the apple?

Burma made a little whimpering noise and extended his trunk toward me. Whimpering was one of the few sounds he made. He didn't speak nearly as much as the others, and when he did verbalize, he didn't make the same sounds they did. . . . . It was as if he didn't speak their language. Of course, that made sense. He'd never been around other elephants, so he didn't even know what sounds an elephant should make.

He whimpered again and extended his trunk as far as possible. He was in danger of touching the wire and getting shocked, and I didn't want him to associate that with me.

I took another quick glance over at Joyce. She still had her back to me.

I reached out my hand, holding the apple. Burma touched the apple with his trunk but didn't take it. Instead he let his trunk play up my arm. I felt a tingle go through my body. Not just from the actual touch, but from the potential danger that touch implied. I knew he could use his trunk to do more than touch me. He could push me backward or grab my arm and pull me forward to the fence and the electric wire, or even over the fence and into the pen.

I should have shifted slightly back. I didn't. I *couldn't*. I couldn't let Burma know that I was afraid. Instead I inched closer.

"I know you won't harm me," I said. Were those words meant to reassure Burma or me?

His trunk continued to explore me. He snuffled as he smelled, ran the little "finger" projecting from the end of his trunk along my arm and then up, gently probing and stroking my face. It tickled. I laughed, and he exhaled through his trunk, which tickled even more.

I dug my hand into the other pocket and pulled out the second apple, so I was holding one in each hand. "Are you sure you don't want these?"

He turned his head to the side and looked at me with one big brown eye. I didn't see an elephant looking at me but a child — a scared child.

"Nobody is ever going to hurt you again," I said. "You're safe here."

I wanted to climb over the concrete wall and under the electric wire and go in and rub behind his ears. I wanted to show him that he was cared for, trusted, safe. I wanted to pick him up and cradle him in my arms, but of course that was as impossible as going into the enclosure. He wasn't a child; he was an elephant who weighed more than a truck. He was an elephant who had injured people, who had killed a man.

Burma took one of the apples with his trunk and put it in his mouth. I heard him give it a big crunch. He took the second apple and did the same.

I took a half step back, then another and another, until there was a safe distance between us.

"Come, Burma, come!" I said. I started down the fence toward the bales and Joyce.

He followed along, paralleling me on the other side of the fence. We were separate but more together than we'd ever been before.

Joyce was just finishing the last few bales, and there was a pile inside the enclosure waiting for Burma. She tossed another bale, looked up at the two of us, and smiled.

"Breakfast is served," she said.

Burma started eating.

"Don't you normally eat your main course before you have your dessert?" Joyce asked Burma.

I looked at her quizzically.

"Shouldn't the apples come after the hay?"

"Usually, I guess." I paused. "How much did you see?"

"I saw as much or as little as you want me to have seen."

"Thank you," I said. "It would just worry my dad."

"With good reason. You aren't actually going into the pen, right?"

"No. Not yet. And I won't until he tells me I can."

"Did he tell you that you could hand-feed Burma?"

"Not really, but that's different. At least a little different."

She paused for a moment. "I'm glad to hear that you're not going in. I know you know elephants better than anybody, maybe even better than Jack, but—"

"I'll be careful even so," I said. "And thank you for saying that. It means a lot to me—it really does. And maybe even more, thanks for keeping this between us."

She slipped an arm around my shoulder, and I had to fight myself to not move away. I didn't want to offend Joyce, and it wasn't her—it was just being close to people. It was funny how I felt more comfortable with the touch of an elephant than the touch of a person, any person other than my father. Maybe I was just more familiar with one species than the other, or maybe one seemed more dangerous. We stood there silently, watching Burma eat.

CHAPTER
Thirteen

AS WE HAD DONE LAST WEEK, I TURNED AWAY THE LAST of the cars waiting to enter the sanctuary. I'd told visitors that the baby needed to be alone. Most people were understanding. A couple of the would-be visitors were less than understanding, offering me more money for admission or responding with choice words and accusations when I told them they had to leave. The more I was around some people, the more I realized why I liked elephants better.

Stacy and Lizzy had been planning to come out today as well, and I had to tell them they couldn't come either. They understood, but I knew they were disappointed. So was I. It would have been nice to see them and show off our new baby.

I had taped the big CLOSED sign to the gate again to turn people away. Of course I'd still have to answer anybody who honked, because we were expecting our partner to arrive today. I still didn't like the sound of that—partner. A backer didn't sound nearly as likely to interfere.

The herd was waiting just inside the fence. They were spending most of their time in a triangle formed by the house, the trailer, and the pond. Trixie kept them close to where she knew Woolly would be fed. Perhaps they still wanted to keep Daisy Mae in sight as well.

I had slept in my bed in the house the night before. Joyce did the first two feedings while I was asleep. She was supposed to get me up to do the next one, but she didn't. I was a little bit annoyed but more than a little bit grateful. Sleep is necessary. How do parents take care of a newborn human baby that has to be fed every few hours? How does a single parent do it alone? Elephants and humans need others to help them.

Joyce had put together a feeding schedule for Bacca, who was offered a bottle every fifth time Woolly got one. It wasn't necessary for him nutritionally — he could survive without formula or milk — but psychologically it was good for him, a nice and caring gesture. Woolly wasn't the only one who'd lost her mother.

I had started to see that Joyce wasn't doing nice things to impress my father or me. She was doing them because she was nice. She'd been spending more nights at the farm since Woolly had been born. I was okay with that. I was okay with her. It wasn't just the elephants who were willing to let her a little bit further into the herd.

I heard an engine. I hoped the driver would see the sign

162

and go away. The noise got louder and louder, and I realized it didn't sound like a car. I looked up to see a big black helicopter sweeping overhead. I spun around, following it with my eyes. What was this idiot doing? The helicopter was so low and loud that it would scare the elephants. Thank goodness they had moved away and were in the cover of the trees.

My father came running out of the house. He was yelling and shaking his fist at the helicopter, which was now hovering over the empty field between the house and the pond. Even from a hundred yards away, I could see that the rotor was kicking up a storm of dust.

I ran to Dad's side. "What is he doing?" I yelled over the roar of the rotors.

"I have no idea, but . . . wait . . . It's dropping down . . . Is he going to *land?*"

No question, the helicopter was coming down.

"Come on!" Dad shouted.

We jumped in the truck, and he gunned the engine and raced toward the chopper. If it did land, he would demand an explanation, and I was certain he would make whoever it was regret ever landing on our property. Seeing his elephants disturbed or threatened was the one thing guaranteed to make my easygoing father angry. Right now he looked like he was going to explode — like a bull elephant about to charge.

The chopper touched down, and we skidded to a stop a safe

distance away. We both raised our windows to keep out the hail of dust and stones that pelted against the vehicle.

"Whoever it is, he's going to pay for the damage to the truck," Dad said.

I had to hope that was the only damage that was going to happen.

The rotors of the chopper got slower and slower until they finally came to a stop, lazily spinning in the other direction. The dust settled down, and there was silence.

"It's time to meet our unexpected and unwelcome guests." My father jumped out of the truck and started toward the helicopter.

Then I remembered. "Wait!" I yelled as I ran to his side. "What if it isn't unexpected guests?"

He kept moving. "You were expecting a helicopter?"

"We *were* expecting somebody," I said. "Our partner, remember?"

"But by helicopter?"

"Who else could afford to come here in a helicopter?" I asked. "When was our partner supposed to arrive?"

He stopped and looked at me. "This afternoon, but I wasn't given a time."

"Then maybe you should be welcoming until we know if it's them," I suggested.

"Until we know, I'll be friendly."

The door to the helicopter opened, and a staircase was lowered down. The first person out was a man wearing a uniform. A flight attendant? Next was a man dressed completely in black. In contrast to his clothing, his hair was almost pure white.

He bounded down the five steps in one leap. He looked around, saw us, and practically sprinted in our direction. He moved really fast for somebody that old. *Wait!* As he neared, I saw he wasn't that old — it was just the hair. He was about my dad's age, maybe a little older, and a little bit shorter than me.

"You must be Jack Gray!" he yelled out as he grabbed Dad's hand and started pumping it.

"Yes, I am. And you're . . ."

"Your partner! I'm JM Limited, which is really my initials. I'm James Mercury." He was no longer yelling but was still speaking way too fast.

"I'm pleased to meet you, Mr. Mercury," Dad said.

"Come on — now that we're sharing a baby, we're practically family. Call me Jimmy!" He turned to me. "And you have to be Samantha — Sammy. You can call me Uncle Jimmy."

That wasn't going to happen. I didn't know him, but I knew he wasn't family.

"So where is our little girl?" he asked — still too fast and excited.

"She's on the other side of the property, in the forest," Dad replied.

"Should we take the helicopter?"

"I think the truck would be better."

"Excellent! Do you think I could drive?"

"Sure, if you want."

"I don't get much of a chance to drive, so thank you."

"The keys are in the truck," Dad told him.

Without a word, our partner sprinted away toward the truck, leaving us behind. What a character!

"He certainly is excited about seeing Woolly," Dad said.

"Baby elephants seem to do that to people."

By the time we caught up with him, Call-Me-Jimmy had started the truck and was revving the engine. My father opened the door, and I slid in first.

"Is this the truck we purchased from the zoo?" Jimmy asked.

"It's the one."

"Is it a good truck?" he asked.

"Very good."

"Excellent! I'm glad we got our money's worth. Which way?"

"Straight ahead, and we'll make a left at the —"

The truck shot backward and then slammed to a stop.

"Whoops, wrong gear," he said. "Let's try this one."

He fiddled with the gearshift. He seemed to be having trouble finding first gear. After fumbling with the gears and moving the shifter around, he finally got the truck into gear — possibly first — and let out the clutch. There was a grinding sound, the truck jumped forward, and then the engine stalled.

"Do you want me to drive?" my dad asked.

"Or me?" I added.

"You're old enough to drive?" Jimmy asked me.

"I'm fourteen — well, almost fourteen — but age doesn't seem to be the problem here."

"Samantha," my father said sternly. I guess that was at least a little rude.

"Wait. You're saying I'm old enough to drive but I *can't* — is that the joke?"

"That was the idea. It was sort of a joke."

He giggled. "That was funny. I don't usually drive. My board of directors thinks I'm a danger to myself and others behind the wheel of a vehicle."

"That's not reassuring to those of us riding with you," I replied.

"But that's in the city. Out here, what could I hit?"

"A tree. The pond. A baby elephant," I said.

"Oh, that's not good. That is very not good. Maybe somebody else *should* drive." He threw the door open, jumped out, and raced around to the passenger side.

"Shift over," my father said.

I slid behind the wheel, Dad moved into the middle, and "Uncle Jimmy" climbed in. I started the truck and seamlessly slipped into first gear, and we were off.

He leaned across my father to address me. "How long have you been driving?"

"Since I was about eleven or twelve."

"Earlier," Dad said. "You drove the tractor when you were nine."

"I meant cars, and by myself, but of course that's all just around the property. It's not like I drive out on the roads."

"But I'm sure you could. You're better than half the people on the road," my father added.

"Driving is very difficult. There just seem to be too many rules to remember, places to look, and things to do, all at once," Jimmy said.

"It's not that difficult," I said as I bumped us along the path.

"Do you think it's wise to have the baby so far from the house?"

"They do mainly stay by the house, but the herd goes where the herd goes," I said.

"But shouldn't she be supervised more closely?"

"We have somebody watching and feeding her," Dad said. At the moment, that somebody was Joyce.

"Excellent! Excellent!" That seemed to be his favorite word. "Is he a veterinarian?"

"She's a lawyer," my father answered.

"A lawyer!" he exclaimed. "I really don't think there should be a need for litigation on this matter! There's no need to get lawyers involved!"

"She's not here as a lawyer," Dad said. "She's a friend — a good friend, my girlfriend."

It was strange hearing him describe her that way. Had I ever heard him say those words about her before?

"She's one of the volunteers who help out here at the sanctuary," he continued.

"Of course. What was I thinking? But you do have proper medical care, correct?"

"Doc Morgan is the best large-animal vet around these parts, and he's here a lot."

"He's *excellent!*" I said. "Just *excellent!*"

"Now you sound like me," he said. "I like that . . . or are you joking with me again?"

"Just a little," I admitted. "But the word does seem to fit."

"The baby being with the herd, I assume, means that she's been accepted as a member of the herd."

"Yes," said Dad. "She has been completely accepted by the entire herd."

"I'm so pleased to hear that. I was concerned."

"Why?" I asked.

"It's just that sometimes it's hard to fit into a group. I personally always found it hard to fit in. Being different is difficult."

"Elephants are different from people," I said. "They are very accepting."

I could see how he might not fit in. And I understood the feeling on a more personal level. Being an Elephant Girl sometimes meant you fit in with elephants more than you did with girls.

"Oh, and I haven't mentioned—I was so sad when you wrote about the surrogate mother dying."

"That was a tragedy," Dad said.

"I couldn't sleep that night, I was so upset."

Hearing that made me like him a little.

Daisy Mae still remained where she had fallen and died. Eventually my father would bring in a backhoe to bury her, but that couldn't happen while the herd was grieving her loss. Individually or together as a herd, the elephants were still stopping by her side. They would touch or caress her with their trunks. Trixie would gently shove Daisy Mae with her head, and Bacca would hold on to her tail. It was all very touching and very sad. We'd wait until the herd let us know it was time.

"Is that the end of the property?" Jimmy asked.

"No, that's the fence around the isolation pen," my father answered. "We have a new bull in there."

"His name is Burma," I added. "He's being rehabilitated before he can join the herd."

"What an incredible thing you do here, to save elephants, to rescue them. It's an honor to be a small part of that, even if it's only financial."

I liked hearing him say that. I didn't know much about *who* he was, but I was getting a sense of *what* he was. He was an animal lover.

"Your financial contributions were a lot more than a small part," my father said. "And this truck and the medical trailer — well, that was beyond generous."

"Nothing is too good for our little girl!" Jimmy exclaimed.

We rounded the corner of the isolation pen, and the herd came into view.

"There they are!" Jimmy screamed. "There they are!"

I slowed down. I never wanted to come too fast or get too close to the herd when I was in a vehicle. I pulled up onto a grassy strip and was about to stop when the passenger door flew open, and Jimmy tried to jump out of the truck while it was still moving. Dad grabbed him by the arm, and I slammed on the brakes.

"What are you doing?" Dad demanded.

"Sorry. I saw the elephants and just wanted to get out."

171

"It's a good thing you didn't see them from the helicopter," I said.

"No, those doors are sealed . . . Another joke. Okay."

He got out and headed rapidly toward the herd.

"Wait!" I yelled, and I was relieved that he stopped. I ran and caught up to him. "They don't know you. If you come up too fast, you could unsettle them."

"Again, even more sorry."

"Just walk with us, and we'll introduce you to the herd."

"Another joke?"

"No joke," Dad said as he joined us. "They need to know that you're not a danger, especially now. A herd gets more protective when there's a newborn, and the death of Daisy Mae has been disturbing enough to begin with."

With Jimmy between us, we walked toward the herd. They had seen the truck and were watching us. Of course they could tell—if not by sight, then by smell—that there was a stranger among us. Joyce had been standing under a tree, a book under her arm, and she gave us a wave. We waved back, and she started toward us.

Behind and between elephant legs, I could see Woolly. She was so little that she could easily have been lost from view, but her distinctive coloring helped me spot her. She was right beside her half brother, Bacca. They shared a mother, but they must have had dissimilar fathers. Woolly looked very different from how Bacca had looked as a baby.

"Oh, my goodness, I see her," Jimmy said. "That's her, partially hidden, right?"

"She's there," Dad said.

"How many people have seen her?"

What a strange question, I thought.

My dad went ahead and answered it. "Well, the two of us and Joyce, of course," he said. "Then there were Mr. and Mrs. Patterson and Nigel and Jenna, who all helped feed her."

"And Doc Morgan and the other two vets, Dr. Grace and Dr. Tavaris," I added.

"So that makes me the eleventh person in the entire *world* to see her," he said.

"I think that's right," my father agreed.

"The eleventh person *alive* on the entire planet to see her."

Dad and I exchanged a look. What did he mean — as opposed to dead people who had seen her?

"Jimmy, this is Joyce," Dad said as Joyce reached us.

"Joyce, the lawyer?"

"I'm Joyce Hepburn, and yes, I'm a lawyer," she said.

"I don't like lawyers."

I stifled a laugh. I mostly felt the same way.

"I must have a dozen lawyers who work for my company,

but I still don't like them. Can we go closer now?" He had finished with Joyce and was looking at the herd.

"Certainly, but you have to stay right with us and move slowly — no sudden movements," Dad said.

We walked toward Trixie. As the matriarch, she was also the gatekeeper and protector. She didn't know this little man with the shock of white hair and had to be certain she could trust him.

"Good morning, Trixie," my dad said.

She tilted her head to the side, and her ears twitched slightly.

"Trixie, this is our friend Jimmy," I said. I wasn't sure if that was the right word, but I didn't think she'd understand backer or partner.

He turned to me. "Friend? That is so nice. Thank you for thinking of me that way."

"Um, sure. Come a little closer," I said.

We stopped directly in front of Trixie. She reached out her trunk, and he jerked back a little.

"It's okay," I said. "Think of it as her wanting to shake your hand."

Even if he didn't fully understand, Trixie did. She extended her trunk again and touched the top of his head. She snuffled around him, inhaling his scent, and then ran her trunk through his hair. She lowered her trunk and delicately ran the "fingers" along his face.

Jimmy giggled. "It tickles."

"I think she likes you," Dad said.

"I like her. Hello, Trixie. Are you helping to take care of our girl?"

His voice was gentle and calm, and he was talking to her much more slowly than he'd spoken to us. It was like he was more relaxed and comfortable talking to Trixie than he'd been with us, with people. I knew that feeling from the inside, and I'm sure my father did.

"Would you mind if I went to talk to the baby?" Jimmy asked.

"Of course not," my father said.

"I was asking Trixie," he said.

I couldn't help but smile. This little man who wanted to talk to Woolly wasn't who I expected our partner to be.

"She said yes," Dad answered. "Samantha, you can take him."

Jimmy reached out unexpectedly and took my hand. Then he reached back and took my father's hand, and my father took Joyce's hand. They trailed along after me. I felt like the engine on a human train or the leader of a herd of elephants.

I greeted each animal by name, and Jimmy repeated the

greeting. Bacca moved aside, and for the first time, Woolly was completely revealed.

Jimmy gasped. "I can't believe my eyes," he said. "She's even more beautiful than I could have imagined."

"She's cute, but still, she's a little odd-looking with all that extra fur," I said.

"No, that's exactly how I expected her to look."

Obviously he hadn't seen a lot of baby elephants before. I'd never seen one as young as Woolly myself.

I stopped right in front of Woolly, and she nuzzled against me, knocking me slightly backward. She was being gentle, but she was still a couple of hundred pounds of clumsy.

Jimmy bent down until he was eye to eye with Woolly. She seemed a little thrown and hid her head behind me.

"She looks perfect," Jimmy said.

"As far as we can tell, she is perfect," Dad said. "She has four feet, two ears, and a trunk — all the basic body parts."

"And she's feeding well?"

"Doc Morgan said she's gained almost seventeen pounds over the last two days," I answered.

"We have a whole roster of people who feed her," Joyce said.

"Joyce figured out all of that," Dad added. He looked at her and smiled — a big, goofy, happy smile. Joyce made him happy.

"Finally, a lawyer doing something I agree with," Jimmy said. He gently placed his hand against Woolly's side.

"She likes being scratched behind the ear," I said.

He started rubbing behind her ear, and she moved a little closer to him.

"Little girl, you are a miracle, a complete and utter miracle, that I never thought I would see with my own eyes," Jimmy said.

"Her name is Woolly," I said.

"Woolly?" he questioned. He straightened up and turned directly to me and my father. "You called her Woolly?"

"It was Samantha's idea."

"It was the perfect name for her," I said. "Don't you like it?"

"I like it a lot. It *is* perfect. I just didn't think you'd figure it out without me telling you . . . I was going to tell you today. I wanted to do it in person after I'd seen her."

"Figured what out?" my dad asked. "Going to tell us what?"

"That she's not an elephant. She's a woolly mammoth."

Fourteen

"COULD YOU REPEAT THAT?" DAD ASKED.

"Yes, please," I said. "I thought you said that Woolly was a woolly mammoth."

"I did, and she is," Jimmy said.

"But that's impossible," I said.

"Mammoths have been extinct for over five thousand years," Dad said, shaking his head.

"That date is generally placed at closer to forty-five hundred years ago, although it was recently discovered that a small population was living on Wrangel Island that died out as recently as thirty-five hundred years ago."

"Either way, they've been extinct for a long time," I said. "They're *extinct*. This can't be a mammoth."

Jimmy looked from me to my dad, to Joyce, and back to me again. He started chuckling.

"So you're joking," I said.

"I think the joke was on me," Jimmy said. "You really didn't know — you just picked a name. I let the cat out of the bag — or really the mammoth out of the elephant — by accident. I was going to break it to you slowly, explain things, before I told you." He gestured toward Woolly. "Mammoths *were* extinct. As you can see, they are no longer extinct."

"This can't be real," I said.

"No, it is real; I believe him," Dad said slowly. "That would explain why Woolly looks different from any baby elephant I've ever seen."

"And also explains why somebody would spend over a million dollars to produce her," Joyce added.

"Actually, when you throw in all the research, the total is closer to seventy million dollars," Jimmy said cheerfully. "But it was worth it. Woolly is real. If seeing is believing, what more proof do you need?"

Woolly looked at me quizzically, like she was trying to make sense of all this talk.

"Why didn't you tell me at the beginning what you were doing?" Dad asked.

"My business interests require me to keep things top secret. We predicted there was around a five percent chance of success, so there was only one chance in twenty that you and I would ever need to have this conversation. Besides, if I had told you, you would have thought I was at least a little bit crazy, right?"

"More than a little bit."

"I see where she gets her sense of humor. Very funny."

"I wasn't trying to be funny," Dad said. "This *is* crazy."

"That would be far from the first time I've had that adjective applied to me or my ideas, and it certainly won't be the last. But really, standing here, looking at Woolly, I would argue that she is the product of a combination of scientific genius and a miracle rather than a defect in my mental stability."

We all stood there staring at Woolly. She stared back innocently.

"But at such vast expense," Joyce said.

"Miracles come at a cost, and really, it's not that much money," Jimmy said. "I have lots of money, but nobody has a mammoth. How much do you think a woolly mammoth is worth to the world?"

My father shook his head. "I can't even imagine."

"That's because it's priceless. Woolly is priceless," Jimmy said. "We are standing beside the most valuable animal in the entire history of the world."

"But how is this actually possible?" I asked.

"It's fairly technical, but in some ways very simple. I developed a software package that could sequence the genome pattern of animals — dogs, cats, even people. All you need is a tissue sample. I have it all outlined on my computer. I was going to show a presentation to you to break the news and explain it all. If you still want to see it, I'll fetch the laptop from the helicopter."

"Helicopter?" Joyce asked.

"He owns a helicopter," I said. "He flew in."

"Technically the helicopter is owned by the company, but because I own the company, I guess it *is* mine. I think we have three of them, plus the corporate jet."

"Wait," Joyce said. She came right up to Jimmy and stared at him. They were almost exactly the same height. "Jimmy, as in short for James . . . Are you James Mercury?"

"Yes, I'm James Mercury."

"James Mercury, the founder and president of JM Limited, one of the top tech companies in the world?"

"Top three, but guilty as charged."

She turned to me and my dad, indicating Jimmy with a wave of her hand. "This is one of the richest people in the world."

Jimmy shrugged. "That's what my accountants tell me, but it's only money — an abstract concept with the sole purpose of allowing us to pursue ideas. Can I feed Woolly now?"

"I don't see why not," Dad said. "After all, she belongs to all of us."

"All of us, and ultimately the whole world."

* * *

WHILE JIMMY WAS DETOURING TO THE HELICOPTER TO get his computer, we went into the house. Joyce, the last to enter, closed the door with a distinct slam.

"My goodness, that's James Mercury," she said.

"Is that his real name or something he invented?" I asked.

"That's his name. He's a genius."

"You wouldn't think that if you saw him trying to drive a car."

"No, he's a genuine, certified genius. He's invented or designed computer programs and systems, apps, medical devices, scientific instruments, and new metallic components and alloys."

"How do you know so much about him?" I asked.

"He's been on the cover of *Time, Newsweek,* the *Economist,* and practically every major tech and business magazine on the planet, as well as being featured on *60 Minutes.* I've even read an unauthorized biography on him."

"So he's more than some rich eccentric who likes animals," Dad replied.

"He's *so* much more. If anybody could clone a mammoth, it would be him," Joyce said. "When he said money is relative, he wasn't kidding. His net worth is somewhere in the neighborhood of eighteen billion dollars."

"You said *billion* with a *b* and not *million* with an *m*, right?" I asked.

"Billion. Aside from being the principal shareholder and president of JM Limited, he has diversified into a variety of high-tech and communications companies."

"Okay, it makes sense to me now," I said.

"You want to explain it to us?" Dad asked.

"He wanted a pet."

They both looked puzzled.

"Half the elephants we get are from private collections. Some rich guy thinks he should have a pet elephant, so he goes out and buys one. He has more money than brains."

"You mean, because this Jimmy guy has so much more money than anybody else, he wants a pet nobody else has," my father said. "That makes Woolly his very expensive vanity project."

"I think you're judging him too harshly," Joyce said. "He's also probably the biggest financial contributor to conservation and animal-rescue causes around the globe. He just bought more than a hundred seventy-five thousand acres of the Amazon rainforest."

"What is he going to do with all that land?" I asked.

"Nothing. He put it in a trust, to preserve it for eternity. He's decided that the best way to preserve the rainforest is simply to buy it."

"I'll admit, that's impressive," Dad said.

"He's made contributions to save endangered animals and protect their habitat, including for elephants in Asia."

"Even more impressive."

"And his efforts to help have extended from developing and distributing vaccines in Third World countries to building hundreds of water projects to funding research to fight diseases and find cures."

"He sounds like an amazing person," I said.

"I guess we wouldn't know him unless he made the cover of *National Geographic*," Dad joked.

"He *has* been featured in *National Geographic* and was on the cover a few years ago."

"That explains it. All we have is back issues," I said. "Our newest issue is older than me."

"But the important thing is that he's a genuine humanitarian and conservationist," Joyce said.

"He's also a little strange," I said.

"He's a full-fledged eccentric, which many geniuses are. I read a pop-psychology sort of write-up about him. He's in a unique category of different."

"I guess you'd have to be to think you should breed a woolly mammoth," I said.

"Definitely. I was wondering why you said Woolly was his expensive pet. Who owns Woolly?" Joyce asked.

"We do!" I said, and quickly turned to my father. "Right?"

"We own almost all of her. Jimmy holds ten percent of the sanctuary, including the animals. The rest is ours."

"So you and Sam have ninety percent ownership of the most valuable animal in the world," Joyce said.

"I guess we do," my father agreed. "I guess we do."

There was a quiet knock on the front door; then it opened, and Jimmy stuck his head in. "May I come in?"

"Since you own ten percent of the place, I'm not sure we could stop you if we wanted to," I said.

"Another joke! Although technically that means I could only come ten percent in — only ten percent of my body could enter."

"Funny," I said.

He tilted his head to one side. "I don't see myself as a funny person." He came all the way in, carrying a state-of-the-art laptop.

"Oh, I'm willing to bet that many, many people find you very funny," I said.

He chuckled. "Many people find me peculiar or unique or different or utterly unusual or funny in a way that doesn't involve humor. You certainly like to make jokes."

"Some of them are even funny," I said.

"Many of them."

"Some people think I'm hilarious."

"And you're different. You and your father run an elephant sanctuary," he said. "For some people, that in itself would define the two of you as eccentrics."

"Or completely crazy," Dad said.

Or define me as an Elephant Girl, I thought.

"And sometimes I think they might be at least a little bit right," Dad went on. "Who in their right mind thinks this is normal?"

"Normal is highly overrated," Jimmy said. "What you're doing is actually noble."

Noble — I liked that.

We all sat down at the kitchen table, and Jimmy opened his computer.

"Open mammoth-genome-sequencing program," he said, and the screen came to life. He was aware of our startled responses. "It's completely voice-activated. It recognizes my voice and will do anything I tell it to."

"Did you invent that?" Joyce asked.

He shrugged. "'Invent' is probably too strong a term. I simply adapted basic voice-recognition software and created an internal app. Within two years, this is how most personal computers will operate."

"That's even more amazing. Sign me up," I said.

"Just what the world needs, more screen time," my father added. He used computers, but he was no big fan.

"I'll make sure you're in the first test-product rollout. If all goes according to schedule, you'll have one in two months."

"You're joking, right?" I asked.

He shook his head. "Remember, I'm not that funny."

"Then — thanks so much!"

"My pleasure. Now, this specific project — the cloning project — began either four years ago, or four thousand, or four hundred thousand, depending upon where you think the beginning is."

"Four hundred thousand years ago sounds like close to the beginning of the beginning, so why don't you start there?" I suggested.

"Very well. Approximately four hundred thousand years ago, the woolly mammoth diverged from the steppe mammoth in Eastern Asia." He cleared his throat. "Early mammoth."

The image on the screen changed to show two elephant-like animals identified as *Steppe Mammoth* and *Woolly Mammoth*. I could see how much our little Woolly looked like her distant relative.

"Northern Hemisphere."

On the screen now was a map of the Northern Hemisphere focusing on the tundra and polar areas.

"The woolly mammoth was very successful and ultimately had a habitat that spread across all of Northern Europe, Asia, and North America. Comparison."

Now the screen showed a woolly mammoth, an African elephant, and an Asian elephant.

"While the mammoth was roughly the same physical size as an African elephant, it had specific adaptations to allow it to thrive in these northern climates: longer fur, with an outer covering of long guard hair over a shorter undercoat for insulation; shorter ears and tail to protect against heat loss and minimize the potential for frostbite; and longer tusks for breaking through snow to graze."

"The ears and forehead look more like the Asian elephant," Joyce said.

"Excellent observation. The Asian elephant is the closest genetic link to the mammoth. Now let's jump forward to about four thousand years ago. A very much alive woolly mammoth was living in Eastern Siberia."

"In Russia?"

"In what is now Russia. It was a healthy female."

"And you know that how?" my father asked.

"Because the entire body was preserved in the ice. Excavation," Jimmy said.

On the screen was a photograph of the body of what was obviously a woolly mammoth, complete with fur. It was surrounded by men wearing parkas.

"Archaeologists believe that she became mired in mud and couldn't extricate herself."

"That happens to modern elephants," Dad said.

"She would have suffocated, then sunk into the mire and frozen."

"So you didn't have only fossilized remains. You had the carcass, the actual flesh of the mammoth," Dad said.

"Completely intact," Jimmy said. "Including blood that was still liquid."

"How can that be possible?" I asked.

"There may have been something in their blood that acted as the equivalent of antifreeze. They could have survived the bleak frigid temperatures on the frozen planet of Mars. I have an entire unit working to isolate this compound and investigate its practical implications and adaptation for use in mechanical systems."

"I'd be surprised if you didn't," Joyce said. "That is amazing."

"But that is not nearly as interesting as the discovery of the frozen carcass itself."

"It had to be like finding a needle in a haystack," Dad said.

"More like finding one of *many* needles in a haystack. Since the 1920s, close to fifty different mammoths with frozen tissue samples have been uncovered. Here are the very first pictures I received. Early excavation," he said.

We all leaned closer to the screen.

A series of photos revealed what looked like a rock poking

out of the mud and the workers digging until the corpse was completely exposed.

"It looks like it's asleep," I said.

"Or just died yesterday," Dad said.

"When I saw these pictures, I knew that I had to purchase and preserve it."

"I know how you could purchase it, but how did you preserve it?" Joyce asked.

"It was transferred to a gigantic freezer so it would remain frozen, preventing decomposition of the cellular material. In other words, I didn't want it to start rotting, so I kept it frozen — sort of like a frozen dinner you'd buy at the supermarket."

The rest of us sat in silence.

"While still frozen, it was examined, a full autopsy was made, slides were prepared, and genetic material was gathered."

"So how did you get from that to Woolly?" I asked.

"That is such an interesting question. It could have gone two ways: creating an elephant-mammoth hybrid or creating a full mammoth."

"Wouldn't you want something that was one hundred percent mammoth?" Dad asked.

"Certainly, but that is scientifically more difficult and of course much, much more expensive."

"So that's what you did, naturally," Joyce said.

"When something is better and more difficult to accomplish, that is the route that *must* be pursued. We were able to harvest woolly mammoth DNA that allowed us to create a clone. Do you know what a clone is?" he asked me.

"A clone is a baby that is genetically identical to either its mother or its father and not a combination of their genes."

"Exactly correct."

I shrugged. "We learned about them in science class," I said. "A sheep was the first clone, right?"

"Dolly the sheep," he confirmed. "She was the first, but subsequently the techniques have become much more refined. With dogs, for example, there is now almost a ten percent chance that the cloned animal will be viable."

"Viable?"

"Born healthy enough to survive and breed."

He had the computer show us a number of screens that were technical stuff about removing the DNA material of an egg cell from a female elephant, replacing it with the woolly mammoth DNA, stimulating the division of one cell into two and two into four and so on, and then inserting it back into the female elephant, who would be the host mother.

"And you implanted a cloned woolly mammoth egg in all three of our elephants?" Dad asked.

"Your three elephants, as well as seventeen other elephants at sanctuaries and zoos around the world."

"You impregnated twenty elephants!" Dad exclaimed.

"Yes. We invested in seven other sanctuaries and zoos as we did here."

"So by making twenty attempts, you were hoping to increase your odds of success," Joyce said.

"Statistically it made the most sense."

I gasped. "Do you mean Woolly isn't the only baby?"

He shook his head. "This was the only egg that was able to reach maturity and become a living mammoth."

"So Woolly is the only one," Dad said. "The only mammoth."

"She is the only living mammoth on the entire planet — in fact, the only mammoth on the planet in over three thousand five hundred years."

"If things went perfectly, there could have been twenty," I said.

"Technically," Jimmy said.

"One out of twenty seems like pretty bad results," I said. "Is that because you did something wrong?"

"That's a legitimate question. In normal cloning, the DNA is taken from a living or recently deceased animal, as opposed to DNA that was frozen for thousands of years. We had to be aware of the possibility that the material had degenerated or degraded. We also knew that the long gestation period of elephants meant a greater risk of things going wrong. We projected a five percent success rate."

"And one out of twenty is exactly five percent," Dad said.

"As predicted."

"So Woolly is a miracle of modern science," Joyce said.

"And that's why she must be watched, cared for, and protected," Jimmy said. "I think it would be best if nobody else is made aware that she is anything other than a baby elephant. Can you imagine how the press would descend on this place if they knew there was a mammoth here?"

"It would be a zoo of a different type," Joyce said.

"As it is, I'm continually hounded by paparazzi. If this got out, I would be the center of an even bigger circus."

"We can keep this a secret," I said.

"In fact, you *have* to keep it a secret," Jimmy said. "Part of the agreement you signed was a nondisclosure clause."

"A what?"

"An agreement that you and Jack wouldn't speak about what you were doing," Joyce explained.

"I'm aware of that," my dad said. "But you don't need that clause. You have our word."

"And as the sanctuary's lawyer, I have professional fiduciary responsibility to keep matters confidential," Joyce said.

"Besides, who would believe us if we did say something?" I asked.

"You'd be surprised what people are prepared to accept as the truth," Jimmy said.

"What about the visitors and volunteers who come in?" Dad asked. "As she grows, I imagine she'll look more and more like a mammoth."

"Good point. I'd like you to suspend the Sunday openings indefinitely, and I will make up the lost income. Would that be agreeable?"

"More than agreeable."

I knew Dad would never have allowed the Sunday openings to begin with if we hadn't needed the money.

"I also want no more volunteers to be allowed on the property."

"We don't need the visitors, but we do need the volunteers, especially in light of all the additional work that's needed to feed Woolly," my father said.

"And Bacca," I added.

"I understand the demands and will compensate for the extra work by offering to pay you a regular salary to be here instead of at your other job," Jimmy said. "If that's acceptable."

"Being here beats working at the diner," my dad said.

"And what did you think of Dr. Grace and Dr. Tavaris?" Jimmy asked.

"Very competent. I was impressed, as was Dr. Morgan. We know that Woolly wouldn't be alive without them."

"Good. I'll have my people contact them, and with your approval, they will become employees of the sanctuary."

"How do you know they'll even be interested?" Joyce asked.

"Enough money motivates most people, and who wouldn't want to become involved in a historic event? They would have the chance to be the personal vets of a woolly mammoth!"

"Woolly already has a vet," Dad said. "Doc Morgan."

"Arrangements will be made for him to be hired on a full-time basis to augment your staff, and we will have them all sign nondisclosure agreements."

"We don't need three vets," Dad said.

"It's all probably not necessary," Jimmy said. "But how could we live with the knowledge that something went wrong and we chose not to have the resources available? We owe it to Woolly. We owe it to the world to take utmost care of her."

It was hard to argue with that logic, maybe even wrong to try.

"I've also arranged for assistance of a different type. There is a contingent of security guards surrounding your property."

"What?" Dad and I asked at the same time.

"The moment I became aware of the birth of Woolly, I had security guards placed inconspicuously around the sanctuary."

"Are they driving white pickup trucks?" Dad asked.

"Yes, I believe they are."

"I noticed a couple of trucks yesterday, but I thought it was my mind working on too little sleep."

"Their assignment was to discreetly secure the perimeter of the property until I had discussed it with you. I thought security would be wise."

"We do have a herd of elephants to protect Woolly," Dad said. "I don't think we need guards."

"They'll protect Woolly with their lives," I said.

"And those lives could easily be taken by men with high-powered rifles."

I felt a shiver go up my spine.

"Do you really think that might happen?" Dad asked.

"I'm trying to think of the worst possibility and prepare for it so that it doesn't happen."

I caught movement out of the corner of my eye and looked out the front window. The herd, led by Trixie, was coming toward the house. Woolly was in the middle of the group, holding on to Bacca's tail. I knew the herd would defend Woolly with their lives if necessary. I didn't want it to be necessary.

"We should keep the guards," I said.

Both Dad and Joyce looked surprised.

"What can it hurt?" I asked.

Dad nodded. "Then we'll keep the guards."

"Excellent. Now, if there are no more questions, I need to be going," Jimmy said.

"You could stay for dinner, even overnight if you want," Dad offered.

"Thank you, but I have too much to attend to at my office. Besides, if I'm gone too long, it might alert somebody to my presence here, or to the project itself."

"What do you mean?" I asked.

"I tend to be followed not only by the paparazzi but by corporate spies. You wouldn't believe the flight pattern we followed to get us here without anybody knowing where we were going. In fact, the last five miles we traveled low enough to avoid radar detection. I even sent my personal bodyguard off in a different direction by car to throw off the hounds."

"Between the guards, the helicopter, and the secrecy, this all sounds like a military operation," Joyce said.

"Yes, it does. And it's one that's going to succeed."

Fifteen

WOOLLY BUMPED INTO DR. GRACE, WHO BOUNCED BACK-ward a few feet, pulling the bottle out of Woolly's mouth. Dr. Grace, with her freckles and very white skin, always wore a big hat and was lathering on sunscreen to protect herself from the sun. Dr. Tavaris, with his olive skin, didn't seem to be worried.

"I never thought I'd be a wet nurse for a woolly mammoth," Dr. Grace said.

"Has anybody ever thought they would be?" I asked.

"Probably not any sane person, but I wish I could be better at it. Why doesn't she take the bottle from me as well as she does from you?"

"I've been doing it longer."

That was true, but I didn't think it was the only reason. We were standing in the midst of the herd, and for a zoo vet, she was surprisingly anxious around the elephants.

Dr. Grace and Dr. Tavaris had been back with us for four days. They arrived only two days after Jimmy dropped his bombshell. They had said they were thrilled to be here again. It was good to have the extra hands, even if they weren't as much help as I would have expected.

"Your father told me that you hope to become a vet," Dr. Grace said.

"That's my plan."

"It's a great career, but you have to know it's harder to get into veterinary school than to get into medical school."

"I'm pretty smart, you know," I said defensively.

"Sorry, I didn't mean to imply otherwise. I think you'd be a natural. So much of this job is more than the science, and you certainly have the feel. You're so good around the elephants."

"Thanks."

"They do make me a little nervous," she said.

"They are big, and you have to be able to read their moods. I try to think like one of them."

"I'll try that. It might make it easier for me to do my share of the feedings."

It was good to have the two of them around. What made the whole thing work, though, was Dad being here full-time. Jimmy was paying him twice as much as the diner paid, and he got to be here with the elephants. He said it was like a dream come true. Dreams made me nervous, because they weren't that different from nightmares.

"Do you want me to do the feeding?" I asked.

"I think Woolly would like that." She handed me the bottle, and Woolly began to suckle almost immediately.

"Her weight gain has been remarkable," Dr. Grace said.

"How much has she gained?"

"She has been averaging 8.3 pounds per day for the past fourteen days, so she has gone from a birth weight of 177 pounds to her present weight of 293.2 pounds."

"That's good, right?" I asked.

"Almost perfect for an elephant, so we assume it's good for a woolly mammoth."

Since finding out what Woolly was, I'd spent my spare time researching mammoths. There was a lot to learn. Once, they filled the Arctic tundra and grasslands. Great herds of mammoths wandered as thick and plentiful as the herds of elephants that once roamed Africa and southern Asia. For hundreds of thousands of years, they ruled their world, the most dominant animal, fearing nothing. Even enemies like saber-toothed tigers — also extinct now — could harm only the baby mammoths, not the adults. That was why the herd was there to protect the babies, the way Trixie and the rest of our herd were there to protect Woolly.

Unlike dinosaurs, which died off millions of years ago, long before humans even stepped on the planet, mammoths may have been made extinct by humankind, at least in part — the same way African and Asian elephants are endangered now. Those mammoths were food to be harvested and eaten. There were no conservation groups or sanctuaries back then.

Mammoths have been extinct for around four thousand years. Maybe that seems like a long time ago, but it was the blink of an eye in the history of time. Mammoths appeared in early people's cave drawings. People in Siberia frequently found mammoth tusks and bodies frozen in ice, snow, and permafrost. Which of course was why Woolly was here.

Even more interesting than the history of mammoths was the future of *this* mammoth. Everything the vets knew — everything my father knew — was about elephants. Mammoths were their close relatives, but did that mean they were the same? Did mammoths have a lower or higher mortality rate? Were there diseases that Woolly was susceptible to but elephants weren't?

Besides, Woolly wasn't just a mammoth — she was a *cloned* mammoth. She was the scientifically manufactured product of a frozen carcass that was thousands of years old. Wouldn't she be especially vulnerable to anything that went wrong? There was so much we didn't know. That nobody *could* know.

On the bright side, we had three vets on staff. Dr. Grace and Dr. Tavaris were living here, in two of our spare bedrooms. It was strange to have two extra bodies around at breakfast, but we were all getting used to it.

Joyce had been spending a lot more time at the sanctuary.

She had to go to work every weekday, but she was there every evening and still there for breakfast some mornings. I was glad to have her around — something I wouldn't have imagined possible even a few weeks ago. My father wasn't much for small talk because he was usually so busy eating, and neither of the vets was what I considered a people person. Joyce was good at starting conversations and keeping them going.

There was a new schedule that divided the feedings among the team members. I seemed to be doing my share plus extra shifts — about every other daytime feeding and some of the night ones. I guess I took extra personal pride in knowing that Woolly was gaining weight because it was mainly my doing.

"I was out for a walk this morning outside the property and talked to one of the guards at the gate," Dr. Grace said. She was particularly chatty today.

"Was he friendly?" I asked.

"Not overly. I don't know if guards have a temperament that's drawn to carrying a weapon or if they're just playing a role, but they aren't the most talkative. And they have no idea what they're guarding."

"No surprise. Jimmy wants it to be a secret," I said.

"He made Dr. Tavaris and me sign nondisclosure agreements."

"All of us had to," I said. "This is serious secretive stuff."

"Very. So what is this Jimmy Mercury like?"

"You've never met him?"

She shook her head. "Hiring us was all done through lawyers."

"He's sort of different." I didn't want to say anything more, but something about him worried me.

"I expect most billionaire-genius inventors are a little bit different."

"My father has nightly Skype sessions with him now."

"We have to send a report to him every night as well," she said.

"You and Dr. Tavaris?"

"Dr. Tavaris, Dr. Morgan, and I. He has the three of us writing separate reports on Woolly's health and status," Dr. Grace replied.

"I guess that means he really cares about Woolly."

Woolly finished up the bottle, and I held it up to show Dr. Grace.

"Congratulations," she said. "You're so good with animals that I'm sure you're going to make a fine veterinarian."

"Thanks. That means a lot, especially coming from you. The feeding just takes time and practice. I've got to go and check the fences," I said.

"I thought we had guards for that."

"They guard them, but they don't repair them."

"That was quite a windstorm last night," she said.

"They happen around here this time of year."

"I don't know about the fences, but some boards were blown off the old barn," she said.

"We're just waiting for that thing to fall down. I should be back in time for the next feeding, but if I'm not, could you do it?" I asked.

"Of course, but no guarantee it will work."

I handed her the empty bottle.

As I started away, I thought I'd like to have company and help on the inspection. "Raja!" I called out.

He turned in my direction and looked like he was studying me.

"Raja . . . come!" I ordered.

Like a big gray dog, he started trotting toward me. He came right to my side, and I gestured that I wanted up. He lowered his trunk, and I grabbed on and put one foot onto the curl at the bottom. Effortlessly, like I weighed no more than a feather, he lifted me up, and I climbed onto the top of his head and slid on down to his back.

"You do have a way with these elephants!" Dr. Grace shouted up.

"It's probably more like they have a way with me, but thank you. Raja, that way!" I called, and pointed toward the gate.

Instantly he complied, and we were off. Normally he wouldn't have gone off by himself, but he was with one other member of the herd — me. I rocked back and forth with each step as he walked. Words can't describe the feeling of sitting on the back of an elephant. Some people get all excited about riding horses, but anybody can ride a horse. Horses are nice and all, but they're so tiny. Actually, a horse could easily ride on the back of an elephant.

I loved riding on the elephants. When I was little, I had fantasies about not taking the bus to school but riding an elephant to get there. I would imagine leaving him in the teachers' parking lot. I imagined him rubbing against the principal's car, maybe even sitting down on the hood. At the end of the day, the car would be scraped and dented, and when the principal blamed my elephant, I'd say, "How do you know it was *my* elephant that did this?"

Up here on Raja's back, I was the queen of this world, or at least a princess. I couldn't help thinking that if I were dressed the way I had been for the dance — new dress, hair all done up, and makeup — this would be as close as I'd ever get to being a princess. Not that I wanted to be a princess. I wanted to be a vet . . . but still . . . I had liked the way I'd looked and the way Brendan had acted around me.

Sadly, I'd only gotten to wear my dress once, for a couple of hours, and it was gone. I wished I could have had it on a little longer, maybe even had a couple more dances. Involuntarily I let out a big sigh. Nothing could be done to change what had happened, and I wouldn't trade some stupid dress for Woolly being born.

Really, there isn't much you can do to change anything that happens in your life. Things just happen, and you get on with it. I guess I'd learned that the hard way from the very beginning of my life.

Reaching the gate, I directed Raja to go to the right, and we started moving parallel to the perimeter, just inside the concrete wall. The concrete wasn't the concern. It was only two years old and as solid as rock. It had cost a lot of money, and at the time, I didn't know anything about us having a partner.

The real worry was the outer fence. The corrugated metal looked strong and solid, but looks could be deceiving and were, in this case. My father had cobbled it together from pieces of metal of assorted sizes, some new but most old, used, and discarded. The panels were held together with bolts and screws and wires. Some were rusty and worn, although most of the rust was hidden under the dozens of different colors of paint.

Raja and I were approaching a spot where the land dipped down so that the fence was low enough to look over. Behind it, I could see a few trees and the rough dirt road that ran parallel to the perimeter fence. As we followed the fence, a white truck came bumping along the path, a little cloud of dust following it. It came to a stop, and Raja stopped too. We stared at the truck, and I got the feeling that whoever was in the truck was staring back at us. Was it the guards or somebody who'd gotten past the guards? Regardless, they weren't seeing anything they shouldn't see. It was just a girl on top of an elephant. . . . Okay, that was a little strange, but not a secret.

The front doors of the truck opened, and two men got out. They were dressed in matching green uniforms and had holstered guns. I certainly hoped they were our guards.

They both waved, and I waved back.

"Nice elephant!" one of them shouted.

"Nice truck!" I called back.

"We're here to patrol the perimeter."

"I'm doing the same thing," I said. "Except you have a truck and I have an elephant."

"Do you want to trade?"

"I'm pretty happy with my ride." I gave Raja a big pat on the head. "Let's go, boy."

They waved goodbye, and we started off. They seemed pretty friendly to me. Dr. Grace could be a little abrupt, and I wondered if she'd said something to ruffle their feathers.

The area just inside the fence had originally been cleared off, but we hadn't had the time to keep the weeds and bushes from growing back in. I could always see the top two-thirds of the fence, but now the bottom was obscured by undergrowth. I wasn't too concerned about the sections where the ground was flat, but there were little dips and a couple of places where small creeks flowed through the property. I had to check carefully behind the underbrush in those spots to make sure that bigger gaps hadn't opened up under the fence.

We reached the point where the isolation pen began. Somewhere behind that wall was Burma. Some progress had been made — my father hadn't slept beside the pen the last few nights. Still, the process was taking much longer than we'd originally expected and hoped. I felt that was partly because we weren't able to give Burma the time and attention he needed. We were giving everything to Woolly.

The herd hadn't come close to the isolation pen yet. That wasn't just chance. Trixie would have smelled the scent of the strange bull elephant and made sure the herd kept a distance. She knew that a bull elephant could be aggressive, and in general she seemed more cautious and vigilant than usual these days. That was probably because of the death of Daisy Mae and the addition of the new elephant . . . *elephant?* That was how they saw Woolly, wasn't it? For them she wasn't a different species or a scientific breakthrough or a miracle or the most valuable animal in the world. For them she was nothing but a little baby elephant who was part of their herd — an orphan who needed their care and protection.

We came up to the gate. I called out "Stop" and then "Down," and Raja responded. "You wait here," I said, and went through the gate of the outer fence, closing it behind me.

Moving forward, I scanned the pen, looking for Burma. As I'd expected, he was among the trees. I'd come to realize he was there not just to hide but to pluck leaves from the upper branches. He was taller than any elephant we'd had before, and he could reach foliage above the browse line established by previous occupants of the isolation pen.

He caught sight of me and almost instantly walked toward me. I enjoyed thinking that he was coming over because he liked me, but his approach probably had more to do with the apples he knew I'd have for him. Thank goodness I'd had the foresight to put three apples in my pockets before I left. There were a couple of crabapple trees in the isolation enclosure that would grow fruit later in the season, and eventually he'd be able to pick the crabapples himself. Would he still be as happy to see me then? More important, would he still be here in two months? I had to believe it couldn't take that much longer to integrate him.

He came up to the concrete wall right in front of me. I pulled an apple out of my pocket and stepped closer to the wall. His trunk moved forward, but instead of reaching for the apple, he touched the side of my face. It was a kind, gentle greeting.

"I'm happy to see you, too."

Burma chirped at me. He was never very verbal, and his noises continued to be different from those made by the rest of the herd. If he had a chance to live in proximity to other elephants, would he eventually learn some of their sounds? I'd read about an elephant in Korea who could mimic human words. Maybe Burma could still learn another language — the language of the herd.

When he was through with the greeting, he took the apple. As always, he was gentle.

Then I saw my father standing off to the side, his arms crossed. He didn't look happy. "Burma really likes apples, doesn't he?" he said as he came up beside me.

"Have you ever met an elephant who didn't?"

"They're all individuals, so I assume some don't. That's the thing about elephants. Just because one acts a certain way doesn't mean that all of them will act the same way. Just like doing something with one elephant is smart, but it might not be smart with another elephant."

"Is that your way of saying I shouldn't be hand-feeding him?" I asked.

"You know the answer to that."

"He's always been really gentle," I said.

"Not always. He hurt two people. He killed a man."

"A man who probably abused him."

"And what about the little girl who was just standing outside the cage and was bowled over and hurt? Did she abuse him too?" my father asked.

"Maybe she tossed something at him, or . . . Probably not."

"I haven't fed him by hand yet. I haven't felt he was ready," Dad said.

"He was ready. You saw me do it."

"I don't want you to do that again. Not now. Not yet."

"Then when?"

"When *I* feel it's time. Maybe not for a month or longer." He paused. "Or never."

"What do you mean, never?" I demanded.

"I'm starting to question if integration is possible. I'm still afraid he could hurt somebody."

"I'm not afraid of him."

"That's what makes me so afraid," Dad said. "You *should* be afraid of him. He could hurt you. He could kill you."

"He just needs more time before he can be released into the sanctuary."

"Then we have to be afraid for the other elephants. It's not just you he could hurt. What about Bacca or Raja or Woolly? He's so much bigger than they are."

"Trixie would protect them."

"He's bigger than Trixie. He could hurt or maim her so badly it could lead to her death. Even if you're willing to risk your life, are you willing to risk theirs?"

Of course I wasn't. That comment made me think, but not give up hope.

"Give him time," I said. "He needs to have the herd closer to him so he can get used to them and they can get used to him. That's how we've done it before. What's the next step to make that happen?"

My father nodded. "I was thinking of taking down a section of the outer fence so they can at least see one another. We could put out their hay up here to encourage Trixie to bring the herd up close."

"Thank you for not giving up on him."

"Nobody has given up on him. We have time. But you have to promise me you won't be getting within his reach again until I tell you it's all right. Okay?"

"I promise. I can still toss him apples, right?"

"I'm not sure I could stop you from doing that if I wanted to."

I took the second apple from my pocket and gently tossed it toward Burma. It dropped to the ground in front of him. He looked at me with those deep brown eyes, and I thought I saw confusion in them, or maybe sadness. Slowly, hesitantly, he reached down, grabbed the apple with his trunk, and brought it up to his mouth. I imagined it didn't taste as good as it would have from my hand.

He turned and lumbered away.

CHAPTER
Sixteen

MY FATHER TOSSED THE LAST BALE OF HAY OVER THE fence and into the isolation enclosure. This was our third day in a row trying the new plan. There was a pile of hay on each side of the low concrete wall. Inside was a pile for Burma, and outside a much larger pile for the herd. As he said he would, Dad had disassembled a long section of the high outer fence so that Burma could observe the herd feeding and they could see into the enclosure.

On the first day, Trixie hadn't wanted to bring the herd up here, but the need to feed was greater than her reluctance. She remained uneasy, vigilant, positioning herself between the isolation enclosure and the rest of the herd. She ate while facing the gap. She knew Burma was there. Even when he wasn't visible, she knew. That first day, in fact, he wasn't visible. Burma's fears and anxiety were greater than his hunger, and he'd stayed off to the far side of his enclosure, hidden in the trees. Just as the herd could smell him, he could smell them. He could also hear them. The herd was seldom silent, and from that distance, his big ears could easily pick up their vocalization. He stayed there, hidden, and didn't eat until they left.

The second day was a little better. He didn't come down to eat but had moved to a place where he could see them and they could see him. As always, Trixie was focused on him, staring in his direction. Bacca and Woolly had remained sheltered within the herd, surrounded on all sides. Raja, however, moved out beyond Trixie and came right up to the fence. He was always curious and teenager-rebellious.

At the end of the second day, when Burma hadn't come down, Dad decided to give him more incentive. He drove the pickup into the isolation enclosure and put half the bales back in the truck. He didn't want Burma to go without, but he did want him to be hungrier the next day so he'd have more reason to come closer.

Now I stood anxiously outside the wall, watching Dad drive in and get out of the truck to toss down the bales. Funny how I thought there was nothing wrong with me hand-feeding Burma, but I was worried about my dad being in the pen with him, even though Dad could flee to the safety of the truck.

We were doing other things differently today. For one, the herd had been held back, to allow Burma to feed first. And it looked like it was going to work, as he trotted out of the trees. He was hungry and eager to eat. With no other elephants visible and no smell in the air, he came to the opening and looked all around, his ears flapping.

The second difference was that the bales for the herd had been laid out in a line, leading toward the wall. The herd could eat their way closer and closer, starting at a safe distance and moving toward where Burma was feeding.

Dad drove out of the isolation pen, and I closed and locked the gates behind him.

"I think the third day is the charm," he called out the window.

I went over to the truck. "We can hope it works."

"It'll work," he said.

"Why do you think he's so scared around the herd?" I asked. "He's bigger than any of them."

"He may not know that. They might look huge to him because he's never seen an elephant before."

"He *is* an elephant."

"Remember, he's an elephant who has lived his life alone. If you'd never seen an elephant before, wouldn't you be afraid?"

"I can't even imagine it. I don't remember a time when I didn't see elephants."

"There aren't too many people who can say that. I remember that amazing picture of your family you drew in kindergarten."

"You kept that picture on the fridge for years, then had it

framed and hung it up. It would be hard to forget." Now it was on the wall behind the desk in his office.

"It was adorable and still is. There were you and me and four elephants," he said.

"How could you even tell they were elephants?"

"You told me. Besides, they were beautiful."

"They looked like gray blobs with long noses," I said.

"You were four years old, so you shouldn't be so hard on yourself . . . although you always have been. I loved that picture then and I love it now, even if it made me sad."

"Why did it make you sad?" I asked.

"Because there were elephants in the picture, but not your mother."

I felt a twinge of sadness and a bigger jolt of surprise. He had crossed into the area we always avoided. I needed to retreat. "There have always been elephants," I said.

"She would have been so proud of you. Then and now."

Wow, he was still going there, and I still didn't want to talk about it.

"There's Trixie," I said, changing the subject completely. She was leading the herd, and Bacca was right behind her. I couldn't see Woolly and felt a rush of anxiety.

Then I caught a flash of brown between gray tree-trunk legs and bodies. Woolly's distinctive coloring and longish fur made her stand out. Even if we hadn't known why she was different, we would have known she was different, but different enough to be a woolly mammoth? That was almost too fantastic to believe, even though I knew it was true.

"Your mother loved the elephants as much as we do," Dad said. "She would have loved that picture."

What had gotten into him this morning?

He climbed out of the truck and put an arm around me. I didn't want to talk about this anymore. "Look, I'm going to go and talk to Burma," I said. I moved slowly, smoothly, until I was close to Burma, separated by the wall.

"I know you see them," I said to the big elephant, trying to sound calm. I wondered if he could hear the stress in my voice.

Of course Burma had seen the herd. He'd stopped eating and was focused on their approach. He could also smell and hear them, as scent and sound carried on the wind. So far, he hadn't run away. His hunger and curiosity were stronger than his fear. He kept his head up, looking at the others, bringing hay up to his mouth, eating and not retreating.

The others weren't getting any closer. Trixie had caught sight of Burma and halted the herd. It was completely against her nature and instincts to lead them into danger, and the strange bull elephant represented danger. Maybe I could do something about that.

I left Burma and headed to the herd. As I passed the last bale, I bent down and grabbed an armful of loose hay.

"Good morning, Trixie!" I called out.

Trixie didn't move, but Woolly, hearing my voice, perked up her ears and ran toward me. I was thrilled that she reacted that way, but a little nervous. She would never hurt me on purpose, but she was more than three hundred pounds of wobbly-legged baby and could easily run me over by accident.

She lightly bumped into me. "Sorry, girl, I don't have a bottle, just hay."

She didn't believe me and felt around with her trunk. She wasn't finding a bottle. All she was doing was tickling me.

I continued toward Trixie, holding the hay in front of me. I stopped a dozen yards away. "Come on, Trixie. Breakfast is served."

She extended her trunk, but we both knew she wasn't close enough to reach the hay. She took a small, tentative step toward me, and then a second and a third. I matched her steps, edging forward. She took the straw with her trunk and brought it to her mouth. That signaled to the others that it was all right to eat. Raja trotted forward, and I gave him some of the hay.

I backed away, and the herd followed me. They weren't being tricked; they saw me as a member of the herd. They trusted me not to lead them to danger — and Trixie really wasn't far away. They reached the closest bales and started eating. I hoped they'd eat their way toward the enclosure.

I started back toward the fence — toward Burma — and

Bacca and Woolly trotted along beside me. Not wanting to let them get too far ahead, Trixie came forward, and some members of the herd came with her. So far, this tactic was working.

I moved back to the truck and joined my father.

"You really are an Elephant Girl," he said.

"Thank you."

From him, that was nothing but a compliment — maybe the biggest compliment he could give. Although he had said that I looked like my mother, that I looked beautiful. That meant something pretty important too. I tried to picture her holding me in her arms.

We stood there off to the side, watching as all the elephants ate.

Burma and Trixie eyed each other anxiously while they ate. He'd never seen elephants this close before, but he probably knew instinctively that she was the leader. She was slightly bigger than the others, and she seemed so regal, so in charge.

There was the sound of an engine, and I saw a truck — a truck I didn't know — coming toward us.

"Who is that?" I asked.

"I don't know, but whoever it is, he shouldn't be here on the property to begin with and certainly shouldn't be here now. We can't have them upset the elephants, or see Woolly."

I hadn't even thought of that.

We sprinted toward the oncoming truck. The elephants,

of course, noticed and stopped eating. I waved my arms, and the truck came to a stop a safe distance away. The engine was turned off, and two men got out. They were both wearing big white cowboy hats and cowboy boots, and they both had thick black beards. Even though they were dressed sort of like twins, the second man, the one who had been driving, was much, much bigger than his passenger.

The driver waved. "Hello!" the passenger called out.

That voice was familiar — very familiar.

"How's our girl doing?" He removed his beard as they walked toward us.

"It's Jimmy!" I exclaimed.

"We weren't expecting you," Dad called out as they got closer.

"Think of it as a drive-by visit."

"Why are you dressed like that?" I asked.

"We're in disguise."

The big guy removed his beard too. He was one of the few people who was as big as my dad.

"Why do you need disguises?" I asked.

"We had to come incognito," Jimmy said.

"But we didn't hear the helicopter — and where did that truck come from?" Dad asked.

"We drove here. Well, James drove."

"He's named James, like you?" I asked.

"I tend to trust people who share my name. I have many Jameses working for me. So, I was a passenger. Apparently if I'd been driving, we would have ended up in the ditch."

"Wouldn't it have been faster to take your helicopter?"

"Much faster, but it would have been too visible. There seems to be renewed interest in tracking down my newest project. Rumors are spreading that I have something big in the works, something some people might call *mammoth*."

"Okay, that was at least a little funny," I said.

"Thank you. My security team heard some intelligence that there was a helicopter positioned to follow mine, so I was afraid we'd be tracked."

"Only you would be followed by helicopter," I said.

"It is a bit peculiar, but we might have been tracked by radar detection or a satellite, or even followed by a small plane."

"That sounds a little paranoid," I said.

"Just because you're paranoid doesn't mean they aren't out to get you," the big James said.

"So I sent the helicopter someplace far away, carrying a fake Jimmy Mercury."

"You have a fake *you*?"

"It's a security measure," James explained. "Not only does it thwart abduction threats, but also it disguises his whereabouts."

"In this case, there have been some very specific rumors. Information has started circulating, arousing interest in my mystery project." Jimmy chuckled. "They're saying that I've created a rural think tank, filled with computer experts working on the human genome and how it can be applied to the prevention of illness and the modification of drugs to treat illnesses."

"That sounds pretty amazing," I said.

"It is. In fact, we have a division working on that exact project, in a country I cannot name. Some of their work had direct implications for this project."

"Do any of these rumors involve Woolly?" my father questioned.

"Not specifically, but people know I'm up to something. That's why I was worried about being followed. That's the reason for the fake Jimmy going off in my helicopter and me coming here in disguise with just one of my — um, associates."

"Do all of your associates carry guns?" Dad asked.

That startled me. "Guns?"

I looked and saw a bulge under James's jacket just below his heart. Was that a gun?

"James is the head of my security force, and yes, he does carry a weapon," Jimmy said. "Now, tell me about Woolly. Tell me everything."

"There isn't anything more to tell than was in yesterday's report," my father answered. "Why don't we just visit her instead?"

He and Jimmy went off toward the herd. I stayed by the truck with James.

"Do you worry about Jimmy being hurt by one of the elephants?" I asked.

"I'm concerned about him and *everything* — but there's not much I can do about it," he replied.

"I thought you were carrying a gun."

"Not that I'd shoot an elephant, but I'm smart enough to know that shooting one with a handgun would only get it mad at you."

"You'd get more than the elephant mad at you."

"I'm not going to shoot anything here, but I have to be prepared to protect Jimmy. What do you think of him?"

"He's nice, but he's — um — well, a little different."

"He's very nice and very different. He's one of the most amazing people I've ever met, and it's an honor to be there to protect him."

"Are there really people following him?"

"Industrial espionage is a reality. People think if they can figure out where Jimmy is going, what he's working on, they can get there faster and get rich."

"This project has nothing to do with being rich, does it?"

"This is about spending millions of dollars for the betterment of humanity. Has he explained the whole plan to you yet?"

"He explained about how he was able to clone a mammoth."

James persisted. "But has he told you the entire plan?"

"I didn't know there was anything else."

"I'll let him explain it to you. I can't do it justice. It's better if he tells you."

I followed James. Jimmy was on his knees in front of Woolly, giving her a bottle. I couldn't tell which of them was enjoying it more. Woolly was playing with the bottle more than drinking from it, and Jimmy was giggling. He was in the very middle of the herd, surrounded on all sides by legs that could have crushed him and trunks that could have picked him up and tossed him, but he appeared happy and relaxed. The elephants seemed calm with him there. That was a good sign—they were good judges of people. They were eating quietly. Trixie was still watching Burma, but she dipped her head down to eat.

"Hey, boss, have you told them your master plan?" James asked.

"I told them a lot, but I don't know if I've told them everything."

"Tell them about your long-range plans."

"Sure. Where do I start . . . where do I start?"

"How about the land purchase?" James suggested.

"I heard about that," I said. "You bought lots of land in the rainforest and turned it into a gigantic nature reserve."

"I did, but that's not the land he's talking about," Jimmy said. "I also purchased a large tract of land from the Canadian government and a First Nations group in northern Canada. It is close to twenty-five thousand acres of tundra and conifer forest."

"That's where the woolly mammoth used to live," I said.

"That's also where the woolly mammoth will live again."

"Woolly can't live up there!" I exclaimed. "She's too small to be alone. She'd—"

"It won't happen for twenty years. By then she'll be very big, and believe me, she certainly won't be the only mammoth."

"Isn't she the only one of the clones who lived?" Dad asked.

"She is the only one so far. Looking back on the success and failure we had, I realized it's just a matter of scale. Twenty wasn't enough. We have to try to clone two hundred mammoths next year. Then two hundred the next year, and so on."

"You're going to create a herd of woolly mammoths," my dad said. "That's . . . that's . . . amazing."

"Not *a* herd. Ultimately, many herds."

I pictured it in my head—herds of mammoths moving together across the tundra. The image was so powerful that it took my breath away.

"So you'd release them, reestablish the species in the wild," Dad said. "That's the dream of every person who ever operated a sanctuary, to allow animals to live safely in the wild."

"We humans drove them to extinction. Now we have brought them back to life. We will protect them. Out there, they will breed and flourish."

"But . . . if they're all clones, that means that they're all identical, which means that they're all girls. How will they breed?" I asked.

Jimmy smiled. "You don't seem to miss much. Remember when your father said that finding that mammoth carcass was like finding a needle in a haystack? Well, I have bought many needles from many haystacks. Five years ago, I let it be known that I would buy—and greatly overpay for—unearthed woolly mammoths. Apparently I started a sort of mini-rush for mammoths. We are now developing six separate clones, three male and three female, to allow for some genetic diversity."

"Is that enough diversity?" Dad asked.

"More is better, but other species have survived a population bottleneck. It wasn't just mammoths that became extinct or almost extinct. Do you know about the cheetah bottleneck?"

"I've read about it," Dad said.

"No. What is it?" I asked.

"The population of cheetahs in the world apparently dwindled to fewer than one hundred animals at one point in our recent history," Dad explained to me.

"Some biologists believe there were even fewer than that," Jimmy said. "So all living cheetahs are the result of that very small gene pool."

"And you think six mammoths would be enough to build a herd from?" I asked.

Jimmy only smiled and shrugged. He gave Woolly another scratch behind the ear and then got to his feet. "We have to get going."

"But you just got here," I said.

"I would love to stay longer, but I can't. We're connecting with another helicopter about seventy-five miles from here."

"You were afraid you'd be followed if you traveled by helicopter," I said.

"I would have been if I'd *left* our headquarters by helicopter. I'll be returning on a second helicopter, which I chartered under an assumed identity and paid for in cash, so there's no danger of being tracked."

"Sometimes it seems like we have to act as if we're drug smugglers or something," James said.

Jimmy chuckled. "The only drugs I use are eye drops for eyestrain."

"You went through all of that to be here for a few minutes?" I asked.

"Seeing our girl is pretty special. Don't you think a whole lot of people would go to that much trouble to see the world's only woolly mammoth?"

"I guess so," I admitted.

I heard something and saw movement behind the fence. I was shocked to see Burma charging toward the wall and Raja, who had been standing just outside, scrambling to get away. In his haste, Raja bumped into Raina, who stumbled. The whole herd shifted and suddenly moved away from us.

The elephants quickly settled down, and the threat of danger was gone. Burma was gone too. He'd turned and run away, disappearing behind the fence. I figured he was heading for the cover of the trees in the far corner of his enclosure.

"What happened?" Jimmy asked, sounding confused and a little scared.

"Raja got too close to the wall of the isolation enclosure and spooked Burma, who charged," Dad explained.

Now Jimmy looked concerned.

"Burma is the elephant we told you about," Dad said. "We keep him apart from the other elephants because he's new and we don't trust him with the herd members yet."

"It looks like there's good reason. Could he harm Woolly?" Jimmy asked.

"Not at all. He's kept separated from her and the others by a concrete wall and electrified wire," my father said. "He can't get out, and Woolly can't get in."

"Why is the herd even up here, close to that elephant?" Jimmy asked.

"We're trying to prepare Burma for the day, sometime in the distant future, when he might be able to live with the herd."

"With the herd, but then he could hurt Woolly."

"He won't be integrated with the herd, allowed anywhere near Woolly or the other elephants, unless we know he won't harm them," Dad said.

"That's reassuring." Jimmy's expression didn't match his words. He still looked worried and uneasy.

"It's taking much longer than we thought. They aren't going to be integrated anytime soon."

"We have to remember that Woolly is what matters. She must always be protected."

Yes, she needed to be protected. I knew that. I wished Burma knew it too.

CHAPTER
Seventeen

"IT'S NOT LOOKING GOOD OUT THERE," MY FATHER SAID as he came into the house. It was late afternoon, about two weeks later, and Joyce and I were sitting in the living room with mugs of tea.

"There's no question it's going to be a big one," Joyce agreed. "We've had a lot of storms the last few weeks."

"More than usual. The winds are incredibly strong already."

"Sometimes all we get is the wind, and the storm blows over," I said.

"We can hope for the best, but we'd better prepare for the worst. We have to take care of Woolly."

"We have to take care of the whole herd," I said.

"Don't Asian elephants in the wild live in the rainforest?" Joyce asked.

"They do, but it's warmer there. Here the winds are blowing in colder temperatures from the north."

"And elephants are susceptible to pneumonia, especially baby elephants," I said.

"But Woolly isn't an elephant; she's a mammoth," Joyce said. "Didn't they live in the far north?"

"They did, but still, we don't want to take chances," my father said. "The herd needs to be in shelter."

"You don't mean the barn, do you?" I asked.

"No, definitely not. Given the shape it's in and the possible strength of this storm, that's the last place we want them to be."

"So where will they go?" Joyce asked.

"The herd can shelter in the woods, and we'll put Woolly in the trailer tonight."

"Are you sure she can still fit?" I asked.

"Dr. Tavaris thinks she'll fit."

I wasn't so sure. In the past month, she'd almost doubled her birth weight and was now 340 pounds. Soon she would be too big for the scale — and the trailer — if she wasn't already.

"How about if we check out the storm on the Weather Network?" I asked.

"Good idea. I think the weatherman is occasionally right."

I picked up the remote and clicked the TV on, scanning the channels for the Weather Network.

"Go back!" Joyce shouted.

I'd seen something too. I went back the other way, and there was Jimmy — a picture of him on the screen behind the announcer. He was wearing his cowboy hat and the fake beard. James was beside him in his identical disguise.

"Turn up the sound!" my father exclaimed.

I clicked it up higher until we could hear the anchorman.

"For a man known to be both a genius and an eccentric, Jimmy Mercury hardly ever disappoints. He was captured here as he left his compound in disguise and evaded the paparazzi known to follow his movements. While he wasn't able to disguise who he was, he did manage to elude them and disappear.

"When Jimmy Mercury starts acting mysteriously, the entire world takes notice. Just what is it that he's trying to keep secret? Is it a new invention or a new idea or a new acquisition?"

"Isn't it obvious that it's a woolly mammoth?" I said to the TV announcer.

"All we know is that when James — Jimmy — Mercury speaks or acts, the world has learned to listen and watch. The holdings of JM Limited soared today, gaining more than ten percent in value as investors flocked to get in on the action. It is estimated that this gain in stock price increased Mr. Mercury's personal wealth by more than one hundred twenty-five million dollars."

"Wow," I said.

"That's pocket change to somebody like him," Joyce said.

"Let me offer my congratulations, James Mercury, but one would think with all that money, you might be able to come up with a better disguise."

"Or a different disguise than you used when you were here a couple of weeks ago," my father said.

"Or use the money to make a lot more woolly mammoths," I said.

Jimmy and James disappeared from the screen. The anchorman started talking about a traffic accident. I turned down the volume.

"He certainly has the money to do what he said he wants to do," Joyce said. "He *could* breed a whole herd of mammoths."

"Will you let him try to breed using more of our elephants?" I asked my dad.

"We only have two females who are the right age and temperament."

"But they couldn't carry to full term this time," I said.

"Maybe a second time would be more successful."

"So you would do that?" Joyce asked. "You'd allow your elephants to be impregnated again?"

"I think Woolly deserves a little brother or sister. Or an identical clone."

"That would be amazing," I said. I pictured two baby mammoths, and a two- or three-year-old Woolly leading them.

"Although technically they wouldn't be brothers and

sisters. They'd be either Woolly clones or clones from another woolly mammoth," my father said. "I guess we should focus on protecting this one mammoth first. Let's try to get her sheltered for the night."

"Don't you want to hear the weather report?" I asked.

"Not necessary. Let's get to work just in case."

* * *

WOOLLY WAS WALKING WITH ME. I WAS USING A BOTTLE to lure her along—giving her a little bit and then taking it away. Trixie wasn't happy with what I was doing. She couldn't stop Woolly from going with me, so she followed, and the herd came with her. Overhead, the skies were getting dark and ominous and the winds continued to pick up, throwing dust into my eyes. It might start to rain any second. We were in a race with the weather, and I wasn't sure we were going to win.

We passed to the left of a large earthen mound, Daisy Mae's gravesite. My father had used a backhoe to dig the grave, push her into the hole, and cover her up. I was on the far end of the property with the herd at the time. Afterward I was happy it was finally done. I was a little bit sad that I hadn't been there, but mostly relieved that I hadn't. It had been hard enough with Peanut, and Daisy Mae meant so much more to me and to the herd. They couldn't see her, but they knew she was down there and still stopped, pawed at the ground, and made chirping sounds.

"You're doing well," Joyce said, coming up beside me.

I started slightly. I hadn't seen or heard her coming. "Maybe not well enough to beat the rain."

"You're getting her there."

"It's not me; it's the bottle."

"It's more than the bottle. She wouldn't come like this for anybody else."

Woolly had sucked down more than half the bottle, and we were much more than halfway to the trailer. It was in sight, not far to go. I stopped and gave her the bottle again, and she instantly began suckling.

The three vets had been working in the trailer while I'd been working on getting Woolly there. They were rearranging things to open up enough space, even unbolting the examination table from the middle of the room and moving it to the side.

My father had told Jimmy about wanting to provide something larger and more permanent in the way of a shelter. Jimmy had said he'd arrange for the materials to be delivered outside the compound, but he couldn't risk having people come in to do the construction because they might discover the secret. Jimmy was pretty concerned about that. After hearing the TV report, I could see why.

The materials were delivered, but my dad would have to bring them inside and do the building on his own. That was just fine with him. We'd done more with less many times before. He could make materials and dollars stretch further than anybody I knew.

I yanked the bottle out of Woolly's mouth. She responded with a gentle headbutt that staggered me backward a couple of feet.

"Are you all right?" Joyce asked. She sounded concerned.

"I'm fine . . . a little surprised, but fine."

"Is that any way to treat your mama?" Joyce asked Woolly.

Woolly reached for the bottle, but I held it away and started moving. "That's the last feeding you're going to get until you're in the trailer," I said.

The vets and my father were waiting outside the trailer. "Lead her right in," my dad said.

The double door was open, and I stepped inside. Woolly stopped at the entrance.

"Come on in," I said, holding out the bottle.

She placed a foot on the lip of the trailer, and the whole thing shook slightly. That unnerved both of us, and she backed off a bit. I went to the doorway and offered her the bottle again. If I could get her suckling, perhaps I could draw her inside. To my surprise, she backed away as I advanced. The rest of the herd were now milling around near the trailer, and Woolly moved behind Trixie.

"Why won't she feed?" I asked.

"Maybe she needs to be hungrier," Dad suggested.

I looked up at the sky. "We might not have time for her to get hungry again before the storm hits."

Bacca came forward and tried to grab the bottle. For a split second, I pulled it away and then realized he had the right to feed too. I could get another bottle for Woolly. I held out the bottle, and Bacca began to suck. He pushed forward as if he wanted to get into the trailer, and the whole thing rocked. There was no way Bacca would fit.

* * *

I FELT THE RAIN AGAINST MY FACE AND HEARD IT PING against the trailer. It was falling lightly. We stood around, watching the elephants stand around. Woolly was still hiding behind Trixie. Fortunately Trixie hadn't moved the herd away, but did it really matter whether Woolly got soaked here or someplace else?

My father, Joyce, and the vets had been trying to come up with another solution. They talked about wrapping Woolly in a piece of canvas or placing a tarp over her, but she wasn't going to stay under anything. We would need a gigantic umbrella and an equally giant person to follow her around and hold it over her.

Someone suggested sheltering her in the storage area for the bales. It had a roof but no sides. Judging from the strength of the wind, the rain would mostly be going sideways, so that structure wasn't going to offer much protection. Whether she got wet from the top or the sides, she was going to be soaked.

The barn was mentioned again by Dr. Tavaris, but it was a definite no as well. It was too old and rickety. There was no sense in shielding Woolly from the falling rain and having falling beams or boards hit her instead. There really was only one possibility: the trailer.

"Maybe we could push her in," Dr. Grace suggested.

"You know that old joke," Dr. Tavaris said. "Where does a four-hundred-pound gorilla sleep?"

"Wherever he wants," Doc Morgan answered.

"We couldn't push her if we wanted to, and I'm not sure Trixie would like it if we tried," my dad said.

"What if we tranquilize her?" Doc Morgan suggested.

"Too risky. She might collapse out here," Dr. Grace replied. "And there's no telling how modern tranquilizers would agree with woolly mammoth DNA."

"What if we started with a small dose and increased to a therapeutic dose that would make her more compliant?" Dr. Tavaris suggested.

"Nobody is going to medicate her." My father's tone made it clear — that discussion had ended.

"I guess we'll have to be patient and hope," Joyce said.

"I can hope, but that doesn't mean I have to be patient." I walked over to Woolly. "I've had enough of you, young lady!" I announced. "You are going to your room, immediately!" I pointed to the trailer.

Woolly obviously didn't understand, but she did look a little bit uncertain. She knew I was trying to tell her something but had no idea what I was upset about. Trixie seemed really interested. She turned her head slightly to the side, and her ears flapped.

"I'm trying to get her in the trailer, and you're being no help whatsoever, Trixie. You're the leader, so help me."

More twitching of the ears and chirping.

I reached out and took Woolly by the trunk. She didn't pull away but instead grabbed my hand. I led her toward the door of the trailer, and she came along willingly. Approaching the door, I didn't hesitate but stepped right in without looking back. I felt the trailer sag and heard Woolly take a step and then another into the trailer. Then she stopped. She kept hold of my hand, and I was dragged to a stop as well. I looked into her eyes and saw fear. She was scared to come in, and I was scared that she wouldn't.

"You have to come in," I said softly. "I'm only doing this to help you. Please."

There was motion from behind, and the dark sky at the top of the door was replaced by an even darker gray. I saw Trixie's big brown eye. She was right there behind Woolly at the door.

The trailer shook slightly, and Woolly bumped forward. Trixie was nudging the baby onward. She *was* helping. Woolly edged forward a half step and then another and another.

Still holding her trunk, I stretched until I could reach the bottle of formula I'd left on the counter. I was just able to grasp it. I brought it back around, Woolly saw it, and that was the only incentive still necessary. She started sucking. I backed away a little farther, and she came forward a few more steps until she was completely inside the trailer. There, visible over top of Woolly, looking in through the trailer door, was Trixie. I could see in her eyes that she understood.

I heard a metallic sound and realized that somebody — probably my dad — had slipped in front of Trixie and was closing the double door of the trailer. The lower halves clanged into place so Woolly couldn't leave. The upper halves were still open. Fresh air and rain could come in, but this far into the trailer, she might stay dry — or at least not get any wetter than she already was.

It didn't take Woolly long to finish up the bottle. I slipped through the little space between Woolly and the wall, and she tried to turn and just about pinned me. I pushed her away. She was more than three times my weight, but luckily I could still move her. The herd and the rest of the people were standing outside in the rain. The people had umbrellas, and the elephants didn't care.

Trixie was still right there, guarding the entrance.

"The baby is fine," I assured her.

Not that she didn't believe me, but she seemed to need to see for herself. She lowered her head so that she could look inside.

"Did you think I was lying?" I asked.

"She's just being a good stepmother," Dad offered.

"More like a grandmother," I said. Either one would be good for Woolly to have. "I guess I have to sleep out here tonight."

"I was planning to do that."

I shook my head. "She came in here with me. It's only fair that I stay in here with her."

"I thought you'd say that. Besides, you're the one she's most comfortable with. I'll bring you the really thick sleeping bag and your PJs."

"Just the sleeping bag," I said. "I think I'm going to stay dressed tonight."

"How about if I do the middle-of-the-night feeding so you can sleep?" he suggested.

"I don't think I'll be getting much sleep lying on an examination table, even with the really thick sleeping bag. I'll be here, I'll do the feeding, and you can get some sleep."

"You need sleep too," he said. "You've been up part of the last three nights."

"How long has it been since you've slept the entire night?"

"Over fourteen years."

That was longer than I had been alive. It probably started about the time he'd found out my mother was pregnant with me.

"I'm going to close one of the upper doors and leave the other open so Woolly can see the herd and they can see her," I said. I swung the door shut, and my father went to get the sleeping bag.

The vets and Joyce had already left. Their red umbrellas were bobbing up the path toward the house. The herd wasn't going anywhere. They were clustered around the trailer, Bacca right outside the door. Trixie had finally moved farther away, but she was still watching the trailer.

The rain was getting stronger by the second. I could hear it drumming against the roof of the trailer and feel it pelting my face through the opening. We'd gotten Woolly inside just in time. The rain was loud and getting louder. Maybe I should have asked my father to bring earplugs as well as the sleeping bag.

CHAPTER
Eighteen

"WAKE UP, SAM. IT'S MORNING."

My eyes shot open, and I sat right up. Joyce was standing beside me. For a second, I couldn't orient myself. Right, I was in the trailer . . . on the examination table. I looked around. There was just me and Joyce in the trailer. "Where's Woolly?"

"She's with the herd. She's okay," Joyce said.

I let out a little sigh of relief. "It was a long night."

"Between the rain and the wind, it had to be a rough night out here."

"I thought the trailer was going to turn into an ark. Or an airplane," I said. "Like a ship in a storm at sea. The only reason we didn't become airborne was because Woolly's weight was like an anchor holding us in place."

The wind was much scarier than the rain. We swayed and rocked all night. A couple of times I felt like a wheel or two had actually risen slightly off the ground. It wasn't a tornado, but I thought about how tornadoes really didn't like trailers, and here I was sleeping in one. I had this bizarre vision of Woolly and me being picked up and landing in Oz. Instead of Dorothy and her little dog named Toto, there would have been Sammy and her not-so-little mammoth named Woolly.

The rain had pounded down, sometimes so strong and so loud that I could hardly hear myself think. As bad as it was for me, it must have been worse for Woolly, with her big ears and extra-developed sense of hearing.

I'd slept in fits and starts. For most of the night, Woolly was pressed against the table. She was frightened. Once when the alarm woke me up to give her a bottle, she wasn't at my side. I found her by the open half door, holding trunks with Trixie. She'd gotten wet from the spray coming in through the door. After I gave her a bottle, I took a couple of towels and dried her off. Then I unzipped my sleeping bag to open it up and draped it over her to try to keep her warm.

"Let's get some breakfast into you," Joyce said.

"I have to give Woolly her breakfast first."

"Dr. Tavaris already fed her."

I felt both relieved that I didn't have to do it and sad that I didn't get to do it. There was something amazing about feeding her, and everybody agreed that she took the bottle best from me.

On the way out, I picked up my sleeping bag. It was damp and dirty and definitely needed to be washed.

I expected the herd to be just outside the door, but they were nowhere to be seen. "Where are they?"

Joyce must have read my concern. "They went down toward the pond, but they're not alone. Dr. Tavaris went with them."

"That's good. I'll get some breakfast and then give Woolly her next bottle," I suggested as we walked toward the house. There were large puddles everywhere, and branches and leaves were scattered all over. "I'll just grab something fast so I can go down to Woolly."

"I'm going to make pancakes."

"Blueberry?"

"I'll make as many blueberry pancakes as you'll eat," she said. "You have to eat. You look like you've lost weight."

"I don't know. I only notice the weight Woolly gains. That's all that's important."

She stopped and took me by the shoulders, which surprised me. "No, it isn't. *You're* important. Sometimes I think you and your father are so involved with the elephants—and now Woolly—that you don't notice anything else in the world."

I didn't know how to reply to that.

"You're important," she repeated.

"There are billions of people in the world, but not many elephants, and only one mammoth."

"There are billions of people, but there's only one Samantha Gray."

I didn't think she'd ever called me by my full name . . . called me Samantha.

"You're important."

"Yeah, but—"

"No buts! *You are important.* Your father is so focused on his elephants that he sometimes forgets the human parts of his herd."

Maybe she wasn't talking about me. Maybe she was talking about herself. "You and my father are good, right?"

It surprised me that I'd asked that question. It meant that I was concerned, that I wanted them to get along. When had all of that happened?

"Yes, we're fine. Wait—this isn't about your father and me. I realize who he is, and I accept that. I'm his girlfriend, but I have a life out there beyond the fence, beyond the elephants."

"But the stuff inside the fence, you still want to be part of it, right?"

"Of course I do," she said.

"Good."

"Good? That's the nicest thing you've ever said to me." She wrapped her arms around me. It felt so nice and warm that I hugged her back.

"It's *you* I'm worried about," she said, releasing me. "Have you been off the property since Woolly was born?"

"No."

"Time for you to take a break. You haven't seen any of your friends since school ended."

"It's not like I can invite them here now."

"You can go to their homes, go to town, and get out. Are you even talking to them on the phone or exchanging messages or anything?"

"I've had some texts." I didn't mention that I'd answered with only a few words, and the texts had stopped coming.

"Summer may seem like forever, but eventually you're going to go back to school," she said.

"Ugh. Don't remind me."

"Somebody has to. You will resume life out there with other human life-forms. How about you and I go into town after I get back from work today, and we'll do a little early back-to-school clothes shopping?"

"I'd like that . . . well, if there's nothing that needs to be done around here."

"There's always something that needs to be done around here, so that's not a good excuse. I always loved back-to-school shopping. My mother and I would go out and . . ." She paused. "Not that I'm trying to be your mother or get in the way of what you and your father usually do."

"We don't usually do anything."

"He doesn't take you back-to-school shopping?"

I shook my head. Was this something else that I'd missed out on?

"Then it's definite. Tonight. You and me."

"Thanks." I was surprised by how happy that made me feel.

CHAPTER

Nineteen

"WE HAVE TO GET THAT SECTION OF THE FENCE BACK UP as soon as possible," Dad said.

The storm had taken down trees and blown over three sections of the outer fence. The decision to stay away from the barn had proved wise, as part of the roof had blown off. The small creeks flowing into the property had become larger streams and in a couple of places had eroded out gullies beneath the outer fence. None of the gaps was big enough to let an elephant through, but some were big enough to let a person look in or even get in.

"There's a lot of work to do," I said.

"I'll start with the places where people can see into the compound. We can't have anybody accidentally seeing Woolly."

"Shouldn't you start with the eroded parts? The guards are keeping people away, and from a distance, Woolly doesn't look that much different from a baby elephant. Aren't you more worried about somebody sneaking in?"

"The guards are there for that, too," he said. "But you have a point. Eroded land means weakened fences. I better get to those sections before they fall down. I can't bring people in to help me, though."

"And how is that different than usual?" I asked.

"I guess it isn't."

"I can help. How about the vets — would they pitch in?"

"Doc Morgan will for sure. The other two work here, but they don't work for me; they work for Jimmy, and he wants them focused on Woolly. While I'm working on the fences, you'll have to do more for the animals."

"Of course . . . Sure . . . No problem."

"It sounds like there *is* a problem," he said.

"I'll do everything that needs to be done; you know that. It's just that Joyce was going to take me shopping for back-to-school stuff after work today."

"We have lots of pens and pencils and paper around here," he said.

"Clothes stuff. Some new clothes. But we don't have to go."

"No, I think you should go." He gave me a questioning look. "Was that your idea or hers?"

"She suggested it, and like I said, we don't have to go."

"No, you're going." He gave me a knowing little smile. "You're starting to like her, aren't you?"

"I think all the elephants are more comfortable around her and like her," I said.

"That wasn't what I asked. Well?"

I shrugged. "She's okay. Better than okay."

"Coming from you, that is *quite* the compliment." He paused. "I think she's okay too." Another pause. "Better than a guy who smells like elephant dung deserves."

"Some of us like the smell of elephant dung."

"Okay, now we've gone too far. You know that you'll always be my number one," he said.

"I thought that was Trixie."

"Trixie's my number-one elephant. You're my number one. I'd give up all of this for you."

I didn't know what to say. Had Joyce said something to him? I'd never dream of him putting me above the elephants.

"You know that, right?" he asked.

"Of course." I believed him. He never lied. But I'd always felt that I was just a member of his herd. When Bacca was born, I had a little brother. Woolly was my baby sister. No, that was wrong. I was more than just a sister to Woolly.

"Joyce told me that sometimes I show more interest in the animals than I do in you," he said.

I snorted and then stopped myself. Joyce *had* spoken to him.

251

"Do you agree with that?"

I shrugged.

"That's not an answer. That's avoiding an answer. Well?"

I had to choose my words. "There are times when the elephants have to be a priority because they need you."

"That's exactly what I said to her!" he exclaimed. "I told her that—"

I broke in. "Sometimes I need you too." I said it fast, before I could change my mind about saying it.

He looked surprised. "I've always tried to be there for you. I'm sure I didn't always do the right thing, and I'm sorry."

"Maybe I should have used words. I didn't want to bother you."

He slipped his arm around me and pulled me across the seat. "You could never bother me. You're my daughter. You're the daughter of my wife. The person I loved more than anything in the world, more than anybody in the world . . . except you."

I felt myself starting to tear up.

"Do you know why I always call you Samantha?"

"Well, I guess because it's my name, but mainly you do it to annoy me."

"Does it really bother you?" he asked. He looked very serious.

"Not really."

"If it had been my decision alone, you would have been called Lara," he said.

"Thank goodness it wasn't your decision." *Wait.* That could mean only one thing. "It was my mother's decision."

"She loved the name Samantha. I figured she was the one doing almost all the work, so she should get to choose. You know that your mother only held you once, right?"

I nodded.

"It was in those brief seconds after you were born and before the doctors realized how much trouble she was in." His voice cracked over the last few words. "And she held you and spoke to you by name. 'Samantha,' she said. 'Samantha.'"

That memory must have been stored in some dim, inaccessible recess of my mind, but I couldn't hear her voice or claim the image.

"And then a nurse whisked you and me away, and your mother was rushed into the operating room."

My father started to cry.

"We don't need to talk about this," I said.

"Yes, we do."

He wasn't the only one close to tears.

"She named you Samantha, and she called you Samantha, so that's what I've always called you. When I call you, when I say your name, I still feel like I'm hearing her voice. Does that make any sense?"

"Yes, but why didn't you ever tell me that?"

He shrugged. "I don't know. I guess it's been like a moment that I still shared with your mother. Now it's time to share it with you."

Part of me wished he'd never told me. Part of me wished I'd known all along.

"Thank you," I said.

He gave me a little squeeze and let me go. "But if you want me to call you Sam or Sammy, I can," he said.

I shook my head. "Samantha is good. Really good."

Now both of us were crying.

"I didn't mean to make you cry," he said.

"I'm not crying," I said, snuffling back the tears. "My eyes are lubricating because there's dust in them."

"It's okay to cry," he said.

"If it's so okay, how come you hardly ever do it?"

"I've cried a lot. You've seen it, but you were much, much too young to remember."

I understood.

"To gain a daughter and lose a wife within a few minutes . . ." he said. "That was more joy and more tragedy than should ever exist in one place at one time." He shook his head slowly. "There's no way to change what's happened, but I'll try harder to know when you're in need and do what I can to help you. But you have to let me know; you have to talk to me."

"I guess we could start now, then. I need something."

"What is it?" my father asked earnestly.

"I need you to fix this section of the fence so that my elephants can't get out, and I need you to do it right now."

He giggled. My big, elephant-sized father giggled like a five-year-old. My tears were drying up.

"I'll do that on one condition," he said.

"What's the condition?"

"I get to go along with you and Joyce on your back-to-school shopping trip."

"But who'll take care of the elephants and Woolly?" I asked.

"We have a couple of live-in veterinarians. I think they can handle things for a few hours."

"I guess you can come with us, but I have one of my own conditions," I said. I paused dramatically. "You have to wait in the mall while me and Joyce go into the stores to pick out the clothes."

"Samantha, that's a deal," he said.

That was a good deal, and I liked that he called me Samantha. Especially now that I understood.

* * *

WHILE MY FATHER WAS WORKING ON THE FENCES, I WAS helping to take care of the elephants and Woolly. I'd loaded the new pickup with bales of hay for the herd. I felt a bit like I was

255

supervising the vets as well as the elephants. Doc Morgan was a good guy, a friend as well as a vet. The other two were just veterinarians, medical practitioners.

They were big-animal vets who had lots of experience. They could diagnose an illness or fix a broken bone or prescribe a medication. We needed them, even if they didn't want to do any of the down-and-dirty work.

Unfortunately, they were clueless about what makes elephants act like elephants. True, elephants are big animals, but the vets continually misread what they were saying and how they were feeling. You have to pay attention to know when you can go closer or when you have to back away, for example. Neither of them could read the elephants, so they were nervous, and the elephants could sense their nervousness and became nervous themselves. Despite the conversations I had with Dr. Grace, she was too anxious for the elephants to feel completely at ease around her. They can always smell the emotions of people who aren't comfortable.

Something else about the two vets bothered me. They were writing daily reports to send to Jimmy, which was okay, but unlike Doc Morgan, they never let my father see what they wrote. To be fair, he hadn't asked, but still, it would have been polite. Maybe there wasn't anything that we needed to see. Maybe there was. Either way, it made me a little uncomfortable around them. Thank goodness they weren't any better at reading me than they were at reading the elephants.

Doc Morgan was being paid by Jimmy, but he wasn't working for Jimmy. He was working for the elephants and for us. The other two were friendly, but they weren't our friends. They were Jimmy's employees.

The truck bounced over the uneven path that led to the isolation enclosure. I was pleased that the herd was up there. They'd learned to associate food with being close to Burma and the pen. It had taken time, but they were finally parallel feeding, the herd on one side of the divide and Burma on the other. They were aware of one another, and it wasn't interfering with feeding on either side.

It gave me hope that someday Burma might be allowed out. As a mature bull, he'd never be a full member of the herd, but if he and they could share the same space, that would be perfect. The sanctuary was large enough to allow him and the herd to coexist and for him to have the run of the whole property, including the pond.

Up ahead was the outer fence of the enclosure. The herd was hovering just outside. The pickup truck that Dr. Grace and Dr. Tavaris usually drove was there too. The vets had been monitoring the herd — really, watching Woolly. The elephants were waiting for their late breakfast. They weren't going to be happy about the delay. For animals who didn't wear watches,

257

they certainly could tell time. Automatically I looked for Woolly, but I knew she'd be there simply because the vets' pickup truck was there. I slowed down, came to a stop right by the vets' truck, and exchanged a wave.

Before I could get out and unload the hay, the bigger elephants, including Trixie, started eating from my truck bed. They crowded around the three open sides. That was fine for them, but there wasn't enough space for everybody. Bacca was off to the back, along with Woolly. Even Raja didn't seem to be able to muscle his way through the older girls. Tiny and Raina could be pretty assertive when it came to food.

I opened the door and used it as a ladder to climb onto my roof. Then I jumped onto the top bales.

"How about a little bit of manners?" I called out.

I wasn't sure they understood my words, but they understood my actions. They all backed off slightly. Woolly was careful to stay out from underfoot. I started tossing the bales onto the ground. They were heavy, and I couldn't heave them far, but at least I could scatter them enough to allow everybody to eat.

The vets were sitting in their pickup truck, watching me work. "You two could help, you know!" I hollered into the open window.

"I'm not getting out of the truck while they're feeding!" Dr. Grace called back.

"It's not necessarily that safe out there," Dr. Tavaris added.

I had the urge to toss a bale into the back of their truck. Maybe even through the window into the cab. That would create an interesting feeding pattern. But I didn't do it. Instead, I worked hard to get all except the last six bales off the truck. Those were for Burma.

I jumped down and pushed against Raina to get her out of the way. She shuffled over so I could pass. That was her being polite, not me being strong.

"You could get trampled doing that," Dr. Grace said out the window.

"Do I look worried?"

I climbed back into my truck bed and stretched up to look over the fence into the enclosure. I couldn't see Burma anywhere.

"Have you seen Burma today?" I asked.

"No, but we haven't really been looking for him," Dr. Tavaris said.

"He's probably hiding in the trees or on the other side of the enclosure," Dr. Grace suggested. "He might still be spooked by the storm last night."

I got in my truck and edged away from the herd, driving slowly, careful not to bump into anybody. I went right to the open section in the fence. There was no Burma to be seen. He could have been in the trees or at the very back of the enclosure.

I had to find him, but first I had to toss the food out right here where we'd been training him to eat.

I climbed out to toss the bales over for Burma. Dr. Tavaris got out of their truck and came over. I had shamed him into it.

"How about if I take care of this part?" he said.

I almost said "Don't bother," but instead I said, "Thanks. I'm going to wander along the fence and look for Burma."

I walked along the twenty-foot gap between the concrete wall and the metal fence. I took a few steps and realized I had company. Woolly was trailing behind me.

"I don't have a bottle for you," I said.

I started off again, and she followed along. She was now tall enough to look over the concrete wall easily. I could have tried to shoo her back, but I liked the companionship. It also felt like a real compliment that she chose to be with me instead of with the herd. I reached back, and she took my hand with her trunk.

"Woolly, you don't have to worry about being alone. You might be the only woolly mammoth in the whole world, but they're working on creating a whole bunch of you."

I looked up ahead. Downed trees had smashed into the concrete wall. I'd have to let my father know. He was so busy taking care of the perimeter fence that he probably hadn't thought about the isolation enclosure. I had to see how bad it was before I called him.

Getting closer, I realized it was worse than I'd thought. The inner wall had been damaged by the falling tree trunks. The wires had snapped, and the concrete was almost completely shattered. The trees leaning against the crumbled remains of the concrete formed a kind of ramp that an elephant could walk up to get over the wall. This could be very, very bad.

I pulled out my phone and dialed. It rang and rang, but my father didn't pick up. I figured he'd left his phone in his truck.

I left a voicemail. "It's me. I'm at the isolation enclosure, and the inner wall is broken. Burma might be able to get over it. I'm east of the gate. Come as quick as you can." I hung up.

I thought about running back to get Dr. Tavaris and Dr. Grace, but decided against it. It was too far, and besides, whatever was wrong, I couldn't count on them to help make it right. What I really needed was to find Burma. All I had to do was keep him away from the section of the fence where he might be able to get out. The apples in my pockets and some gentle encouragement should be enough to do the job.

I walked along the fence toward the gate. As I went, I yelled for Burma at the top of my lungs. He could have been in the back corner, or he could have been hidden among the trees and undergrowth toward the back. The pen was big, but so was he, and there was no place where he could completely hide from me if I looked for him hard and long enough.

Woolly trailed obediently behind me. She was incredibly

cute and good-natured. It was amazing to raise an elephant — well, a mammoth — from birth. It was a lot of work, but it was totally awesome.

I thought about Daisy Mae often. Not as much as in the beginning, but still a few times a day. I liked to think that she would have been proud of me. I was doing what I said I'd do. I was raising her baby.

I was relieved to see that the rest of the fence and the gate were still intact. I was a little worried about the gate, although I had no logical reason to be. The gate was solid metal — steel — and was stronger than both the corrugated metal fence and the concrete inner wall. A truck could hit it or an elephant could ram it, and it wouldn't give.

I kept calling for Burma, hoping that my voice and the associated promise of apples would lure him into the open. So far, no luck.

I turned and looked back the way we'd come. Moving toward me along the fence — in the gap between the fence and the wall, where we were — was Raja, followed by Bacca, Trixie, and the entire herd. They'd never been in that space before. I had to figure that Trixie's concern for Woolly had overcome her fear of getting too close to Burma's enclosure. If Burma came out now, the herd would be forced to stay close to him until they came to the gate, where the space opened up again. That could be a good thing.

I heard an engine and hoped my father had come to help. I was disappointed to see the vets' pickup truck. They pulled in right beside me.

"It's obvious that they really consider you part of the herd," Dr. Grace said through the open window.

"You already knew that, didn't you?"

Dr. Tavaris chuckled.

"So where is — Oh, my God!" Dr. Grace exclaimed. I saw her eyes get huge, and I turned around.

There was Burma. He was standing no more than thirty yards away, on the outside of the enclosure — on *our* side of the outer fence. He was motionless and silent. The wind was blowing toward him, so the herd, still some way down the fence, couldn't hear or smell him. They didn't know he was there.

"Get into the truck," Dr. Grace said, starting to open the door.

I pushed against it to close it again. "Unless the rest of the herd can get into the truck, I'm not going anywhere."

"He's dangerous," Dr. Tavaris said. "You know his history. He's hurt people, he even —"

"If he gets angry, do you think being in a truck is going to protect you?" I asked. I was scared, but I couldn't show it. I had to be calm.

"We can outrun him," Dr. Grace said.

"We're not running anywhere without Woolly. We have to protect her."

"We have to protect ourselves," Dr. Tavaris said. "We don't even have a tranquilizer gun with us. It's back at the trailer. Maybe we should go get it."

"Don't go anywhere. One of you call my father, and the other take off the lock and chain and open the gate to the isolation enclosure. Then get ready to use that truck."

"Use it for what?"

"To get between Woolly and Burma if you have to — Wait! He's moving."

Burma slowly stepped forward. His ears were twitching. Was he nervous or excited or just scared?

"Please get in the truck," Dr. Grace whispered. "We have to go."

"No. I'm staying here."

Dr. Tavaris was on the phone. "It's going to your father's voicemail."

"Leave a message. Then one of you can get the gate for me."

Woolly stood close to my side, staring at Burma. She knew he was an elephant, but she also knew he wasn't part of her herd.

"He's coming closer," Dr. Grace said, stating the obvious.

"He's not that close, and not as close as he's going to be in the twenty seconds it's going to take you to open the gate."

"What good will that do?"

"Just do it."

"How are you going to get him back in the enclosure?"

"I'm going to take him by the trunk and lead him back in."
I needed something more to convince them. "If you don't do
what I'm telling you to do and something happens to Woolly,
I'm going to make sure Jimmy knows who's to blame."

They both looked worried. Dr. Tavaris climbed out of the
truck. Looking back over his shoulder at Burma, he hurried
over to the gate in the concrete wall. He fumbled with the
lock, took it off, pulled the chain free, and threw open the two
halves of the gate. They bumped against the fence with two
clanks and bounced back slightly. He ran back to the truck
and jumped in.

Now I had to figure out how to get Burma through the gate
and back inside the enclosure. It would have been so much
easier if Woolly hadn't been with me. I could have just —

Wait. I didn't have to get Burma inside the enclosure.
Maybe I could get *Woolly* inside the enclosure and close the
gate behind us. If we moved quickly, we could get there. I'd
lead her in, and we'd be safe. The two vets could drive away
faster than Burma could run. We'd all be safe.

Then Raja and Bacca came out from between the fences,
followed by Trixie and the rest of the herd.

And Burma charged toward us.

CHAPTER
Twenty

I FELT MY HEART RISE UP INTO MY THROAT. I WAS FRO-
zen in place, rigid with terror.

Then Burma skidded to a stop. I stumbled back a few steps.
My whole body was shaking — a combination of the terror I'd
just experienced and the fear that was still there.

Burma stood stock-still. Raja and Bacca and Woolly all
scrambled away, retreating into the safety of the herd. Trixie
had moved forward and was now standing directly between
Burma and the rest of the herd, as well as me and the vets and
their truck. She had always seemed so big, but now, no more
than a dozen yards from Burma, she was obviously much
smaller than he was.

Burma pawed at the ground with his front feet, raising
and lowering his head so his tusks were menacing. Trixie was
motionless. She had to know that if he charged, she would be
gored, wounded, possibly killed, but she stood her ground.

"Get in the truck!" Dr. Tavaris stage-whispered at me. He was trying to keep his voice calm and quiet. It wasn't working.

"No."

Trixie couldn't stand alone against Burma. She didn't have to. I walked forward.

With each step closer, Burma appeared bigger and scarier. When I was right beside Trixie, I stopped. She angled her head slightly toward me, and I could see the fear in her eyes. I was sure that she could see the same fear in mine.

I was now so close to Burma that I could actually feel his breath. He was puffing, expelling air through his trunk. I could also look into his eyes, and what I saw was *his* fear. It wasn't just that we were afraid of him. He was afraid of us, and that was why he was behaving this way. I had to let him know he didn't have to be afraid.

I had to be calm. I couldn't show fear. I couldn't let Burma smell my fear. I took a deep, slow breath, summoned every fiber of courage I had in me, and inched forward. My feet felt like concrete, so heavy that I could hardly move them. Slowly I reached into my pocket and pulled out an apple.

I held the apple up so Burma could see it. "I brought you a treat," I said. My voice was so hoarse and strained that I didn't recognize it. I was afraid Burma wouldn't either, and I repeated my offer. This time it sounded like me.

Burma continued to lower and raise his head, and he lifted his trunk into the air. If he grabbed me, he could toss me through the air or crush me. Those tusks would kill me in a second. I had to fight the urge to turn and run, but what good would that do? He was so much faster than I was that he could run me down. I could go only one direction — forward.

I edged two small steps closer. I held the apple out a little bit farther. "Burma, this is for you." I tossed it up in the air and was amazed that I still had enough focus and coordination to be able to catch it.

Burma raised his head and turned it slightly to the side. He wasn't pawing the ground. He wasn't thrusting his tusks. He still looked scared, but maybe less so. Confusion and uncertainty were there, too, in his eyes.

I took a little bite from the apple. "It's a very good apple."

I edged forward until I thought I was close enough for him to reach out with his trunk and take the apple. On cue, Burma extended his trunk. He was going to take the apple or toss me like a rag doll. I had to trust him. I had to trust that I understood what he was saying.

Ever so gently he took the apple from my hand, pulled it away, and placed it in his mouth. I heard it being crunched. I pulled out a second apple. Burma took this one from me without hesitation. One pocket was now empty. The second held two more apples. That would have to be enough.

"I know you're afraid," I said to Burma. "I know how you feel. Believe me, I know how you feel, because I feel the same. I want you to be safe."

I started moving again. This time I was heading slightly off to the side of Burma, to the side closest to the enclosure and away from the herd. As I walked, I reached into my pocket and pulled out the third apple. I made sure Burma could see the apple in my hand, but I didn't offer it to him, keeping my arm down by my side.

I looked back at him. His head swiveled as he looked first at me, then at Trixie and the herd. He was still afraid, still uncertain.

"Come, Burma!" I yelled as I started walking away, toward the enclosure. This time my voice was strong and decisive. This wasn't a request. This was an order.

And he listened! He started walking after me, his head still turned so that he could keep an eye on Trixie. He trotted behind me as I started to make a big semicircle around the herd and cut back toward the gate.

With each step, we were getting farther from the herd and closer to my goal. We were a little more than halfway around the circle. I offered Burma the third apple, and he took it from me. It was gone in the blink of an eye and a loud crunch. Still walking, I pulled out the fourth apple, the last apple. This one would have to do the trick.

We reached the gate, and I walked through it into the enclosure. Burma hesitated at the entrance and came to a stop. Again, his head swiveled back and forth between me and the herd. I had been so focused on Burma that I hadn't noticed that Trixie had moved as well. She had shifted around so that she was still between Burma and the rest of the herd. She was a good mother, a wonderful matriarch. Even if she was as afraid as I was, she was still going to care for her family, to put herself in danger to protect them. Wasn't that exactly what I was doing for my herd too?

"You'll be safe in here," I said to Burma. I held up the apple.

Burma stayed motionless. I felt frustrated and anxious it wasn't going to work. Going this far and no farther was like going no place. "Burma, come!" I ordered.

He put his head down like a scolded child and came into the pen after me. I waited until he was almost on top of me, and then—very deliberately, very visibly—rolled the apple along the ground. The red gleamed against the brown of the trodden earth. Burma kept moving, following the apple past me and farther into the pen.

Quickly, quietly, I ran back toward the gate. I was surprised, but pleased, to see that Dr. Grace and Dr. Tavaris were each holding one side of the gate and swinging them closed, leaving just enough of a gap for me to slip through. Dr. Tavaris looped the chain around the two sections, and Dr. Grace snapped the lock in place.

"Are you all right?" Dr. Grace asked. Her voice was shaky.

"Yeah, fine; good."

"That was the most amazing thing I've ever seen in my entire life," Dr. Tavaris said.

"That was the bravest thing I've ever witnessed," Dr. Grace said.

"He was scared. Just like the rest of us."

Burma came slowly toward the gate. The two vets moved away, beyond his reach through the bars. I didn't. Burma couldn't think I was afraid of him any more than he could think I had tricked him. I moved right to the gate, climbed up on the lower bar, and reached toward him.

Burma extended his trunk and touched my hand. I rubbed his trunk. He could have pulled me in, he could have pushed me back, he could have grabbed me and thrown me into the air. Instead, he lowered his head and allowed me to rub behind the closest ear.

"You're safe now."

There was no fear in his eyes. He was calm. He was glad to be back inside the pen. He wasn't feeling threatened, so he had no need to threaten anybody else.

"Okay, I was wrong," Dr. Tavaris said. "What you're doing *now* is the most amazing thing I've ever seen."

"It's not that amazing," I said. "He's not afraid anymore, and neither am I."

And more important, maybe I never needed to be afraid of him again. Something good might come from this.

As I stood there on the gate rails, I felt a nudge and looked down. Woolly was right by my side. With my attention focused on Burma, I hadn't seen her coming. Before I could shoo her away, Burma reached his trunk through the bars, and the two touched trunks.

I didn't know if I should be terrified or thrilled. Here was Burma establishing contact with a member of the herd, but it was with Woolly — the most valuable animal in the world. This was more than I could have dreamed and more than I could have feared, all at once. There was nothing I could do but hold my breath and watch and hope.

"Sam, you have to do something," Dr. Grace said quietly.

"There's nothing I can do. . . . Wait. . . . There's something."

I gave Burma one more rough scratch and jumped down off the gate. For a split second, I was worried — what if Woolly didn't come when I walked away? What if Burma wouldn't let her go? But Woolly trotted after me, thank goodness. Risking my life was one thing. Risking hers was unthinkable.

"Now we have to clear away the fallen trees and repair the gap so he can't get back out," I said. Quickly I told them where the fallen trees were. "You need to get to the gap and move those trees . . . push them aside with the truck and then use the truck to block the gap."

"What if Burma goes right to the gap while we're working?" Dr. Tavaris asked.

"You'll just have to move fast," I answered. "I'll lead the herd away. We'll go down to the trailer. Woolly needs to be fed anyway. All right?"

They nodded in agreement, got back into their truck, and drove between the fence and the wall, heading toward the gap. I started off, trailed by Woolly, then Bacca, then Trixie and the rest. Burma was still standing at the gate, following us with his eyes. Somehow leaving him seemed wrong. The only thing that would have been more wrong would have been opening up the gate and having him join us.

Twenty-One

JOYCE AND I WERE SURROUNDED BY THE HERD, AND Woolly was greedily taking a bottle from me. "The important thing is that you're all right," Joyce said.

"The important thing is that *everybody* is all right," I countered.

"No. It's good that the whole herd is fine. It's great that Woolly is okay. But you're the most important."

"Thanks for saying that and for understanding. I hope my father is as good about it."

"Do you want me to tell him what happened?"

My immediate gut response was to say yes, but I didn't say it. "It has to come from me."

"I thought you might say that, but how about me at least being there when you tell him?"

"I'd like that."

"Sometimes it's good to have a lawyer around, even when you're not guilty of anything."

I heard the engine before I could see the truck bouncing over the crest in the road. My father was driving much faster than usual. That probably wasn't a good sign.

"I have a feeling he might already know what happened," Joyce said.

"Yeah, I was thinking that." If he had gone to where the wall needed repairs, he had run into Dr. Grace and Dr. Tavaris, and they would have told him everything. It would have been better if I had been the one to tell him. I could have left out the scary parts. . . . *Wait*. It was all scary parts.

The truck slowed down and came to a stop, and he jumped out. He looked even larger than usual, and he looked angry. I wasn't used to seeing him angry, especially at me. I felt more frightened than when I'd faced Burma. That was silly. . . . wasn't it?

"What were you thinking?" he yelled.

Reacting to his tone of voice and his anger, the elephants eased away, opening up a clear path between us.

"You could have been killed!"

"I guess so," I mumbled.

"You *guess* so? That elephant has killed before. You know that."

"I knew he wasn't going to harm me. I could see it in his eyes."

"To get close enough to look in his eyes, you had to be close enough to be killed!"

He had a point. At that distance, I had been too close to get away.

"You promised me you wouldn't feed Burma by hand, and then you went and did this!"

"What would you have done if you'd been there?" Joyce asked.

He looked like he hadn't even noticed her before she spoke. "What?"

"If it had been you instead of Sam, what would you have done? Would you have walked away?"

"Of course not."

"Wouldn't you have done exactly the same thing?" Joyce said.

"Whose side are you on, anyway?" he demanded.

"I'm not on anybody's side. I'm just saying that if she were my daughter—"

"She isn't your daughter!" he snapped. "You have no idea what it would be like to lose your daughter!"

Joyce looked hurt. "I'm sorry. . . . I was just trying to help."

"You can help by leaving my daughter and me alone to talk. This is a family matter." His voice was cold.

Joyce looked hurt. I knew that look, because I'd caused it

before. She turned to walk away, but I grabbed her arm. "No, I want her here," I told Dad. "And you should apologize."

"You want me to apologize to you?" He sounded dumbfounded.

"Not to me, to Joyce. She didn't deserve that attitude or what you said to her."

"It's all right," Joyce said. "I understand."

"It's *not* all right. You did nothing wrong. Maybe I did, but you didn't." I turned directly to my father. "Well?"

"I'm . . . um . . . sorry, Joyce." His anger had been replaced by what looked like embarrassment or remorse.

"It's all right," she said. "You're upset because something could have happened to the most important person in the world. I understand."

"I *am* sorry," he said. "You know that sometimes I understand elephants better than I understand people. Especially now, especially when I'm so angry and scared and—"

I laughed. "It doesn't matter how or what or when. You always understand elephants better than people," I said.

He shrugged and gave me a meek little smile. "Still, you shouldn't have done what you did."

"I know. I probably shouldn't have. It was probably more stupid than brave, but what else could I do?" I asked. "I did what you would have done."

"Maybe better than I would have done it."

"Maybe you should hug each other," Joyce suggested.

My father looked taken aback for a second, then wrapped me up in his big arms. I reached out and pulled Joyce into the hug.

CHAPTER

Twenty-Two

I PEEKED THROUGH A HOLE IN THE FENCE BESIDE THE front gate. There had to be a dozen trucks out there, almost identical except for the colors and big letters on the sides identifying the TV stations they belonged to. Thank goodness the guards had kept them at a distance from the property.

Of course the guards couldn't stop the helicopters. We'd had flyovers by three different TV helicopters during the past hour. They had searched the property from the air and buzzed the herd, spooking them. My father was so angry that I thought he would have taken a shot at them if he'd had a gun. Fortunately he didn't have a gun.

I was pretty sure the helicopter crews hadn't seen Woolly. She and Bacca were in the food storage area, eating straw and being bottle-fed by Dr. Grace and my dad. There, under a roof, they were out of view from the air. Obviously the newspeople had discovered that something was happening here, but we wanted to keep Woolly hidden as long as possible. We didn't want them taking any pictures of her.

Hearing the sound of a helicopter engine, I moved away from the fence and scanned the sky. I bent down and picked up a rock to throw before I realized just how stupid that was. I let the rock drop to the ground.

The sound got louder and louder, and then a dark shape shot past overhead. I recognized Jimmy's helicopter. It was headed toward the house, and I ran after it. It slowed and started to lower to the ground. I stopped at a safe distance but wasn't far enough away to escape the dust and pebbles kicked up by the rotors. I shielded my face with my hand. The rotors slowed down, and the breeze and debris subsided.

The door opened, and Jimmy climbed out. He wasn't in disguise. There would have been no point, since the newspeople knew he was doing something here. As Jimmy started down the ladder, a second man, wearing a suit and carrying a briefcase, appeared in the doorway. He had *lawyer* written all over him. I didn't like lawyers, except for Joyce.

"We weren't expecting you, but I'm glad to see you!" I called out.

"Glad?" Jimmy echoed. "Well, it's all in the interpretation. Is Woolly all right? . . . Well, is she?"

"She's fine. She's in the food storage area. Helicopters kept buzzing the herd."

"That won't be happening anymore. I had my lawyers file an injunction, and the judge granted a temporary order banning all aircraft from flying lower than ten thousand feet within five kilometers of our property."

"Wow, that's amazing."

"If you have the right lawyers, almost anything is possible."

"He's a lawyer, right?" I asked, indicating the man standing beside him.

"Yes, he is. This is Mr. Sawyer."

"Is his first name James?" I asked.

"Of course it is. I assumed you knew he was a lawyer because of the suit and the shiny shoes. You can practically smell a lawyer," Jimmy said. He looked directly at the man. "No offense."

"None taken," he said.

"I have learned that in life, lawyers are essential. They have a function."

"So do cockroaches and mosquitoes, but that doesn't mean that I have to like them," I said.

Jimmy gave his strange laugh. "I like you."

"I like you, too," I said.

"And that makes this more difficult."

"What do you mean?"

"We need to speak to your father. Where is he?"

"He's with Woolly in the food shelter."

"It's over this way, correct?" Jimmy asked.

"That's right."

Jimmy started off with those fast little steps. I had to struggle to keep up with him, and the lawyer fell behind. His shiny shoes had to be getting dusty. I hoped in his hurry he'd step in a big elephant turd up to his ankle.

"How did they find out about Woolly?" I asked Jimmy.

"They don't actually know about Woolly."

"Then why are they here?"

"They know something important is taking place here, but they don't know exactly what it is. We've been monitoring the news reports, and so far they are in the dark," he answered.

"But how did they know to come here to begin with? You know it wasn't us that let the cat out of the bag."

"I know. You and your father are honorable people. It could be somebody in my organization, but not one of the people directly involved in the project, or the press would know more. It could also be somebody who pieced together my travels or an industrial spy."

"But you don't know who or how," I said.

"Not at this moment, but I will figure it out and — There's my girl!" he exclaimed. Woolly and Bacca were poking their heads out of the storage shed.

He ran toward them. I hurried to catch up. His sudden

approach seemed to spook them, and they both disappeared inside the shed. I ran after him and grabbed him by the hand. "They're upset by all that's happening. We need to walk in calmly."

"Yes, yes, of course. You are very wise around elephants."

"I try."

"And brave. Very brave."

"There's nothing brave about being around Woolly and Bacca."

"I'm talking about what you did with that bull elephant yesterday. You were willing to protect Woolly with your life."

Of course, the vets had told him about it. There was never any doubt he was going to be told.

"It wasn't as brave as some people might have thought. Things get blown out of proportion sometimes."

"I don't think putting oneself between Woolly and a charging bull elephant *could* be blown out of proportion."

I shrugged. "Wouldn't you have done the same?"

"I'm afraid not. I'm willing to risk my money, but not my life. I am rather risk-averse about that," he said. "I need you to know that sometimes we must do things that we don't necessarily want to do." He paused. "Some decisions are wrong no matter what you do."

I was confused. What was he saying — or not saying?

We entered through the gate, and Woolly came over to greet us. To my surprise, she seemed happier to see Jimmy than to see me. She nuzzled against him, and he giggled.

"She really likes you," I said.

"She should. Technically I am sort of like her father, since I created the gene sequence program that allowed her to be cloned. And of course the mother is" — for a split second I thought he was going to say me, but he didn't — "a mammoth that has been dead for close to four thousand years."

"It's good to see you," my dad said, coming up to us.

"Yes, good."

Dad shook Jimmy's hand and then caught sight of the lawyer. "And you are?" he asked the man. He didn't sound friendly.

"Mr. Sawyer. James Sawyer."

"He's a lawyer," I said.

"Why would you bring a lawyer with you?" my father asked.

"It's okay," I said reassuringly. "He did some injunction thing that stopped those helicopters from buzzing us."

"Oh — then I'm happy to meet you and very grateful."

"He's not the lawyer who did that," Jimmy said. "I have a bunch of lawyers." He paused and looked quizzical. "What should you even call a group of lawyers?"

"What?"

"You know, there are herds of elephants and pods of whales and packs of wolves and . . . That's it: they are like wolves. I have a *pack* of lawyers who work for me."

I laughed. "Maybe they should be like geese or crows. A gaggle of lawyers or a murder of lawyers."

Jimmy giggled the way he always giggled.

"Why do you have this particular lawyer with you now?" my dad asked.

"I had to bring him because of what happened with the bull elephant."

"You want him to sue the elephant?" I asked.

He giggled again. "You are always so good with jokes. You are very funny."

"Why is he here?" Dad asked again. His tone and expression were so serious that I felt a chill.

"You and your daughter are good people," Jimmy said.

That didn't seem like a bad thing to start with.

"I am very grateful to both you and Sam for all that you've done for Woolly."

"It's nothing more than we do for all our animals. Woolly is family."

"She is a member of your family who was almost killed yesterday. I can't allow Woolly to be placed in such danger ever again."

I gasped. "Are you saying we need to get rid of Burma?"

He shook his head, and I should have been relieved, but I wasn't.

"I protected Woolly," I said. "I put myself in the way."

"And that's what makes this even harder." He turned to his lawyer. "Please."

The lawyer put down his briefcase. He opened it and pulled out an envelope. "May it be noted that I am formally serving you with these papers," he said, handing my father the envelope.

"You're suing us?" my father asked in disbelief.

"Of course not! I would never do that," Jimmy said.

"Then what *are* you doing?"

"I'm buying you out."

Twenty-Three

JOYCE HAD STUDIED THE ORIGINAL CONTRACT WITH Jimmy that my father had signed and was reviewing the papers that he had just been given. He had called her right after Jimmy flew away. If you fight fire with fire, I figured you'd fight lawyers with lawyers. Jimmy had a pack — or a murder — of them, and we had only Joyce.

"So what does this all mean?" Dad asked.

"This," she said, holding up the papers, "is his formal offer to buy your sanctuary."

"It isn't for sale."

"That doesn't matter."

"Of course it does. You can't just buy somebody's place without them agreeing to it. A man's house is his castle."

"Yes, it is. Unless he signed a previous agreement saying he'd have to sell. And you did that."

"I signed an agreement that he could become my partner

and buy ten percent of the sanctuary, not that he could buy me out."

"You signed both. It's right here." She flipped a few pages and pointed to the bottom. "This is a mutual buy-out clause. You signed it."

"I wouldn't have agreed to that," Dad said.

"You signed the contract, so legally you *did* agree."

"But I didn't know it."

"I just wish I could have been there to look at it before you signed it."

"Me too, but it was more than a year before you came here as a volunteer, before we met — well, before everything about us."

"What is that mutual buy-out thing?" I asked.

"It's a clause. In simplest terms, both parties to this agreement — your father and JM Limited — have agreed that upon written notification, one partner can buy out the other."

"Even if the other partner doesn't want to be bought out?"

"Yes. If one partner makes an offer, the other party has to proportionally match or exceed it."

"I'm lost," my dad said.

"You own ninety percent of the property, and he owns ten percent. If you wanted to buy him out —"

"I can do that?" my father asked.

"You can."

"Then let's do that. Instead of him buying me out, I'll buy him out. End of discussion."

"But where would we get the money to do that?" I asked.

"We could take out a bank loan."

"It would have to be a very big loan. Let me explain," Joyce said. "A proportional bid means that you would have to match what is offered. According to these papers, he's offering you nine million dollars for your share of the —"

"Nine million dollars." I gasped. "He offered us nine million dollars?"

"Yes, the amount is right here in the offer," Joyce said.

"But we're not taking it," Dad said. "It doesn't matter how much he offered."

"Yes, it does," Joyce said. "That's what the proportional offer means. Since he offered you nine million dollars for your ninety percent ownership, you'd have to offer him one million and one dollars for his ten percent ownership."

"But there's no way we could pay him that much," Dad said. "There's no way the bank would loan me a million dollars."

"Wait — what if you told them you had a woolly mammoth that's practically priceless?" I suggested.

"That might work if I could convince them," my dad said.

"But you couldn't tell them anything about Woolly to

begin with," Joyce said. "If you told them, you'd violate the nondisclosure agreement and Jimmy would just take everything without even having to pay."

"That's right. . . . I hadn't thought about that," he said.

"And that's why he offered you so much money," she said. "He wanted to make sure that you couldn't match his offer."

"There has to be another way."

"You know I'd lend it to you myself if I had it," Joyce said.

"And you know I wouldn't take it even if you did."

"Wait! Can't we just use all the money he's offering and take our herd and set up another sanctuary?" I asked. "We could do that with nine million dollars."

"You could buy property, but you couldn't take the elephants with you. Woolly and the rest of the herd are all part of the chattels of this property," Joyce said.

"What does that mean?" I asked.

"He's part owner of the property, including the elephants and Woolly. His offer isn't just for the property but for the herd."

I didn't know what to say. I was stunned. But my mind was racing. "So. . . . if we can't buy him out, we'll have to leave the farm, leave our house. . . . leave our elephants. . . . leave Woolly behind, right?"

Joyce nodded.

"And you're saying we're powerless to do anything?" Dad said.

"I'm sorry, but I can't see a way out."

"That's not right," he said.

"It has nothing to do with what's right, only what's legal. Maybe I can appeal it through the legal system, tie the thing up in the courts."

"Could that work?" Dad asked.

"We could at least make it so difficult that he'll want to settle and possibly allow you to take at least some of the elephants."

"Some of them?"

"Maybe we could negotiate so that you could take Trixie and Raja and possibly one or two of the others."

"We can't do that. They're family. They need to be together. Woolly needs them," I said.

"Especially if she doesn't have us," my dad said. His voice was flat, almost without emotion. He looked defeated.

"What if we talk to Jimmy?" I said. "Maybe we can convince him not to do this."

"I tried," my father said. "He's not answering my e-mails or phone calls."

"When litigation is possible, it's common practice to have all communication go through lawyers," Joyce said. "He's insulating himself so he doesn't have to face you. That's the way terrible people do terrible things."

"But that's the problem. I don't think Jimmy is a terrible person, even if this is a terrible thing he's doing," I said.

"I don't agree. He tricked me and betrayed us and our elephants," Dad said. "He is a terrible person."

"No," I said, shaking my head. "He's not. He's different, kind of strange, but he's not terrible."

"I don't believe that," my father said. "If we can't stop him, what happens to us?"

"You'll have to leave."

"When?" I asked.

"According to the terms of the contract, you have forty-eight hours to match his offer. If you fail to do so, you'll have another twenty-four hours to vacate the premises."

"But that's only three days!" I exclaimed.

"The clock started ticking when the papers were served. You have less than seventy-two hours," she said.

"But where are we going to go? Where are we going to live?"

"You'll have nine million dollars in your bank account. You can go anywhere in the world."

"The only place I want to be is here," I said. "That's all I ever wanted. This is my home."

My father's whole body shuddered. "We'll build another home," my father said, his voice hardly a whisper.

"No. We can have another house, but we can't have another home."

"Home is where your family is," Joyce said.

"And I'm leaving almost all of my family behind." I stood up and headed for the door.

"Samantha!" my father called out.

I froze in place.

"Where are you going?" he demanded.

"To start saying goodbye."

CHAPTER
Twenty-Four

I SAID GOODBYE TO MY EMPTY ROOM AND CLOSED THE door behind me. It was the only bedroom I'd ever had in the only house I'd ever lived in. In an hour, it wouldn't be mine anymore.

For the past three days, we'd been scrambling to get ready. Everything we owned had been packed up and carried out the door — my entire lifetime of memories plus my father's memories of the years before I was born. Times he spent here with my mother. His memories and mine were everywhere.

I stopped at the open door to his bedroom, my parents' bedroom until the day I was born — the day she died. She wasn't in the house during my lifetime, but she had been here once. Would her memories be only the boxes we'd packed, or would some of them remain even in an empty room in a house we didn't own, lost to us forever?

I struggled, trying to decide whether it would have been better to have my own memories of her. Would that have made leaving harder? Probably. No, definitely it would have been harder, but I would have taken the pain if I could just have had some of those memories.

Would it have been easier to leave our house behind if I'd never had the chance to know Trixie and Raja and Bacca and the others? What about Woolly? She'd been in my life for only a short time, but she had a bigger place in my heart than any of the others. Not because she was a mammoth, but because I was there from the beginning of her life. I felt bad about all of it, but what troubled me most was the promise I'd made to Daisy Mae that I would take care of her baby. It was a promise I couldn't keep.

I knew I had to leave, but I had to decide how to do it. I opened the front door and hesitated. Should I look back or just walk away? I let the two options play around in my head until I knew. I wanted to remember our house as it was before, full of furniture and the future, not as it was now, empty and finished.

I closed the door behind me and walked away.

I couldn't let reality overshadow my memories. I had to try to be happy about what was and not sad about what was gone. Easy to think, harder to believe, but I'd have to try.

The big moving truck was parked right in front of the house. It was packed with all our possessions. We'd had help loading it. The money—that immense, unbelievable sum of money — hadn't helped us stay, but it had made moving easier. It had paid for the truck and the packing and the place where we were going. It was a small house with a nice yard, right in town, just a block over from my two best friends, who said they'd meet us at the house and help me set up my room. That was so nice, and I needed kindness right now.

It was a rental, only until we found something more permanent. My father was looking for either a house or some land where he could build one. The property had to be at least three hundred acres, a place with lots of open fields and a forest and streams that ran through and a pond, or a place to dig one. It would be big enough to hold twice as many elephants, and nobody would ever be able to take it away from us because it would be entirely ours, and money would never be a problem again.

We already had the first elephant, Burma. Arrangements had been made for him to leave the sanctuary soon and be housed at another park until we could take him in. I was sad that he'd have to go through two more moves and because what happened with him set off the catastrophe. I couldn't allow myself to blame him, though. None of it was his fault. He had been abused and had lived through so much. And despite it all, he showed he could be gentle, even when he was afraid. At the same time, I was happy that he would finally have a home with us. We could at least make the rest of his life good.

In the meantime, we were going to get a puppy. My father let me choose the breed, and I had decided to get an Irish wolfhound. I wanted the closest thing I could get to an elephant. Tomorrow we were going to look at a litter of wolfhound puppies that had been born three weeks ago.

I walked down toward the pond, where the herd was. My father and Joyce had already gone to see them and say goodbye. Say goodbye . . . that's what I was doing, saying goodbye to them. Saying goodbye to my family. Forever. No visits, no contact, we'd been told. We'd never be allowed back on the property. I'd never see them again. Well, maybe. I had already thought about sneaking past the guards. I knew every place where I could get under the fence. I could see them, even if I couldn't let them see me.

The herd was surrounding my father and Joyce. The elephants were dripping wet, so I knew they'd just come out of the water. Raja was still in the pond. He was always the first in and the last out. I'd never float in that pond again. I'd never be mad at him again for flipping me over. I felt myself starting to tear up, but I choked back the tears. There was no point in crying.

Trixie was the first to notice my approach. She dipped her

head slightly, quizzically. She was trying to figure things out. She knew something was different. Not just the moving — she could probably smell our emotions. Woolly was in the middle of the herd and hadn't seen me yet.

The two vets sat in their truck off to the side. Their reports had set this outcome in motion. They knew that and felt bad about it. They had apologized repeatedly and told us how awful they felt. No matter how bad they felt, I felt infinitely worse.

I came close, and my father wrapped an arm around me. "How are you doing, Samantha?"

"Terrible. The same as you. How are they doing?" I asked, gesturing toward the herd.

"They know something is wrong, but they don't know how wrong."

"I wish we could tell them," I said.

"We never needed words before, but we do now," he said.

"The worst thing is, they'll think we just ran off and abandoned them."

"They won't even have a body to mourn," he said.

I thought back to how they'd mourned over Daisy Mae and Peanut.

"What's the longest you've ever been away from them?" Joyce asked.

"I think three days," I said.

"It was Samantha's grandmother's funeral, her nana." My father looked at his watch. "It's almost time to go. We have to say our final goodbyes."

"I'll leave you two alone," Joyce said.

I reached out and took her hand. "You don't have to go."

"Yes, I do. You need to be alone for this."

She gave my hand a little squeeze and walked away.

Joyce's movement must have caught Woolly's attention. She raised her head, then her trunk, and ran toward us. She was coming fast. For a split second, I was afraid she'd bowl us over, but she came to a stop right in front of me. She reached up with her trunk and felt all over my face and then my body. I realized she was glad to see me but would have been happier to see a bottle. Why hadn't I thought to bring one?

I heard a truck door open and saw Dr. Grace and Dr. Tavaris coming toward us. I felt a surge of anger. I didn't need another apology. All I needed was for them to leave us alone. Then I saw that Dr. Tavaris was carrying a big bottle of formula.

Woolly saw the vets and the bottle, but she stayed right beside me. Maybe she wanted to be with me even more than she wanted the bottle.

"We hate to trouble you, but we were wondering if you could do this feeding," Dr. Tavaris said.

I took the bottle from him. Instantly Woolly fumbled

around for it, and I helped her get it into her mouth. She started slurping the formula down, bubbles rising up in the bottle to replace it.

"Thank you for letting me feed her," I said.

"No, thank *you*," Dr. Grace said. "She always takes the bottle from you better than from anybody else."

"I wish I could come back and feed her."

"If it were up to us, you'd be here every day and none of this would be happening," Dr. Tavaris said.

"You know how bad we feel. We talked about quitting," Dr. Grace said.

"You can't do that!" I protested. "With us gone, all she has is the two of you and Doc Morgan."

"That's why we didn't," Dr. Tavaris said. "We're so sad about everything. I don't understand why he won't even let you back on the property."

"It's probably better for the elephants this way. Having us come and go would be confusing," my dad said.

"I wish we could at least know how they're doing," I said.

"We can call you all the time to keep you up to date on what's happening," Dr. Grace said.

"Won't that get you in trouble?" Dad asked.

"Technically, yes. We're not supposed to talk to anybody about anything that goes on here," Dr. Grace said. "You know, the nondisclosure agreement."

"But what Jimmy doesn't know can't hurt anybody," Dr. Tavaris added.

"I really appreciate what you're saying," I said, "but I don't think you should do it. You mustn't risk your jobs. Not just because of what would happen to you, but because you need to be here for Woolly. It would be even worse for her if you two had to leave as well."

They both nodded.

"We're going to leave you alone now," Dr. Grace said.

"Thank you," Dad replied.

"We will stay in touch," Dr. Tavaris said. "Even if we don't talk about what's happening here, we're still allowed to call friends to find out how they're doing."

"And you are our friends," Dr. Grace said. "People we admire."

I reached out a hand to say goodbye. Dr. Grace pulled me close, and Dr. Tavaris threw his arms around both of us.

"We'll do our best to take care of the herd," he said.

"And to keep your promise to Daisy Mae. We'll care for Woolly. We'll watch over her. You have our word," Dr. Grace said.

"We may work for Jimmy Mercury, but we have a higher oath to care for the animals in our charge. Woolly will be cared for."

"Thank you. Thank you both."

They nodded and walked back to their truck.

"Now it's time for the hard part," I said.

"I said my goodbye to them before you got here. Do you want me to stay with you while you say yours?" Dad asked.

I shook my head. "It might be better if I was by myself."

He hugged me. I felt safe wrapped in his arms. He gave me an extra squeeze and then let me go.

"It's going to be all right," he said.

"Will it?"

"I don't know how, but it will."

Tears were starting to form in his eyes as he turned to walk away. I understood that he didn't want me to see him being weak when he felt that I needed him to be strong.

I wanted to talk to each member of the herd. It wasn't important who I started with, but I knew who I wanted to end with.

Woolly had finished her bottle and trailed along behind me as I went to the first elephant, Bacca. I offered him a scratch behind his left ear — his favorite spot. He was still just a toddler and wouldn't understand. I wondered if he'd even remember me once I'd been gone a few months.

I went from one elephant to another until only three remained.

"Raja, I have to say goodbye. I hope you'll understand that this isn't something I want to do, but something I have to do."

He lowered his head and gently rubbed his forehead against me. I could feel the wet through my clothes. The cool felt good.

"I wish I could have seen you grow up. I'm hoping in time you'll stop being such a blockhead."

He rubbed a little bit harder.

"We're both teenagers. We'll still have time to meet again, one way or another. I promise I'll remember you, and you have to promise to remember me. Elephants never forget, and neither will I."

I gave him one more scratch on his trunk and walked away. He stayed put, and Woolly followed me.

As I moved from elephant to elephant, Trixie watched me. She stood off to the side but never took her eyes off me. It was as if she knew that I needed privacy with each elephant but still wanted to be part of my goodbye to the herd. Was she looking for my reaction or those of the other elephants?

I walked toward her, and she started to walk toward me. We met in the middle. Woolly, of course, trailed right behind. She was trying to suckle from my hand.

"I don't have another bottle," I snapped.

Instantly I felt bad. Not just for speaking sharply to her but because I realized that was the last bottle I'd ever give her. "Sorry," I told her.

"Well, Trixie, it's all up to you now. We're not going to be here. Not me or my father. You're the only one in charge now.

I guess you always were the only one in charge. Thanks for letting me be part of your herd."

Trixie lowered her head slightly, turned it to one side, and stared at me. She made a soft clicking sound and then puffed at me. What was she trying to say? As always, I tried to read the emotions in her big brown eye. She wasn't sad or confused, and she certainly wasn't scared or playful, the emotions I knew. Was she feeling calm? Accepting?

"You've always been a good mother and grandmother and a good matriarch. Woolly probably is going to need you more than any of the others ever did. They wouldn't let you or the rest of the herd go with us because they thought Woolly needed all of you. She does. Now more than ever."

I was fighting to hold back the tears. Trixie didn't need to see me cry. Nobody did.

She reached out with her trunk and gently ran it along the side of my face. It felt the same as my father hugging me — safe and reassuring. I reached up and wrapped my arms around her trunk, giving that hug back.

"Goodbye, Trixie. I know you'll be okay without me. I just hope I can be okay without you." I released my grip and walked away.

There was only one goodbye left, and I wanted us to be alone for it. Woolly trailed after me as I walked. I stopped when we were halfway between Dad and Joyce, who were waiting for me on the top of the rise, and the herd. I looked one way and then the other. Both groups were watching us.

I leaned down so that Woolly and I were eye to eye. "I know you're not going to understand anything I say or anything that's going to happen."

In answer, she lowered her head slightly and bumped into me.

"I want you to know that you're going to be all right. I'm not really your mother, and even if I was, I was all right without *my* mother. I survived, and you can too. I had only my father. You have your whole family here to help you. They'll take care of you the way my father took care of me. You lose some things, but some things stay."

And then you lose them *too*, I thought but didn't say. I had thought I'd be part of the herd forever.

"It's time for me to go." I gave her one more scratch behind the ears, wrapped my arms around her, and then released her, turned, and started away. I kept my eyes forward, not looking back — and I was bumped from behind and almost knocked over. There was Woolly.

"Go back," I said loudly. "Go to your herd!"

I shuffled backward a few steps, and she shuffled forward to fill the gap. She tried to take my hand, and I pulled it away.

"No, I have to go!"

I looked back at Trixie, somehow hoping she had an

answer, but she stood still and stoic. She didn't have an answer either.

But maybe I did. I walked over to the waiting, watching vets.

"Do you have another bottle?" I asked.

"We have two more in the truck. Do you want to give Woolly another one?" Dr. Grace asked.

"No, I want *you* to give her a bottle."

Dr. Grace climbed out, holding a bottle. I took it, and Woolly quickly started sucking. I was grateful and sad. I handed the bottle to Dr. Grace, and Woolly continued sucking. I turned and walked away, eyes straight ahead. There was no point in looking back.

CHAPTER
Twenty-Five

"THIS WAS ON YOUR NIGHT TABLE, RIGHT?" LIZZY ASKED, holding up a framed photo that she'd taken from a box.

It was one of my favorite pictures. It was me and my father standing in the middle of the herd.

"Yeah, that's where it was, but just leave it in the box."

"No," she said. "I'm not doing that."

"What?"

"I'm not putting it back into the box. Forget it." She walked around the bed and put the picture on the night table. "This is the perfect place for it."

The real perfect place was in a different room in a different house, but there was no point in telling her that. She was just trying to help. She and Stacy and Joyce had spent all day yesterday and this whole morning helping us get unpacked and set up. Stacy had gone home a little while ago. I didn't want to unpack. Taking things out and putting them in place meant we were living here. I wanted to live where we had been or in the undetermined place where we were going.

My father had already started looking at properties. The money we now had in the bank gave us options he'd never thought possible. Lots of options, but none of them involved going home, so I didn't much care. In the meantime, we had to live somewhere.

I picked up the picture and felt myself starting to tear up.

"It's okay to cry," Lizzy said.

"Who said I was going to cry?"

"I think *I'm* going to cry, so why shouldn't you? You're tough, but even an elephant doesn't have that thick a skin."

I knew I wasn't that tough.

"So now that we're alone, are you going to tell me what really happened?" Lizzy asked.

"I can't do that."

"Sure you can. We're friends, and I won't tell anybody," she said.

"I can't. We signed something called a nondisclosure agreement, so I can't tell anybody anything, not even my best friends."

"I know some stuff already."

Everybody in town thought they knew something. I didn't say anything but gave her a questioning look.

"I know that you were paid a lot of money to give up the property," she said.

"How do you know that?"

"It's a small town with one bank. I heard it was a million dollars."

"You shouldn't listen to rumors," I snapped. "I can't tell you much, but I can tell you it was definitely *not* a million dollars." It was *nine* million, so I really wasn't lying to her. Not much.

"Sorry. Then I guess you aren't looking to buy a big property outside of town," Lizzy said.

I shrugged. "That one's true. We are looking to set up another sanctuary."

"So you must have gotten some money . . . enough to buy a new property."

"We are, but you know it wasn't our idea to leave and start again."

"I know how terrible it was for you and your father to leave the sanctuary."

"It's been awful. Not just leaving the property but leaving our family — our elephants."

She gave me a big hug. It felt so good.

"Thank you. I needed that."

"That's what friends are for."

We continued to unpack. I was grateful that she dropped the subject right there.

"There are lots of rumors about what's going on back on the property," she said.

Apparently she hadn't dropped it. That didn't mean I was going to say anything.

"I've heard some of them," I said.

"Whatever it is, it's the biggest thing that has ever happened in this town. I can't believe all the reporters and news trucks," she said.

"It is pretty unbelievable." They were everywhere — not just outside the gates of the sanctuary, but throughout town, including in front of our new house. I'd hoped they'd get tired of it and go away. Instead there seemed to be a bigger crowd today than there had been the day before.

"I've been watching the news," Lizzy said. "Some of the stories are pretty unbelievable."

"And bizarre."

There was speculation that Jimmy was developing a special energy project, that he had figured out how to convert animal poo to fuel, that he had developed a mind link so he could talk to elephants, that elephants were being trained to detect cancer and other diseases using their acute sense of smell. That last one made sense — at least from a biology point of view — although what were they going to do, staff hospitals with elephants?

There was also one story that was too close to the truth. Supposedly Jimmy's people were studying the genetic sequencing of elephants so they could clone them and repopulate Africa and Asia. Close but not on target.

"Can I ask you one more question?" Lizzy asked.

"You can ask me anything as long as you know I can't answer."

"When are you going to get your new puppy?"

I smiled. "Okay, that I can answer. It will be another five weeks."

"Why so long?"

"They're only three weeks old, and they need to stay with their mother until they're eight weeks old," I explained. Eight whole weeks — I wished I could have been that lucky. At least we'd have some pictures.

"Puppies are the cutest things in the world . . . well, except maybe for baby elephants."

I felt an ache in my heart.

"I wish I could have seen him — the elephant, I mean," Lizzy said.

"Her. She's a girl."

"She. You called her Woolly, right?"

I nodded.

"Do you have a name for the puppy yet?"

"I have to get the puppy before I name her," I explained.

"I guess that makes sense."

"Do you have a picture?" Lizzy asked.

"I didn't think to take one. Do you want to come with us next week when we see the puppies again?"

"I meant the baby elephant."

"I don't have any pictures," I lied.

"Do you think I believe that?"

I hated lying to her. "None that I'm allowed to show. I'm sorry, I'm really sorry, but you have to stop. There's nothing more I can say or show or answer. Please."

She nodded.

I couldn't talk, and my father couldn't talk, but Jimmy had been doing a lot of talking. Of course, none of what he'd said was true. He'd held a big press conference and tried to convince the reporters that there was "nothing to see." But the newspeople didn't leave, and more of them came.

Jimmy's mystery project was in the newspapers, on the radio, on TV news, and on every talk show. Crowds continued to gather around the property, hoping to catch a glimpse of whatever it was that was happening. I saw in one of the newscasts that Jimmy had hired a lot more security people to ring our property — what used to be our property.

Of course, we were part of the story. It had been easy for people to find out who had owned the sanctuary and to get our telephone numbers, as well as follow us when we left with the moving truck. Reporters wanted to know what we knew, why we weren't living at the sanctuary anymore. My father had been offered money — a lot of money — to tell "his story," but it was nowhere near the money we were getting for *not* talking.

I went over to the window and opened the curtain slightly. There were a couple of TV vans parked across the street, and I counted more than a hundred people. Some were reporters; others just curious locals and even some who had driven hundreds of miles just to be part of what was going on. Some of them held signs that called us "traitors" and "sellouts" for leaving the sanctuary and our elephants. That hurt. I wished we could let them know the truth.

There was so much I wanted to say, but I couldn't say anything. If we violated the nondisclosure agreement, we would forfeit the money. We'd have no elephants, no sanctuary, and no money to start a new one.

Two uniformed policemen were also stationed outside our house. They were stopping people from coming up and knocking on our door, either to interview us or to bother us. The first evening, people pounded on the door and peered through the windows and called our phones. Now the police kept outsiders from getting to the house. We'd mostly kept our phones turned off since then.

Lizzy came up beside me and looked out the window.

"It's really a circus out there," she said.

"A circus without elephants," I said without thinking, and then felt bad for both of us.

"I thought the policemen were going to search me for bombs when I tried to get into your house," Lizzy said.

I let the curtain fall back shut.

"I wish they'd all just go away," I said. I wished the whole situation would all go away like a bad dream, and I'd just wake up and —

There was a loud knock at the front door, and we both jumped.

"Somebody must have gotten past the police," Lizzy said.

"Yeah, but they're not getting any farther."

I went straight for the door, with Lizzy trailing after. I got there as my father and Joyce came out of the kitchen.

"I got it," I said.

I pulled open the door. James, Jimmy's chief of security, was right outside.

"Hello, Sam," he said. "I was wondering if we could talk."

"No," I said, and slammed the door in his face. That felt good.

"Very nice," my father said from behind me. "I might have slammed it harder."

There was another knock at the door, quieter this time. I pulled the door open again.

"Jimmy sent me to ask if—"

"Does he want to take *this* house away from us now?" I questioned. "I'm getting a puppy soon. Does he want to take that away too?"

I slammed the door again with so much force that the picture we'd just hung on the wall fell to the ground and the glass smashed.

"That was more like it," my father said. Joyce applauded.

Once more, James knocked. I pulled the door open a third time.

"Please, I understand exactly how you feel," he said.

"Wrong again!" I went to slam the door. He put his hand out and effortlessly held it open.

My dad was there in one leap. "My daughter owns that door, and if she wants it slammed, it's going to be slammed. Move your hand or you're going to lose it."

James was big and had a gun. My father was big and was as strong as an elephant. I didn't like where this was going.

"Wait," I said. "Let's hear him out."

"Really?" Dad asked.

"For a few seconds."

"That's all I need. And sorry for blocking the door," James said as he removed his hand. "Do you want to slam it one more time before we talk?"

"No need. I'll probably slam it right after we talk," I said

"Can I come in so we can have some privacy?" He gestured to the crowd on the sidewalk, watching and listening.

I motioned for him to enter.

He came in, and I gently closed the door behind him.

"Well?" Dad asked.

"Jimmy tried to call you."

"Our phones are off."

"I thought they might be. Jimmy's hoping you can come out to the property so he can talk to you. It's important."

"If it's really important, tell him to send his helicopter to pick us up," I said.

"He did."

"What?"

"We landed in the school playground, one block over," James said.

"We were informed that all communication had to go through his lawyer," Joyce said.

"This is personal. It's about Woolly."

"What about Woolly?" I asked anxiously.

"You'll have to talk to Jimmy about that. Please, will you come with me?"

Dad and I exchanged looks and nodded in agreement. If it was about Woolly, we had no choice.

Twenty-Six

"I'VE NEVER BEEN IN A HELICOPTER BEFORE," I SAID.

"Me neither," Dad admitted.

Lizzy had gone home, and a whole security team had escorted us through the newspeople and protesters and gawkers to the helicopter. It was unnerving and a little bit scary. These people couldn't get to us, but that didn't stop them from taking pictures and shouting comments. They followed us, bumping into one another, yelling out questions, and snapping photos, until finally the door of the helicopter closed and shut them out.

I didn't feel safe until the helicopter had taken off, and then I didn't feel safe in a different way. Going straight up, like being on a ride at the amusement park that kept going higher and higher, was a strange sensation. I didn't like heights. Raja's back was about as high up as I ever wanted to be.

"This is a pretty fancy helicopter," Joyce said.

"Jimmy likes his toys," James said.

"Is that what Woolly is to him, a toy?" I asked.

"Of course not. He cares for Woolly. You know he's not a bad guy."

"He forced us to leave our home," my dad said.

"He did that by paying you a small fortune, much more than he had to, in order to buy you out," James said defensively.

Joyce had said the same thing. My father was clear that even if Jimmy had offered us half that amount, we wouldn't have been able to match it.

"I don't care about the money. He took away our elephants," I said. "He took away our family."

"I know," James said. "I told him that was wrong."

"You did?" Joyce asked.

"Somebody has to tell him things he doesn't want to hear. Sometimes he gets so wrapped up in a project that he loses sight of everything else. For what it's worth, he was so upset that he didn't sleep that night."

"Neither did we," Dad said.

I remembered that Jimmy had reacted the same way when he learned that Daisy Mae had died. He did care about the elephants—I knew that.

I felt it in my stomach as the helicopter decelerated and started to drop. I peered out the window. From the air, our sanctuary looked big and lush and—"The barn is down!" All that remained was a pile of beams and barn board.

"Jimmy thought it was a danger, so he had a crew come in and take it down."

"But what if they saw Woolly?"

"He had it done when the herd was on the other side of the property, eating. You'd be surprised how fast twenty people can demolish a building."

I scanned the property below for the herd. I still hadn't seen them.

"Hang on," James said. "Landings can be a bit bumpy."

Lower and lower we went, and then the pilot spun us around to face the other direction. A small bump, and then we were on the ground. The roar of the rotors grew quieter. As we undid our belts, the pilot and copilot came out of the cabin. They moved some levers, opened the door, and lowered the stairs.

"Ladies and gentlemen, please." The pilot gestured to the door.

I followed Joyce through the door and onto the stairs. I stopped partway down. There in the distance was my house — my used-to-be house. At the bottom of the helicopter stairs stood Jimmy.

"It's good to see you!" Jimmy yelled as I approached him.

"Yeah, it's a pleasure to see you, too, a *real* pleasure," I said.

Joyce got right down to business before we even got down to the ground. "What do you want with my clients?"

"I want them — I want Sam to feed Woolly."

Dad had reached the lowest step. "You sent a helicopter to get us so my daughter could give Woolly a bottle?"

"Yes, exactly, that's what I want and why I sent the helicopter. Woolly hasn't eaten since you left."

"But it's been almost two days," I said.

"Is she sick?" Dad asked.

"Initial medical examinations have been completed, and the results show no issues. The doctors assure me it's nothing physical. They believe she is just grieving. Please come. She needs something to eat."

A truck was waiting off to the side. We all piled in — me and Joyce and Jimmy in the back, and my father beside James in the front seat. "Are we going to the woods?" I asked.

"They're up by the isolation enclosure," Jimmy said.

"That's the last place I thought they'd be," I said.

"It's not my choice; it's Trixie's decision," Jimmy said. "She keeps taking the herd up there."

"That's because we were feeding the herd by the enclosure," Dad said.

"Yes, Dr. Grace and Dr. Tavaris explained that, so we started to feed them near the house. They eat and then go up to the enclosure."

I almost said, "That's so they can get as far away from you as possible," but I didn't . . . and was that the reason?

"I thought you didn't want them anywhere near Burma because he's so dangerous," I said.

"I've brought in a crew, and they've started to make the fences and barriers higher and stronger as well as taking down the barn. No need to worry about Burma right now."

"You could have done that without removing my clients from their home," Joyce pointed out.

"I wanted to make sure Woolly was safe immediately, but I also wanted the enclosure to be sturdy enough that I wouldn't have to move Burma a second time before he settled with you."

"But you didn't mind having to make my clients move."

"I am sorry about that. I believed it was necessary."

We drove past the pond. I couldn't help but think about all the wonderful memories it held for me. Now somehow the water looked dark and cold.

"I have a question," Joyce said. "Was this really about you being afraid of Burma harming Woolly, or was that just the pretext for exercising the clause in the contract to buy out my clients?"

Jimmy didn't answer.

"Was it?" I asked.

He let out a big sigh. "I was genuinely afraid that Burma could harm Woolly. I believe that was realistic. I also believed it was necessary to have full control over the project before injecting even more money."

"So it *was* primarily about us leaving," Dad said. "Was that always part of your plan? Is that why the clause was in the contract to begin with?"

Jimmy shrugged. "I'm a businessman. I know my saying 'I'm sorry' means nothing, but I am. Have you had any luck with finding a new property?"

"It wasn't going to happen in two days," Dad snapped.

"Good — it hasn't happened. That's good."

What could he possibly mean by — "There's the herd!" I yelled.

They were all right next to the enclosure fence. That was where we'd peeled the fence away, but it had been put back up. Trixie, as always, was the first to notice us. She stopped feeding and raised her head to observe our vehicle approaching. And then I saw Woolly. She was holding Trixie's tail with her trunk. I noticed how they were all close together, each elephant no more than a dozen feet from the next. Was that just coincidence? Or were they afraid, were they grieving us being gone, were they confused?

James pulled our vehicle in next to the vets' truck. Dr. Tavaris and Dr. Grace hurried to meet us as we climbed out.

"Thank goodness you agreed to come!" Dr. Tavaris exclaimed.

"She hasn't fed since that bottle I gave her the day you left," Dr. Grace said.

I felt my heart ache. My poor Woolly. I'd let her down. I'd let Daisy Mae down.

"She's had nothing at all?" my father asked.

"Maybe a few drops."

"She's got to be severely dehydrated."

"It's almost reached a critical point," Dr. Grace said.

"And you're sure there's no internal blockage?" my father asked.

"As certain as we can be. It's pretty hard to give an elephant a scan without sedation, and we're concerned about sedating a woolly mammoth, for obvious reasons. We are fairly sure that it's psychological."

"So you think she's not eating because we left?" I questioned.

"That's our best theory, and the way to test it is for you to give her what she needs. She needs liquids. Can you give her a bottle?"

"Go and get me a bottle and I'll do it."

"We have one in the truck."

"Bring it to me," I said. I headed for the herd. My father was at my side. Jimmy and Joyce were a few steps behind us.

"Trixie! Woolly!" I yelled.

Trixie raised her head, and her ears perked up. Woolly released Trixie's tail and turned to face me. I ran toward her as those stubby, stumbling, plodding legs came running toward me.

She came right up to me and practically bowled me off my feet. The only thing that stopped me from falling over was that I wrapped my arms around her.

"Woolly, Woolly, Woolly, my little baby!" I cried.

She started chirping and touching me all over with her trunk. I hugged her tight, trying to reach all the way around her head but not quite managing it.

I looked up and realized that the whole herd was surrounding us. Trixie was with my father, Bacca was right beside her, and Raja had pushed in so that Woolly was shuffled slightly over to the side. We were in the middle of the herd. Our herd.

"Here comes the bottle," Jimmy said.

Dr. Grace waded through the herd and handed it to me. She seemed to have overcome her fear of wading into the herd.

"Take this, Woolly," I said.

I expected her to take it instantly — she had to be starving and incredibly thirsty — but she didn't. She was ignoring the bottle — no, worse, deliberately pushing it aside so she could rub her trunk against my face.

"She's not drinking," Dr. Grace said.

"This isn't what you said would happen," Jimmy said.

"If she's not taking the bottle from Sam, then something else has to be wrong," Dr. Tavaris said. "Something physical."

"We have to do a full GI-system scan and —"

"No, you don't," my dad said, cutting off Dr. Grace. "You don't understand. She wasn't taking the bottle before because Samantha wasn't here. Now she's not taking the bottle because Samantha *is* here."

"What do you mean?" Jimmy asked.

"She misses Samantha so much that she'd rather greet her than take the bottle, even though she's so desperately hungry and thirsty. She wants Samantha even more than she wants the bottle. Just wait."

"That makes perfect sense," Joyce said.

All eyes were on me and Woolly. Not just the humans, but the elephants as well. They knew how bad this situation was. Woolly continued to chirp at me. She continued to rub my face with her trunk and then lowered her head and rubbed it against my body. How long was this going to go on? Was my father right?

"It's time to eat now, Woolly. Please." I pressed the bottle against her mouth. She pushed it away, and I pressed it back toward her. "Come on, Woolly, take the bottle."

I placed it directly against her mouth. She took it and started suckling, so loudly and so powerfully that it felt like she was going to swallow the bottle and my hand.

Dr. Grace and Dr. Tavaris cheered, and Joyce started to cry. My father and Jimmy were beaming. I was so filled with emotions that I didn't know what I was feeling, but I knew what needed to be done.

"She's going to be finished soon. Can you please get me a second bottle? And maybe even a third."

CHAPTER

Twenty-Seven

WOOLLY DOWNED FOUR BOTTLES BEFORE SHE DECIDED she'd had enough. For good measure, I gave one to Bacca, who was equally receptive and grateful. Even Raja might have taken a bottle if I'd offered him one.

The herd finished feeding and headed toward the pond for their evening dip. We followed. I wished I'd brought my bathing suit along.

"I'm so relieved and so grateful," Jimmy said. We stood at the edge of the pond and watched them wade into the water. "I think we need to talk about some sort of arrangement."

"Arrangement?" Joyce asked.

"Your last arrangement kicked us off our property and out of our house and took away our elephants," Dad said angrily.

"Yes. I believe I miscalculated."

"Miscalculated?"

"That's the word you use for taking away somebody's family?" I demanded.

"I was wrong. I thought Woolly's family was the other elephants. I didn't realize it was the two of you, but especially you, Sam. You're Woolly's mother."

"So because you didn't realize that, you thought it was all right to get rid of us and to make some stupid, heartless lawyer do it because you didn't have the guts to do it yourself?" I turned to Joyce. "No offense meant."

"None taken."

"Well?" my father said.

There was a pause before Jimmy spoke.

"James told me it was wrong," he said. "I should have listened to him."

James nodded.

"So what exactly is this arrangement you have in mind?" my father asked.

"Or will your lawyers talk to our lawyer about it?" I asked sarcastically.

"No. I want to talk to you now, directly. What I am suggesting is that you move back to your house and resume the role of caring for the herd. You will receive a large salary—both of you—to do so. And you will keep the nine million dollars."

"So you want us to come back here and care for the herd as your employees, is that right?" I asked.

"Exactly."

"Wow," I said. "That's really—"

"Not going to happen," Dad said.

Everybody, including me, stared at him in disbelief.

"What do you mean?" Jimmy asked.

"I'm not going to work for you, no matter how much you pay me."

"Woolly needs you and Sam."

"Yes, she does, but she needs Sam to be her mother, not some employee who gets paid a few dollars to care for her and can be fired at any time."

"I wouldn't do that," Jimmy said.

"Don't you mean you won't do it *again?*" I asked. Dad was right.

"I won't. You have my word, and believe me, it will be far from a few dollars. We can talk about any salary you want. Name your figure."

"You don't get it. I'm not working for you no matter what the salary is," Dad said.

"That's just crazy!" Jimmy exclaimed.

"You'd know a lot about that subject," I said.

"Another joke?"

"No. What's to stop you from waiting until Woolly is weaned and then kicking us off our property again?"

"She has a point," my dad said. "Joyce?"

"We can try to negotiate something, but there's no legal document that can't be challenged if you have enough money and enough lawyers — and he has both."

"It seems like you'll have to just trust me," Jimmy said. "Besides, there's no choice, really. If you walk away, Woolly will die."

I looked away from Jimmy to my dad. Dad was looking at me. I studied his expression, looked deep into his eyes, trying to figure out what he was thinking. I knew he was doing the same with me. Then he winked. I didn't think anybody else saw it. Elephants don't need words to communicate, and sometimes people who work with elephants don't need words either. There was only one way out of this.

"Dad, we have to go."

Without hesitating, he nodded and took my hand, and we turned to leave.

"Wait!" Jimmy called out, and we stopped. "You can't be serious. If you leave, Woolly is going to die."

"Then she'll die," Dad said. He sounded so hard, so harsh, so cruel, that I winced, but I knew what we had to do.

Both Jimmy and Joyce looked completely shocked.

"You can't mean that," Jimmy said.

"Yes, I do. We're leaving," my father said.

"You're bluffing."

"I don't bluff."

Jimmy turned to me. "You won't be able to live with yourself, knowing that Woolly died because of you."

"I'll live with myself just fine. Besides, I won't be the one responsible; you will. You're the one who did this."

"But I've changed my mind," Jimmy said.

"I haven't changed mine," I said. "Dad, let's go."

"Your conscience will get the better of you," Jimmy said. "You'll be back tomorrow or the next day or the next at the latest."

"Even if I did change my mind in three or four days, it would be too late. She'd be dead," I said.

"Maybe it's the right thing. We shouldn't be creating life. Maybe nobody should be playing God, not even you," Dad said.

Jimmy let out a loud sigh. "You don't believe that, do you? I know you'll come back."

"If we leave, we're not coming back," Dad said. "You know we're as stubborn as an elephant."

"The saying is 'as stubborn as a mule.'"

"You don't know much about elephants, do you? You think everything is just a business deal," I said.

"Everything is. Look, do you have a counteroffer?"

"Counteroffer?" Dad asked. He looked over at Joyce.

"Yes. You don't like my offer, so what do you suggest instead?"

I worked hard not to smile. Jimmy was weakening. Maybe our "arrangement" could be made to work. I did have something to suggest. It was the fantasy I'd been playing with in my head before I went to sleep the last couple of nights. Right now, it was nothing more than a fantasy. But maybe . . .

"Well . . . I do have something in mind."

"Let's hear it."

Joyce was looking back and forth between us as if we were in a tennis match.

"If we do move back, it's going to be our house again. You have to give us the house and all the property."

"Of course! You can even have the adjoining land, the five hundred acres that wraps around the property."

"You already bought that?" I gasped.

"I like to move fast. That's such a small matter that I can give you all of that and —"

I cut him off. "Keep listening; there's more. As you suggested, my dad gets to keep the nine million dollars."

"That's not even an issue. Go on."

"We don't come back as your employees. We come back as your partners."

Jimmy furrowed his brow. "You want to be partners again?"

"Wasn't that what we were before you chased us away?" Dad asked.

"Well, yes, but what sort of partnership are you talking about now?"

"An equal partnership. Fifty-fifty. You can't make any decisions we don't agree with, and we can't make any decisions you don't agree with," I stated firmly.

"That's an unreasonable request. It's worth far more than the settlement you have already received."

Jimmy was getting upset, and his voice sounded strained. Had I pushed him too far?

"Jimmy, you kept saying that money was no object," Joyce said. "What's a few million dollars to you?"

He didn't answer right away. He looked like he was thinking. What could I do to move him in the right direction?

"And it's not like you're going to lose Woolly. I think it's important for you to be here a lot," I said. "You have to be more than just a business partner. You have to come to the sanctuary whenever you can. After all, you are Woolly's father, right?"

He smiled and nodded. "I still think you two might be bluffing," he said.

"Can you afford to take that chance with the most valuable animal in the world?" Joyce asked.

"You people are pretty good negotiators," Jimmy said.

"Does that mean we have a deal?" Dad asked.

Jimmy turned to James. "What do you think?"

"Sounds like a good deal for everybody," James replied.

I had to stop myself from leaping up into the air. Dad had his arm around Joyce, and both of them were beaming.

"Oh, and there's one more thing," I said.

Everybody turned toward me, even the elephants.

"Go on," Jimmy said.

"You have to try again with Raina and Tiny to create brothers and sisters for Woolly. If new mammoths are born, they have to stay here with their family," I said.

"That was part of the plan already, so it is no problem. I can certainly agree to that," Jimmy said. "I can agree to all of it."

Wearing a huge grin, Jimmy shook hands with Dad, with me, with Joyce, and even with James. "I'll have my pack of wolves contact your wolf to make the arrangements."

"That's great, except Joyce isn't a wolf," I said. Joyce was holding Dad's hand now, and I took her other hand. "She may be a lawyer, but she's not a wolf; she's an elephant. She's a member of our herd."

Afterword

ROOTED IN THE REALITIES OF ELEPHANT BIOLOGY AND behavior, *Elephant Secret* adeptly integrates the science of elephants with the art of nonviolent elephant management. While introducing the elephant protagonists of the story, Walters provides a glimpse into the exceedingly complex social relationships between elephants, including, perhaps most important, the deep lifelong bonds between mothers and calves.

Incorporating interesting facts about elephant biology and behavior, such as elephants being neurologically advanced at birth, needing to consume large quantities of vegetation daily to obtain the nutrition they require to survive, being uniquely adapted to the specific environments they inhabit, and grieving the death of family members, *Elephant Secret* provides a credible and informative window into the remarkable world of these animals.

The sanctuary setting of the novel depicts a form of nonviolent elephant management in which the human protagonists integrate themselves as much as possible into the social fabric of the elephants in their care. And the stories of the individual rescued elephants reveal to the reader some of the abusive elephant management practices these animals experienced in their pre-sanctuary lives, including elephant chaining, the forced separation of mothers and young, and the numerous health challenges faced by elephants in the restrictive confines of zoos.

As the story progresses, it reaches an unexpected, but seemingly plausible, turn of events, exploring a new and controversial field of science that not too long ago was considered to be nothing more than science fiction. Will the secret in *Elephant Secret* materialize in real life? Many people think it will. In the meantime, Eric Walters offers an accessible account of the practicalities of the science and the ethical debate associated with it. These topics offer an opportunity for critical thinking about a variety of different wildlife conservation and animal welfare challenges, and will spark discussion about what the future should hold.

All in all, an engaging, entertaining, and informative story. I loved *Elephant Secret* and highly recommend it.

Rob Laidlaw
Founder and director of Zoocheck
Recipient of the Frederic A. McGrand Lifetime Achievement Award for Animal Welfare

AUTHOR'S
Note

THIS NOVEL IS FICTION, BUT IT'S NOT SCIENCE FICTION. The science in it is factual, starting with the established fact that woolly mammoths existed. At one time, massive herds of mammoths flourished throughout the northern part of the entire Northern Hemisphere. They were the dominant animal, the top of the ecosystem, for hundreds of thousands of years.

Our early ancestors hunted mammoths and recorded these hunts in cave paintings. While human hunting may have played a role in the decline of the species, changing climates after the last ice age reduced woolly mammoths' habitat, and this is thought to have been the primary cause of their extinction. Asian elephants are the closest living relatives of mammoths, sharing many characteristics, including domed heads and smaller ears than African elephants. In fact, they share 98 percent of their genomes.

We have only fossilized remains of dinosaurs. From

mammoths, we have skeletal remains and actual carcasses. Mammoths would become ensnared in swamps, sink below the surface, and die. Their frozen remains are still being unearthed in the far east of Russia, and there have been more than thirty skeletal discoveries in Michigan alone. In 2015 a find in Michigan included numerous bones, including the skull and tusks.

In 2007 in Siberia, the best-preserved mammoth ever discovered was unearthed: a calf less than two months old, believed to have been in the permafrost for more than 40,000 years. Despite the length of time she spent frozen, she was intact, including eyes, trunk, internal organs, and skin. The discoverers called her Lyuba. Scientists proceeded to do genetic sampling and performed an autopsy to look at her digestive tract and organs.

The idea of bringing extinct animals back to life has fascinated scientists for hundreds of years. Dinosaurs aren't good candidates for de-extinction, because the extreme passage of time has eliminated genetic material from their remains. Mammoths, on the other hand, have provided the DNA necessary for cloning to take place.

Cloning, creating an exact replica of a biological unit, stopped being science fiction and became science fact with the birth of Dolly the sheep in 1996. The techniques that produced Dolly have evolved since then. Today there are companies that will — for a price — clone your favorite dog or cat. So why not a mammoth?

Skin cells are the best type for cloning, and Lyuba's remained intact. Despite some deterioration, scientists were able to decode and sequence more than 70 percent of the mammoth DNA. While this is insufficient to create a complete clone, it is believed that a woolly mammoth could be successfully cloned within fifteen to twenty years of this writing.

Lately, efforts have been made to create a hybrid woolly mammoth–Asian elephant clone. As recently as February 2017, a Harvard team predicted that within two years they would be able to produce a hybrid embryo — a vital first step in producing a living, breathing animal that will be the closest thing to a woolly mammoth on the planet in more than 3,500 years.

People have a natural love of elephants, perhaps because elephants share so many of the characteristics that we think make us human. They feel empathy, they grieve the loss of a family member, they live in family groups, they are playful, they have long memories, and they are self-aware.

Like people, elephants are complex and social animals. They communicate with one another through vocalization as well as nonverbally. Their sense of smell, the most acute in the animal world, is a key to their ability to communicate and their awareness of their surroundings. If you had the sense of smell of an elephant, you'd never need to ask somebody where they'd been, who they had been with, what they'd eaten, or what their emotional or physical state was — you'd know all of that with one sniff.

I think of myself as a "method writer." I like to live what I'm writing about. Of course I was unable to hang out with mammoths, but I was thrilled to spend time with elephants. I walked among the largest herd of freely grazing Asian elephants in North America. The experience was amazing and powerful and almost magical.

I spent a great deal of time with a young elephant named Hannah. She kept running her trunk over my face, trying to push her trunk into my mouth, and trying to steal my glasses. The matriarch of the herd saw us together and came over to investigate. She came right up, towering over me, and then lowered her head to look me in the eyes. I got the feeling she was telling me, "Don't mess with my girl." I guess I should have been afraid of this massive animal, who weighed more than two full-size cars. She could easily have picked me up and tossed me or simply crushed me. Instead I saw a sense of calm in her eyes that let me know I had nothing to fear.

In *Elephant Secret* I have tried to present a realistic picture of the interaction between Sam, her father, and their "family" of elephants, and to introduce the idea that cloning and de-extinction of woolly mammoths exist as a scientific probability. A woolly mammoth will walk this planet — not today and not tomorrow, but soon. I hope you look forward, as I do, to that day.

* * *

This book is dedicated to those making science fiction into science fact so that one day we all may have the opportunity to see woolly mammoths grace our planet once more.

SELECTED

Bibliography

Books

Dunn, Joeming. *Dolly: The 1st Cloned Sheep*. Illustrated by Brian Denham. Minneapolis: Magic Wagon, 2011.

Elephants! An Explore Series Book: Wild Animals Edition. CreateSpace, 2016.

Hehner, Barbara. *Ice Age Mammoth: Will This Ancient Giant Come Back to Life?* Illustrated by Mark Hallett. Markham, Ontario: Scholastic Canada, 2001.

Laidlaw, Rob. *Elephant Journey: The True Story of Three Zoo Elephants and their Rescue from Captivity*. Toronto, Ontario: Pajama Press, 2016.

5 Elephants. Markham, Ontario: Fitzhenry and Whiteside, 2014.

Lister, Adrian, and Paul G. Bahn. *Mammoths: Giants of the Ice Age*. Berkeley: University of California Press, 2007.

Madison, Jordyn. *All About Elephants: A Children's Book of Fun Facts and Pictures*. Amazon, 2014.

Marsh, Laura. *Great Migrations: Elephants*. National Geographic Kids. Washington, D.C.: National Geographic Children's Books, 2014.

Shapiro, Beth. *How to Clone a Mammoth: The Science of De-Extinction*. Princeton: Princeton University Press, 2016.

Documentaries

"Amazing Life Mammoths of the Ice Age Discovery Documentary 2015 HD." YouTube video, 1:00:10, from *Nova* episode "Mammoths of the Ice Age," televised by PBS on January 9, 1995. Posted by "Discovery Channel Documentary," June 22, 2015. www.youtube.com/watch?v=Pna2A8tKFfg.

Woolly Mammoth: The Autopsy. Written and directed by Nick Clarke Powell. Released November 23, 2014.

Articles

Andersen, Ross. "Welcome to Pleistocene Park." *Atlantic Monthly,* April 2017.

Wade, Nicholas. "The Woolly Mammoth's Last Stand." *New York Times*, March 2, 2017, D4.

Internet

Smith, Oli. "Scientists to Bring the Woolly Mammoth Back to Life After Ground-Breaking Discovery." *Express,*

October 9, 2015. www.express.co.uk/news/science/611035/
Scientists-bring-woolly-mammoth-back-LIFE-discovery.

Woollaston, Victoria. "In Ice Condition: Amazingly Preserved Woolly Mammoth Found Frozen in Siberia After
39,000 YEARS Goes on Display in Tokyo." *Daily Mail,* July
9, 2013. www.dailymail.co.uk/sciencetech/article-2358695/
Woolly-mammoth-frozen-Siberia-39-000-YEARS-goes-
display-Tokyo-woolly.html#ixzz4ffXs0iHB.